DEATH INTERFERES

AN RC FRANE/GRETA ROGERS MYSTERY

BY

B. ROBERT ANDERSON

PublishAmerica
Baltimore

First printing

At the specific preference of the author, PublishAmerica allowed this work to remain exactly as the author intended, verbatim, without editorial input.

ISBN: 1-4241-0676-1
PUBLISHED BY PUBLISHAMERICA, LLLP
www.publishamerica.com
Baltimore

Printed in the United States of America

Dedication (as always)

To my wife, Joyce S. Anderson

DISCLAIMER

This is a work of fiction. Names, characters, places and incidents
are either the product of the author's imagination or are used fictitiously,
and any resemblance to any actual person, living or dead,
event or locales is entirely coincidental.

Also by B. Robert Anderson

Freezing to Death
Dying to Meet You
Jogging to Death

Professional Selling
Professional Sales Management

1

"You wanted to see me?"

"We haven't spoken before. But, I know you know who I am."

"Of course. That's the only reason I agreed to meet."

"Maybe I should have said, you know who I was."

He didn't allow himself to smile. As if people changed because they changed their names, or their jobs. Who can account for what people do and how they change. Something happens, an accident, a child is born, a death in the family. Maybe an unexpected inheritance that spells freedom from work. Rarely, very rarely that a person decides to alter his life style. But, it happens.

"My recollection is that you were a police lieutenant. Homicide."

"Over twenty years. Only the last eight in Homicide."

"Did you tire of looking at all those dead bodies?"

Remembering the easy ones, those with a single bullet hole, was not too painful. But, the vision of a body sinking into the Delaware River somewhere in the path of steaming ships or those who arrived in the city piece by piece in boxes of frozen shrimp, not to mention the bad ones torn asunder by a maniac bent on revenge for reasons only a twisted mind could conceive.

Those were the tough ones.

"Yes," he responded. "The bodies began to get to me."

"Every job has its' downside."

"Guess that's why I decided to find another line of work. Too young to sit home and watch TV."

"Still, it's a shame not to utilize what you spent twenty years learning."

"That's exactly why I came to visit with you."

He nodded. "That's why you came to visit me? Knowing what kind of businesses I'm in. Interesting."

"Mr. Pentram, I know some of the things you do. Not all. But, a person with my background might prove useful in your operations."

"RC, I hope you don't mind if I call you that. Lieutenant Frane doesn't fit anymore. Besides, I have some knowledge of your background. Among the tidbits is the story of how your mother insisted on naming you for Robinson Crusoe. Have you lived up to his reputation for survival and her expectation of your life?"

Frane felt put upon. His life was constantly questioned because of the name that circled over his head like a halo about to drop and strangle him. He never discovered what possessed his mother to link him with the fictional, shipwrecked adventurer. By the time he was old enough to risk the question of her choice, she was gone; the cancer advanced at breakneck speed.

Facing the steady stare of John Pentram he responded, "I've never been certain what she might have expected."

"So, this career change is one of your own making. A need to move into a different venue."

"That's the way I feel about it. Time to do something, maybe a little less exciting, a little less demanding. Putting bad guys in jail makes sense, but after a while it takes a toll."

Juliani's Restaurant was a neutral setting for this meeting. When Pentram told them he wanted a little privacy they were led to the small room behind the kitchen where a white tablecloth, Lenox china, and silver service were used. Pentram pointed at the heated coffee pot and said, "Another drop?"

Sensing the need to be cooperative Frane said, "Yes. It's strong, but good."

"You said you know a little bit about my businesses. The question is where do you think you might fit in?"

"Let's put it this way. My strengths are in the line of investigating. You do business with a variety of people. Is it possible that you want some background on these people?"

Pentram philosophized, "Surely you realize I have many avenues to determine the reliability of the people I deal with. I'm not sure how you would add to my already formidable resources."

"True," answered Frane. "On the other hand they tend to be effective in different ways. I would bring a high degree of professionalism. Unlike any you currently employ."

"Does that imply you are looking for a job?"

"Not exactly. I am a consultant with unique skills and knowledge. Not a nine-to-five person; certainly someone to confer with on matters of importance."

"You sound quite sure of yourself; of what you can offer."

Taking a sip of the coffee that was now almost cold he answered, "Yes, on both counts."

In an expansive manner Pentram asked, "And what do you perceive your services might be worth?" He added, "Just as a matter of conversation."

Frane leaned back and crossed his legs as he explained. "I will be available twenty-four/seven. Naturally with some degree of notice. Try to minimize the emergency situations. And I am thinking of an agreed upon annual fee."

"You sound like a lawyer."

"Except that my work will be more diverse."

"No hourly rate?"

"No. An annual fee, payable in twelve equal installments."

"How about if the client wants more of your time?"

"My clients are reasonable. Whatever it takes to keep them satisfied. If it gets out of hand, we'll both know."

"Interesting," mused Pentram. "What you're saying is you're on call all the time. And no limit to what you will do?"

"Within the law, of course."

"Of course."

"So, what is the annual fee? Just a question, you realize."

"$108,000."

"Strange number. Seems like a lot more than police lieutenants make."

"True." Frane didn't want to go into lengthy explanations. Simple answers seemed best.

"Would I be the only client?"

"What I assure you of is availability when needed. I would never say another client has first call. Most assignments would not be of an emergency nature. Still, if that happens, I'll be there. Oh, and no clients who might be competitors."

"No other costs?"

"Only in the event you want me to travel to some distant point. Plane trips, overnight hotel bills, food, that sort of thing."

"Suppose I'm not satisfied?"

"Twenty-four hours notice and I'm gone. Works both ways."

"What does that mean?"

Knowing he was reaching positive territory Frane added, "If I'm not satisfied, I have the option of leaving. Same terms."

This was new ground for Pentram. He was unaccustomed to a negotiation in which the participants had equal rights. The idea that someone he was paying could leave of his own free will was a curious thought. More than curious, it was not really appealing. Most of all the prospect of facing a subordinate who might challenge his authority was upsetting. Not a man to turn away from a challenge he said, "Let me think about this. Maybe come up with a list of activities in which your services would prove beneficial."

"While you're considering, please keep in mind that I would need immediate access to you. When I have something to report or a piece of information that might prove of interest. Maybe even a new business opportunity."

"Seems like a different kind of consulting arrangement, a little extraordinary."

"Here's my first bit of consulting. If you want ordinary, I'll be happy to gather some names for you. If you want extraordinary, look no further."

2

Cops have their own watering holes. Places to congregate after hours to have a few drinks before going home. Talk over the days' events, who shot who, big arrests, or just old-fashioned belly-aching. Stand-at-the-bar comfortable, smoke filled, reeking and always friendly.

When he left the police department, Frane also left the old hangouts behind. In his role as a consultant this was part of his new persona. That is why he met Sergeant Greta Rogers at the Ritz Carlton, across the street from City Hall. The startling new addition to the Philadelphia hotel scene offered two places for a casual drink. The vast open Rotunda that serves as the main entry and a more private club-like dining room set off to one side where dim lights and dark woods blend. In the late afternoon it was the perfect place for quiet conversation and tall drinks.

"I miss you," she said.

"We'll probably see each other more now than before."

"No way. We used to be together all day and sometimes afterwards."

"It'll be more fun to just concentrate on the afterwards part."

"Hey, I still have to work for a living."

"Give it a little time and you can become a consultant."

Frane and Rogers had worked together for over five years. She made Sergeant when she passed the test for Homicide and sought out Frane. Word throughout the department defined him as the "Dour Lieutenant." She knew he was good at his work and that meant she would have to find ways to turn "Dour" into "Not so dour." Heavy concentration in that area led to a deeper understanding, especially after hours.

"How does it feel being out there all by yourself?"

"It's only been a couple of months," he answered. "Takes a little getting used to."

"Nobody to order around," she laughed.

"That too."

"Can we afford drinks in this place? Pretty fancy."

"I'm still figuring out where I am. Already have a couple of small clients and now I'm after a very big fish. Big bucks. Put it all together and we can even have dinner here."

Twenty years on the force had given Frane buckets of confidence. Only after he got up that first morning with nothing to do did the full effect of his decision register. No one to talk to, nobody to call, no Captain Bailey yelling for him to come into his office. All alone trying to think of ways to make a living. Scary.

"What kind of clients?" she inquired.

Still unaccustomed to his new role he needed someone to confide in. The realization that consulting meant keeping your dealings with a client secret created a dilemma. He measured his words because he trusted Rogers.

"Couple of small jobs tightening security for a distribution company. Since we spent so much time with those grocery companies, I approached one or two with the idea that I could advise them on ways to make their plants more physically secure. Most of them have so many leak holes, it's amazing they're still in business. Also, I'm thinking of doing the same thing with a couple of big retail operations. Teach them to lock the doors at night."

"How does that measure up against a late night call that some bastard has shot an innocent citizen?"

"Hard to say. Nobody has called me with a real rush job. Especially in the middle of the night. How are things at the Round House?"

"Usual stuff. A murder here a murder there. Miss the place?"

"As a matter of fact I do. Every minute there was action. Something had to get done, some piece of work, some phone call. Plenty of action. This consulting work is slow and easy. I just sort of lean back and make a short list of things I have to do and maybe a shorter list of things I think I ought to do."

Rogers signaled the waitress for another round. The shadows of the lounge hid them from the world. A perfect setting for a late afternoon encounter that could lead to an early evening tryst; a couple of Tanguery and tonics smoothing the way.

"Can we talk about us for a moment?" she asked.

"Good idea. How about we go to my place and continue the conversation."

Reaching out to take his hand she challenged him. "Like I said, I miss you."

"We've had some good times together. Every reason to continue."

"Think it might go beyond these once-in-a-while meetings?"

Frane retreated. Being completely on his own was a radical move. When he told his father he was leaving the force the old man mumbled his objections. Captain Bailey was stunned. And Greta Rogers felt her life was coming apart. Five years in close harmony, losing a partner had been a shock to her nervous system.

A jiggling on her hip by the silenced cell phone jarred her. Instinctively she slid the instrument from its case, looked at the number calling and raised the phone to her ear. "Rogers."

"There's been a shooting, Sergeant. Captain wants you to take it over."

"Where?"

"Near the Food Distribution Center. In back of a restaurant; Juliani's. Do you know the place?"

"Been there a couple of times. What else?"

"Nothing at this time. You're the first one I called. I'll get the ME there as soon as he can break away."

"I should be there in ten minutes."

Looking at Frane she said, "Gotta go. Homicide waits for no one."

Before he could respond there was a jiggle on his cell phone. "Stay a minute," he said. Pushing the answer button he said, "Frane."

"You know who this is?"

"Yes. You're my number one concern."

"I have a small piece of work for you."

"Good."

"For openers I want you to do some investigating. It might take a month. Not full time you realize. So, I'll pay you for one month and we'll see where that takes us."

Gritting his teeth, Frane recognized the risk he was about to take. It had to be his way or no way. "If you want to engage me according to our recent conversation, I'll be there in minutes."

"I want a trial run," Pentram demanded.

"You can have a trial run based on the terms I outlined. You always have the option to cancel whenever you wish."

The quiet at the other end was ominous. A tough former police lieutenant facing off with a tough boss of undefined businesses. "This is not the way I usual give assignments."

"And it's not the way I usually accept them," answered Frane. "That makes us equal." Softening his tone, "We're both engaged in a learning experience. See if we can be happy together."

Another silence that carried with it a need for some kind of concession. Finally, "You know my address?"

"Yes."

"Stop at the house. There will be a check for one month in advance. Then, go to Juliani's. A man was shot. I want to know who did it."

"That's police work."

"Oh."

"I'll be at your house in ten minutes."

Clicking off he looked at Rogers who had been standing during the entire conversation. "You headed south?" he asked.

"Yeh. You headed south?"

3

Thirty-five years ago Charlie Brewer was known as, "The left end and guard." He sat on the left end of the bench and guarded the water bucket. From this choice seat he watched all the action on the football field and rooted for South Philadelphia High School. Early that December he gawked in amazement as Thurman Arthur tore through the line of his team. The big black kid from West Philly High was unstoppable. Just plain ferocious in his approach to the game. Just as he was ferocious in his hold on the drug business in West Philadelphia. Only now that he was well established, "More mature," he liked to say, the ferocity had turned to a calm certainty about how he ran his business.

Looking back to that cold winter day haunted Brewer. He remembered with clarity Arthur's twists and turns and pumping legs. It was a moment in his life that he cherished and nurtured. A turning point when he was able to separate himself from the natural inclination to root for his team into complete marvel and admiration for a great performance. West Philly scored four touchdowns that day to win 28 to 10. Arthur crossed the goal line three times, standing up.

Ironically, the deft ball handling of Bob Vogt, one of only four white players on the West Philly team almost went unnoticed. Not nearly as big as Arthur, he called the plays and ran the team with the sophistication of a chef making an omelet. Break a few eggs, mix in some cheese and mushrooms, simmer in a hot skillet; and then gently flip the edges to insure perfection.

Brewer wanted to approach Arthur to express his admiration. But, when you grew up in South Philadelphia you never crossed the line against your own team. Especially against West Philly. And certainly not to praise a black player. That was then. Three-and-a-half decades later many things had changed, but Brewer was still wary of visiting neighborhoods in West Philadelphia when he had to make deliveries.

Vogt got a scholarship to Villanova, Brewer made it through two years at Temple University, and Arthur took his degree in the College of Hard Knocks. Their paths crossed multiple times over the years. Vogt as Arthur's lawyer and Brewer as one of Arthur's loyal workers. Three disconnected boys who grew into a business relationship that transcended all the unnatural barriers of religion, education, and color.

When Arthur needed a lawyer, what better source than his former quarterback. Calling legal plays required the same skills as calling football plays, plus knowledge of the law. "I'm gonna try to do exactly what you tell me," Arthur said. "Cept when I think you're wrong. You know, sometimes you call a bad play. Most of the times we win."

"This isn't football," Vogt said. "So far you've got me doing easy stuff. That's okay. Writing a will isn't much of a challenge. Some of the partnerships you're involved in don't really need much legal work. Probably there will come a time when you have to really trust my judgment."

"Thing is this," Arthur said. "Some of the things I do, you don't want to know about. When the time comes, if it comes, we may need a different kind of lawyer."

"Is that why you made me your executor?"

"I did that because I trust you, man."

"So, there are other things I don't know about. Who's the executor of those holdings?"

Arthur smiled. "When you need to know, you'll know."

4

All the attention was focused on "Chips" Brewer who lay dead next to the dumpster behind Juliani's; Sergeant Greta Rogers of the Philadelphia Police Department, Thurman Arthur, his employer, Bob Vogt, lawyer for Arthur, John Pentram, silent partner in Juliani's Restaurant, and RC Frane, consultant to John Pentram.

Yellow crime scene tape cordoned off the area around Juliani's Restaurant. The body lying beside the oversized green dumpster had a single bullet hole behind the left ear. A signal that this had not been an accidental shooting, rather a planned event designed to send a message.

Standing outside the tape, RC Frane found it difficult to investigate when he couldn't get close to the victim. It was only eight weeks since he left the Homicide Division and decided to become a consultant. A check for $9,000 was safe in his left front trouser pocket, close to the three $20 bills he always carried. The first monthly payment from John Pentram spelled a lot of security. Now he had to earn his keep by finding the killer without all the help he was accustomed to.

"No need to hang around," said the Blue Coat.

"What?"

"This is a crime scene. Body over there. Unless you have some business here, why not just move along."

"Any idea what happened?"

"Yeah. Guy took a bullet in the head."

"Sergeant Rogers, the woman in the tight pants and leather jacket. Want to ask her to step over here for a minute."

"You kidding? When she's looking for the perp?"

"Try," Frane insisted.

It was a strange juxtaposition. Half an hour ago they were having a drink together, planning a night of wine and TV. Now, he was on the outside pleading for a chance to get close to the victim. At least find out his name.

"Sorry to bother you, Sarge. Guy over by the tape says can you come over and talk to him."

Without looking Rogers knew who it was. "Officer, any idea who he is?"

"No, mam."

"Tell him he can come over and look at the body."

The surprised officer motioned to Frane to join the crowd.

As he slid under the tape there was a twinge, almost of remorse for the time when the show was his. Now he had to seek permission to get close to the victim. Asking questions was sure to be another challenge.

"Took you long enough to get here," she admonished.

"Had to stop and pick up a check from a client. Now we have enough cash to go away for a weekend. Got any plans?"

"Listen, Mr. Whoever you are," she almost laughed. "What's on your mind besides murder?"

"If we concentrate on murder, we'll have time to get away. How does Bermuda sound?"

"Must be some helluva client. Care to mention his name?"

"Come on, Sergeant. You know consultants have to retain a high degree of confidentiality. Hope the check clears."

"I'm glad you not dealing with the types who do everything in cash."

"Yeah. Me too. So, who have we got here?"

"We?"

"Sorry. Lost track of time."

"Wallet says Charles Brewer."

"Address?"

"17th off Lombard. Neighborhood boy."

"One bullet?"

"I think so. You better get out of here before Homer arrives. He'll have a fit."

"You figure the ME won't want to talk with me? Ask for my opinions? Just because I'm a civilian doesn't mean I can't be helpful. For instance, why the early evening? What does this guy do for a living? Any money in his wallet? You know the drill."

"Is this a lesson in crime detecting?"

"Just one last question. Wanna meet me around nine o'clock?"

"Usual place?"

"I'll stop by the State Store and get a bottle of that new Merlot. Fact is maybe I'll get a couple of bottles. After all, this check won't last forever. So, I'll stock up a little."

"Will you get the hell out of here so I can get some work done!"

Frane took a closer look around the body of the victim. No struggle, very little blood. His immediate reaction was in favor of a very professional hit. With a backward wave of the hand he ducked under the tape.

The officer sidled up to Greta Rogers and asked, "Who he?"

"Him? Oh, he used to be a cop."

There was a time when Frane pulled into any convenient curb and left his car. Today he had to hunt around to find a space near Brewer's home. The two-block walk bothered him as all the little perks of being a Police Lieutenant slipped away. Trying to interview the widow, assuming there was a widow, meant he was stepping ahead of the police. Not a good idea. But, then again, he was merely a consultant. Nothing official. Just a business card.

The row house was set in brick and clumped between two similar houses. It was odd that a small iron shoe-scrapper was on the bottom step. Reminiscent of the time when the streets weren't paved and mud had to be removed before entering the house. It was a predictable Philadelphia Row House, 16 feet wide and three stories high, with a small yard in the back.

No surprise when Rose Brewer opened the door. She had a wrap-around apron over a simple blue dress, the one she wore to work. Dinnertime was approaching and this unwanted interruption would only delay her rush to set the table and baste the potatoes alongside the roast.

"Yes."

Frane was at a loss for words. Being a consultant was not like being a Police Lieutenant. He had no right to tell her about her husband, "Chips."

5

"Mrs. Brewer, my name is Frane and I'm a consultant. Is your husband at home?"

It was a terrible way to start, but he could think of no other approach. After years of intruding on people's lives with bad news the impact never softened. At least in this instance he played a different role and took refuge in the notion that he wasn't lying, just using some deceit until the proper authorities could deliver the ultimate information. *Learning to be a consultant took on new meaning. He didn't like it, even though he knew cops were allowed to lie when trying to get a confession, so why not consultants.*

"Chips needs a consultant?" she questioned. "Ha, that's a laugh."

"Sorry," he fumbled. "I'm a consultant and my client wanted to get some information that your husband might be able to supply. That's sort of what I do. Nothing serious, just a couple of questions. Any idea where he might be at this moment?"

"You sure you got the right guy?"

Trying to make it more professional, Frane took out his black note pad, flipped through a couple of pages and said, "Charles Brewer, wife Rose

Fable, son John. Have I got the right place?"

"You got it right, mister, but what's Chips got to do with a consultant?"

"The point is Mrs. Brewer, it's not me, it's my client. I'm just doing my job."

"So, who is this client? Must be a big shot, has himself a consultant."

Groping for a new way to proceed, Frane said, "Your husband was supposed to be making a delivery for my client. He is late. I'm trying to find out what happened. Can you help me?"

Still standing in the doorway she held firm. "You gotta come back later when he's home. I don't know nothing about his work."

"Any idea when he might get home?"

"Probably for dinner. Around seven. If you want, come back."

Holding up his hand Frane added, "One last thing. Is your son John around?"

With a snort she answered, "Yeah. Try the pool hall around the corner."

It had been a long time since Frane had a door shut in his face. Consultants, he decided don't get the same amount of respect as police officers. He would have to find some new techniques.

Knowing that Brewer surely would not be home for dinner, he walked toward Locust Street to find the pool hall. Growing up in the Eastwick section of the city he realized that the pool halls of his youth were no different than the pool halls of South Philadelphia. They existed as places where young men could congregate, smoke, drink a beer, claim sexual conquests that were mostly fiction, and in general avoid work. Lately they had also become the destination of small time drugs. As he walked through the door the reek of marijuana mingled with the sour smell of beer all cloaked in a slight haze of cigarette smoke. To his surprise, there were even women present. Sign of the times.

Using his best-relaxed approach he went to the counter where time and cues were available and asked, "Any tables open for a singleton?"

"Plenty of space," answered the heavyset man. "Take that table in the far corner. You meeting anybody?"

"Tell you the truth, I'm supposed to meet Chips Brewer. His wife said I could find his son John. He around?"

"That's him, the one in the plaid shirt."

"Thanks."

As he loosened his tie, Frane moved toward John Brewer. "Hi, John."

23

Cigarette dangling from his lips, he said, "Hi, yourself. Wanna shoot some pool?"

"I'm not much good. Been a long time, but for fun, sure."

Brewer laughed. "You some kind of high type hustler?"

"Nah, just a guy at the end of the day. Let's play for fun and talk. I stopped over at the house and your mom said I could find you here."

"You got a name?"

"People call me all kinds of names. Try RC."

"RC? What kind of name is that?"

"Secret. I'm a consultant looking for help. Supposed to talk with your father, but he wasn't around. Guess he works funny hours."

As he lined up to break the rack he said, "So what do you want with me?"

"Trying to follow up on a delivery your father was supposed to make. You work with him at all?"

The balls scattered across the table, one of them dropped in the far right pocket. John Brewer proceeded to sink six more balls, demonstrating he was a player, but also allowing that he wasn't perfect, a come-on to the unsuspecting.

Frane really couldn't play; he took his turn and missed. Brewer took this as a fake, expecting any moment an offer to put some money on the table.

"So, any idea where your father is?"

As he proceeded to pocket five more balls, John Brewer paid little attention to Frane. Finally, when he missed another shot he said, "My old man and me, we don't really hit it off. He keeps wanting me to work with him. But, that doesn't seem like such a hot idea."

"Exactly what is it he does?"

"That's what I mean. Who knows?"

24

6

As instructed, Frane took the Market Street Elevated train to 52nd Street. He felt safe even though this was a tough neighborhood, changed from earlier times when he worked here in a supermarket. That store was now converted into an oversized music depot. Hard Rock challenged the trains running overhead.

He crossed Market Street and headed for Chestnut Street, secure in the knowledge that he was being followed. He spotted two men in dark suits on the far side of the street. They were set apart because they both wore jackets, not exactly the attire one expected in this area. Ahead he saw another man similarly dressed. He assumed this would be his guide.

"Evening, Mr. Frane." A serious greeting emphasized by the bulge in his chest, symbol of an over-sized .57 Magnum.

"You were expecting me?" Frane asked.

"Yes sir. I'm supposed to be your escort. Shall we go?"

The man was of average height and weight and moved with the light step of a boxer. He walked half-a-step to the right of Frane making sure that his own right hand was always at the ready to reach in and grasp the weapon.

Daylight did not matter in this neighborhood. The sound of a shot would go unnoticed because there was no one anxious to take note.

When they reached Walnut Street the man motioned to the left. Three houses in from the corner an old dilapidated structure stood four floors above the six steps up from the pavement. Scattered on the front porch was an assortment of rocking chairs standing guard in a disorderly array.

Without knocking the door opened and Frane stepped inside. Two men led him down the hall into what had once been a living room. A fireplace surrounded by an ornate wood carved mantle was covered with pictures of football action shots. Oriental carpets were spread around the room and a couch of another era faced two mohair stuffed chairs. Seated in one was Thurman Arthur.

He hoisted his large frame that showed the consequence of steak, potatoes, and wine. "Welcome, Mr. Frane. How can I help you?" He pointed to a chair.

"Thank you for seeing me," Frane answered. Scanning the color pictures he added, "I was a little behind you in high school, but those pictures certainly tell your story. What ever happened to your career?"

Arthur seemed pleased to be remembered. "That was sure a long time ago. I was good, but not good enough for the big time. Bounced around for a couple of years, got my comeuppance playing sandlot ball and finally decided to pursue some other avenues. Understand you have just made a change in your career."

Frane was surprised that his departure from the police force had reached across the community. "Didn't know I was so well known," he laughed.

"Guess it depends on your line of work. People in my business try to keep track of what's happening down at the Round House."

A woman who might have been a waitress entered the room, approached the two men and asked, "Can I get you something to drink?"

Arthur extended his hand to Frane. "Coffee, tea, something stronger. We have a selection of liquor or beer. Maybe a glass of wine."

"Coffee sounds good. Straight."

"I'll have my usual. Late afternoon is tea time."

Frane took this in stride. Teatime for this man who was supposed to run West Philadelphia. Drugs, bookmaking, a touch of prostitution, and then there were the legitimate businesses needed to cover the flow of money. Cash businesses like restaurants and bowling alleys, small stores like cleaners and possibly a little loan sharking on the side.

26

"So, what can I do for you Mr. Frane? You looking for a job? Guess we can always use an experienced hand."

"Nice of you to ask. However, I'm now a consultant. I'm working for some clients to help them with security. And to do a little investigating. Not like the old days. Easy stuff. Which is why I'm here."

"You investigating me?" Arthur said with a tone of surprise.

"Just the opposite. I'm here to ask for some information that might point me in the right direction. I have a client interested in finding out about someone you probably know."

It was almost laughable the way Arthur reacted. His jaw dropped slightly in a display of shock. "Why me? You a big time detective asking me for help."

Based on his long experience in police questioning, Frane ignored the question and went right on. "Thing is, I'm trying to learn something about a man named Brewer. Charles Brewer, nickname, Chips."

Arthur looked toward the door as the woman entered pushing a cart with a teapot, coffee pot, two sets of cups and saucers, and an assortment of cookies. "Just a touch before dinner."

After taking his cup of tea Arthur said, "Yes, I know Brewer. What can I tell you?"

Before reaching for his coffee Frane said, "I'd like to know what kind of work he does. For instance, did he do anything for you?"

Arthur changed the direction of the conversation. "This client of yours who wants to know this stuff, has he got a name?"

Frane reasoned that he was now confronted with a major ethical decision. Years doing police work offered the opportunity to shade the truth, not lie, but hold back information when interviewing a potential culprit. In fact, there were times when outright deceit seemed appropriate if the crime was serious. His new role as a consultant presented similar situations. Did revealing the name of a client transcend the line of confidentiality? Was deception acceptable? Is there a difference between protecting a witness to a crime and secreting the name of a paid customer?

"I see you're troubled, Mr. Frane. So, let's be realistic. If I help you, I may be hurting myself by showing my cards to somebody sitting at the table. Now that's not good poker. Is it?"

Frane forced a laugh. "This is a new game for me, I'm just feeling my way along. Here's what I know. Brewer was a small time player. Did favors, ran errands, made himself useful. Not just to one person, but maybe two or three. As long as there was no conflict of interest."

Arthur sat up sharply in his seat. "Was?" he blurted.

Sensitive nerve, Frane thought. "Oh, I neglected to mention. He was found with a bullet hole behind he left ear a couple of hours ago. Does that make a difference?"

7

Ridge Avenue is one of the strange streets in Philadelphia. In a city noted for its checkerboard design, Ridge runs diagonally from downtown north, until it reaches the river and changes names. Along the way are side streets, enough to be confusing, and secret enough to hide a body. In a desolate part of a busy city there are plenty of places where crime goes unnoticed because it is unreported. What's one body more or less?

Pearl McCabe lay curled in a doorway a block from Columbia Avenue where it crosses Ridge, apparently sleeping off too much to drink. Other doorways were home to drinkers and druggies resting after a hard night. Disinterested passers-by were unaware of the bullet hole behind her left ear. Her sleep was permanent.

As the sun came up and the day opened, the sleepers stirred and rose to get out of the way before the shopkeepers arrived. Only Pearl McCabe didn't move. Out of friendship for a neighbor and ready to explore the possibility that she had more than he, Harold nudged Pearl in search for money to get coffee. Adhering to the honor that exists among street people, when she didn't move he looked through her pocket book and found a dollar. That was all he took. He neglected to tell the police about the dollar. Existence on the street dictates a fair level of comradeship.

"She doesn't look like any kind of bum," said Wilson.

"Any ID in her bag?" asked Rogers.

"Would you believe this? A drivers license, owners card, maybe fifty, sixty dollars, social security card; looks to be a normal citizen. Also, she's well dressed. What do you think happened?"

"Sure not robbery. How about the bullet behind her ear? This was a professional hit. But, why here and why now?"

"There's an address in her bag. She lives maybe ten blocks from here."

"As soon as Homer Longstreet gets here, we'll go around and see her house. Also, that creep Schindel ought to be here soon. I don't see anything much, only that the body was planted here. Shot somewhere else and brought here. Let's go. Leave a couple of blue coats to watch the scene."

As they pulled away the Medical Examiner appeared. Thinking better of leaving, Rogers had Wilson pull to the curb, got out and walked back to talk to Longstreet.

"Morning, Homer. Look what we found for you."

"Another body, another day. They do keep popping up."

"Is that a smile on your face?" asked Rogers.

"Sure is. The Phillies won last night. That's enough reason to celebrate."

Pointing to the corpse, Rogers said, "What do you think?"

"I think the lady is dead. Don't know anything else. Was the body moved?"

"From what I can see of the scene she must have been brought here and posed as a sleeping drunk. But, her clothes make you think there's more to this. Let me know about alcohol and whatever else you think is important."

"My dear Sergeant, you know I'll do the best I can. Which, as you also know is perfection. You should expect nothing less."

Smiling, Rogers said, "If I didn't love you I could soon learn to hate you. Keep trying." With a wave of the hand, she was off.

Wilson moved the car close to the address on Pearl McCabe's driver's license. The two officers surveyed the street, a residential area in a modest neighborhood. Rogers felt out of place, a white woman stood in contrast to the surroundings. They rang the bell and waited.

"What 'dya want?" The man was short, needed a shave, and wore underwear sagging below his belt line. A bulging stomach added to his otherwise revolting appearance.

Holding up her badge, Rogers asked, "Is this the home of Pearl McCabe?"

"What's it your business?" he snorted.

"Sir, we are the police. Either answer my question or we'll take you downtown and ask you there."

"I need a lawyer?"

"No, you do not need a lawyer. We just need some information. Let's start over. Is this the home of Pearl McCabe?"

"Yeh."

"That's good for a start. What is your name?"

"McCabe."

"You the husband?"

"Yeh."

"We have something serious to discuss with you. Mind if we come in?"

"Suit yourself." Turning he walked through a short hallway and turned into the living room. An oversized couch, two chairs, the obligatory TV set, fairly clean room adorned with several framed prints probably from the local Woolworth. He motioned to the two seats before collapsing on the couch.

"Mr. McCabe, we have some bad news for you. Your wife, Pearl McCabe was found not too far from here. She had been shot."

"Damn, I told her to get out of that business. Dangerous."

"What business was that, Mr. McCabe?"

"She was a collector."

"Collector?"

"Worked for some guy, went around collecting money and then giving it to him."

Wilson was taking notes. "Got a name for the guy?"

"Nah. She been doing it for a couple of years. Till she did some stuff for somebody else."

"Who might that be?"

"How the hell I know. She kept all that stuff to herself."

"What do you do, Mr. McCabe? That is, what's your job?"

"I'm sort of a mechanic. Do odd jobs here and there. I work for myself."

"We'll need you to come down to the morgue to identify the body. What's your phone number? We'll call to tell you when."

8

Two men followed Robert Vogt into the elevator. Before he realized what was happening the door closed and the carriage moved down and stopped in mid-descent. Snapping to attention he exclaimed, "What's the matter with this damn thing?"

The taller of the two quietly said, "Don't be upset. We're getting off at the ground level. We have just a moment to talk."

"Talk? Who are you? What's this about?"

"Easy, Mr. V," the shorter man said. "We'll talk. You listen."

"First. Forget about Chips Brewer. He's not in the game anymore." He added, "And forget about Pearl McCabe. She's gone."

Vogt edged to the back of the elevator. *He thought in terms of the times he was a star quarterback. Step back, dodge, move around, stay in the pocket, and command your eyes to see the whole field. Then, when you think you spot an open receiver, throw the ball. If no one is open, look for a hole in the line and run. Remember to slide, don't get tackled. Don't get hurt; be prepared for the next play. It might yield a touchdown.*

The two men stood silently. Again the taller one said, "There are three other people we have to know about. We want those names. Now!"

"I don't know what........."

The shorter man slapped him across the face—hard.

"Make is easy on yourself, Mr. V. Just tell us the names."

It takes a good quarterback to know when he is about to be sacked. Caught behind the line, no way to escape. Defenders all gone. Monster linemen about to crash into his body, maybe do some real damage. Best to just curl up and take your hits. Only thing they wanted was three names.

"Got a pencil and paper?" he asked.

"We got good memories. The names!"

"James Kennedy, James Curtin, and James Duncan."

"See," the taller man said. "That didn't hurt. You could just have said 'The Three Jimmies.' We all know about them. So, we'll just get out on the bottom level and you can head back to your office."

"Sorry I had to hit you," added the shorter man. "Anyhow, have a nice day."

As the elevator rose gently to the 12th floor, Vogt recovered slowly. He touched where the sting remained on his face from the hard slap. The words, "Chips Brewer is not in the game any more" began to penetrate his consciousness. "And Pearl McCabe is gone." Troubling questions. Also, not a good way to start the day.

He took a sharp left turn down the paneled corridor to his office. "Get me the morning papers," he snapped at his secretary, Arlene South.

The occasional clients who visited Vogt in his office were always impressed with her calm efficiency. Her desk was clear, the computer station sat to her left, the monitor hidden from view. A warming smile implied an easy-going disposition, long legs leading the way to a slim waist, magnificent breasts, and a head of dark brown hair surrounding a perfect oval face. What remained hidden from view was a lust that emerged after work, and sometimes even surfaced in mid-day. This was not one of those days.

When she returned with the papers he said, "Call Henry Kriger at The Orchid Room and tell him I'll be in for lunch at 12:30."

Turning to the newspapers, he spread them across his desk and searched the headlines. On Page Two of the Inquirer he spotted what he was looking for.

Murder Victim Found
Behind Julianis' Restaurant

The body of Charles "Chips" Brewer, 48, was found late yesterday afternoon lying in a pool of blood in an alley behind Julianis' Restaurant three blocks from the Food Distribution Center in South Philadelphia. There were no witnesses to the crime and police are mounting a house-to-house search.

Brewer was a known figure in the community, having grown up in the area. There was no information about what he was doing behind the restaurant. Sergeant Greta Rogers of the Homicide Division is heading the investigation and she said, "We are looking into a number of different avenues. The victim was shot once in the head, something like a gangland style murder."

There was no need to read further. Vogt knew Brewer. What he didn't know was why he was murdered. He also didn't know who did it.

South appeared, carrying a silver tray with a small silver coffee pot. She poured a cup of steaming coffee and handed it to Vogt. "Is there anything I can do," she offered.

He looked at her closely. "You are a marvel of all that's good," he smiled. "But, this is different. Something is happening and I don't know what."

"Sure I can't help?" she asked.

"Just having you around is a comfort."

Reaching out, she ran her finger around his ear and then touched his lips. "I can distract you from whatever the problem is."

He took her finger into his mouth and then held her wrist as he slowly withdrew her hand. "Oh, you are good."

"Maybe later," she said softly.

Kissing the palm of her hand he added, "I sure hope so."

9

Trenton, New Jersey lies thirty miles north of Philadelphia. One of the bridges linking the two states carries the logo, "Trenton Makes, The World Takes." The home of some major manufacturing companies including the steel complex of the Roebling family, it is an old city. Famous for the historic site of Washington crossing the Delaware River with his bedraggled army to defeat the British during Christmas of 1776. It is also the state capital, a place where political battles are still being fought.

The face of the city has changed with the times, but many original buildings still stand, a sign of stability. Ethnic neighborhoods remain as protection against shifting events. Heavily populated Polish sections are matched by heavily populated Italian areas. Each has its unique meeting hall complete with facilities for congenial eating and drinking. Friendly local places for gathering and sharing, all marinated in the aromas of ethnic foods.

On any given day a select group of men sit in one corner of Roman Hall to take a glass of wine with lunch. For them, the chef comes out of the kitchen and asks, "What would you like today?"

Harry Waterhouse usually sets the menu. "I feel like a small antipasto, some gnocchi, more bread and olive oil, a bottle of Chianti from Orvieto, and maybe a canoli for dessert."

The four men sitting at the round table nodded in agreement. Whatever Harry wanted to eat was fine with them. In fact, whatever Harry wanted was fine with them. He was the boss. Without question.

"Gentle, but firm persuasion," was his motto. "Find a way to find a way," another rule to live by. After twenty years in the business his word was his bond and his rule.

Once, he was asked how he came by the name, "Waterhouse." His response joined the other anecdotes surrounding his reputation. "It's my name." Not very exciting, but certainly the final word. It defined a man who had decided who he wanted to be. There was no past, only a future. Or, as some of his associates said, "Don't ask."

When Frane walked through the door everyone was surprised because he was an interloper. No one showed any overt interest, some merely spoke in Italian to inquire of a waiter, "Who he?"

As if guided by a diagram, Frane walked directly to the table where the five men were seated. "Good afternoon, Mr. Waterhouse."

The four men examined the visitor with practiced eyes, measured him for bulges in his pockets and then sought some assurance from their leader. He quietly said, "It's alright. This is Mr. R.C. Frane, an acquaintance from Philadelphia. He and I are going to have a small talk. Will you excuse us, gentlemen?"

Adhering to protocol, Frane waited till the men left to find seats at a distant table. "Thank you for seeing me, Mr. Waterhouse."

Signaling to a chair on his right, Waterhouse said, "Will you have some lunch. I'm sure the chef has enough gnocchi. Perhaps a glass of wine?"

The formality of the setting was strange for Frane. He knew that he had to accept the offer. To break bread with the man who ran most of what was running in Trenton was an honor. Some might think of it as a command. But the way had been paved by a phone call from John Pentram.

"I understand you are a retired police lieutenant," Waterhouse said.

"That's correct. Spent twenty years on the job. Now, I'm a consultant."

"Just what does a consultant do?"

"Right now I'm doing some investigating."

"Oh?"

"Let me try again. I'm getting information for a client. He wants to know some things. I'm trying to satisfy his interest."

"Isn't that like being a cop all over again?"

"Yes and no. In the old days when I gathered information it was intended to catch a murderer. That was then."

"And now?"

"I'm assigned to find out certain facts. My clients then have the information they need to make decisions."

The waiter interrupted the conversation. "I brought a large antipasto so you and your special guest can help yourselves. Plenty of fresh bread and a dish of olive oil with garlic and olives. Good for soaking. Gnocchi when you are ready. Shall I pour some wine?"

When he left Frane asked, "With lunches like this, how do you keep yourself in such good shape?"

Waterhouse had the appearance of an aging athlete. Six feet tall, broad shoulders, 180 pounds, all fitted into a dark blue double-breasted suit. A starched white shirt, foulard tie, and silver cuff links jutting out of the sleeves. His full head of hair showed a few streaks of gray.

"I guess it's because I lead a good life. Exercise, watch my diet and try to behave myself."

"Sounds like the perfect formula for success."

"And you, Mr. Frane."

"I took up jogging two years ago. That helped me get my weight down and now my body is more responsive. In a number of ways."

"Your client called and asked if you could meet with me. How can I help?"

"Yesterday a man was shot in Philadelphia. I'm trying to get a fix on who he worked for, why he was shot."

"Is your client interested in that?"

"He instructed me to do some research. I have no knowledge of why he wants this information."

"I assume you're speaking of Chips Brewer?"

"You knew the man?"

Waterhouse moved his fork through his antipasto. Snared a piece of Provolone and lifted it to his mouth. "To be quite fair and because you represent an important man, yes, I knew him. But, only in the broadest sense. In the same way that I know dozens, hundreds of people."

"Any idea who he worked for? What he did for a living?"

Waterhouse answered cautiously. "I know very little, other than he ran some errands for people. Picked things up, carried messages. Nothing terribly serious."

"Among the things he picked up, could they have been bags of money? Or even drugs?"

"These are areas in which I have no knowledge. The man didn't work for me, so I can only guess what he was doing."

"Mr. Waterhouse, this is Trenton, Brewer was taken out in Philadelphia. My earlier experience suggests that people in the same lines of business usually have a sense of what goes on in other areas. You said you could only guess what Brewer was about. I'd appreciate you best thinking on this question."

Thoughtfully, Waterhouse responded, "Mostly the world has changed. This may come to you as something of a surprise, but there are people of power who have learned that using their skills they can do better in the world of business than in the more risky activities that attract the attention of the law enforcement community. My own thoughts are that Brewer didn't share that notion."

Frane nodded. Took a sip of wine and said, "Chianti is good in the afternoon."

"My dear Mr. Frane, Chianti is good whenever you drink it."

10

Captain George Bailey was his usual self. Despite all the training in how to get the best out of his people he often reverted to his natural authoritarian behavior, the result of a father who drank and a mother who died too soon. There were three Bailey children and George the oldest did his best to save his brother and sister from the Saturday night onslaughts when his father stopped off at the corner bar for a few drinks before coming home. He protected Thomas and Mary, taking the blows they might have received. Love hardened to hate with each thump or smash or slap across the face. By the time he was sixteen and tall enough to confront the aggression, the hate had blotted out any remaining love.

"Now listen up, Sergeant. This looks like an easy case. There's no doubt this was a mob hit. Who ever heard of an ordinary white-bread killer shooting the victim behind the left ear! Get real, find the damn perp!"

"Yes sir," was the best Greta Rogers could think to say. In the past RC Frane took all the flak from the Captain. Now that he left the department she stood in his place, lacking the title. Bailey had indicated that he wanted her to run the team. In time, a promotion might be in order.

"What do you know about this guy, Brewer?"

"He's small potatoes. Works for some of the heavies around town; sort of a part-time runner. Picks up packages that might have money. We don't know yet. Would you believe his wife wasn't sure what he did to make a living?"

"What did you pick up at the site? Anything resembling a clue?"

"If I was reconstructing what happened I'd say that the two of them walked around to the back of the restaurant and the perp took out a .22 and just shot Brewer."

"Any other ideas?"

"We haven't had much time to go through his check book and bank accounts. But, there is one interesting thing. He has a new Cadillac. Doesn't go with the two story row house he lives in."

"Maybe he was buying it on time. Or renting it."

"Any way you look at it we're talking about $500 a month, at least. Where does he get the dough to cover that?"

Bailey muttered, "Maybe you better find out."

Back in her office, the one that belonged to Frane, she sat with Peg Wilson and Milt Thomason. The two officers had worked with Rogers and Frane on a couple of earlier cases and she had requested their help. They constituted a team, three against the world.

"Let's talk," she started. "What do you think? You first Peg."

Wilson was anxious for success. The thought of being back on a beat gave her the incentive to read the manuals and prepare to take the Sergeants test. Rogers encouraged her, remembering her own drive to get ahead. Preparing this black woman for promotion would be a feather in her helmet. Besides, Wilson was tall and slender and could hit the soft ball a mile. Good for the inter-departmental competition.

"Nobody makes a living running errands. Picking up collections whether from the local bookie or a horse joint just doesn't pay enough. I'm thinking this guy was moonlighting. Somebody caught on and wanted to send a message, in case anybody else had a similar idea."

"What kind of moonlighting?"

"Maybe something on the side, picking up in somebody else's back yard. Stepping on toes that hurt."

"How about you, Milt?"

"Drugs. Gotta be drugs. You don't get shot for stealing a few bucks or bumping another carrier's territory."

40

"You mean pushing junk?"

"How about this?" Thomason added. "He makes a deal with somebody out of the area. That could be a real no-no. Peddling for a mover, say from Atlantic City."

"Then, of course, there's Pearl McCabe. She gets it the same way; her old man says she's a collector. Same job description."

"So, you're thinking that a local shooter gets the word to take both of them out because they're bringing stuff in from afar. Interesting. But who?"

"It's just a thought. When you get to knocking somebody off there has to be a really important reason."

"Let's work on that premise. Talk with your snitches; see if any junk is coming into the market from out of town. What else have we got?"

Wilson said, "I talked to the manager at Julianis'. He said Brewer just had a drink at the bar and another man joined him." Opening her notebook she found a page and added, "Says the other guy was new, but heard the name Jim used."

"They leave together?"

"Yeh. The second guy ordered a drink and never touched it. Then they left and maybe half-an-hour later is when we got the call. Found Brewer out back."

"Do we know who Brewer was working for?"

Now Thomason jumped in. "I nosed around with some of the patrons who were drinking in the afternoon. Word is this guy in West Philadelphia, Arthur; Thurman Arthur was paying the bill. He's into a bunch of stuff looks legal. He's involved in lot of businesses, restaurants, bars; that kind of thing. Never heard about any rough stuff. Course, that doesn't mean a thing. Never been charged. You know him, Peg? He's from your old neighborhood."

"I wouldn't exactly say I know him. He played football, big star. We used to hear about him. Got a nice reputation, quiet, strong."

Rogers had been taking notes. She looked up and said, "How about you two go to see this man. Ask around, see if he knows anything."

"Okay, boss. What you going to do?"

"I'm off to see the widow."

1 1

"You want me to come in to see you?"

"Let's meet in the park. You know where?"

"Sixth street side?"

"In about ten minutes. Can you make it?"

"I'm half way there. I'm at 36th and Chestnut headed into town."

"Good."

Frane knew the spot because Captain Bailey had met Pentram there on a number of occasions. Washington Square, across from the tomb of the Unknown Soldier, out in the open, one man on each end of the park bench. Nice day, late afternoon. Perfect.

The black Lincoln Town car pulled slowly into the no parking zone and Pentram got out, looked around, and walked into the park. Frane decided not to get up to greet him. Instead he sat cross-legged and waited.

Seating himself comfortably at the other end of the bench Pentram said, "Good afternoon."

"Thank you for the inside number. Haven't got much to report, but I wanted to get more instructions."

"Go."

"I met with the man in Trenton. He was cordial, gave me time, but didn't have much to say about Brewer. Before that; I met with the man in West Philadelphia and got a similar response. They both acknowledged that they knew Brewer as a small time runner. Beyond that, not much."

"What's your impression of these two meetings? Other than what they said to you?"

"It was almost scripted. They both said almost the same thing, as if it was rehearsed. My read is that they are both holding out. Just what, I'm not sure."

"Could Brewer be working for them, maybe on a part-time basis?"

"My guess is that Brewer needed money. Fancy car, couldn't get into his house, but I did get to meet his son. Wife is out of it, she didn't even know who he worked for or what he did. Can I ask if he was working for you?"

Pentram turned the question over in his mind. "We both realize we're touching on strange ground. I'm not accustomed to sharing information with people who work for me. And you are not accustomed to sharing information with people who might turn out to be suspects in some crime. So, let's define our relationship a little further."

Frane agreed. "So far I have not told anyone who my client is. Except that you arranged the meeting in Trenton. I have explained that I am gathering information so my client could make whatever decisions he or she deemed necessary. That is why I have asked for this meeting."

"Nor have I informed anyone that you are doing research for me. Should this be kept secret?"

"That's up to you. You are the boss."

"How do you work with your other clients?"

"They're not quite as sensitive as the work I do for you. Sometimes I even ask one to write a reference so I can meet a new prospect. However, as a consultant, I'm not exactly an employee. My thoughts are sought after."

Nodding understanding, Pentram continued, "Here is what I would like to do. Our relationship should be held confidential. Periodically we will meet, try to stay away from telephones, to discuss other requirements. When you have something to tell me, certainly get in touch. In the meantime, here is what I know and a little of what I think. Yes, Brewer was collecting for me. I have substantial holdings, money invested with small business people who repay on a regular basis. All these records, by the way are legal and computerized."

"May I ask, are the interest rates out of proportion?"

"Since these are bona fide business deals there are no interest rates. I share in the profits of the business. Perhaps you will gain a better understanding of my business involvements as we go forward."

"But, you see fit to have someone collect your share of the profits on a weekly basis?"

"Makes better business people out of my partners."

"And you said something about what you think."

"As you may imagine, the work of collecting is rather routine. Doesn't take much talent. Just pick up the money, leave a receipt, and bring it to my accountant. That leaves a lot of time on the collectors' hands."

"Since you have shared some of this rather confidential information, can I ask how many businesses you're involved in?"

"No, you may not ask. But, I'll help your thinking. Suppose there are ten, and each shows that my share of the profit for the week is, oh, say $300."

"Sounds reasonable."

"Then, let your imagination run away. Say, 20, or 30, and so on."

"Makes you a conglomerate of small businesses. Not exactly GE, but a similar model."

"I didn't realize that your consulting work extended that far."

"I'm still learning. You must have some organization. Keeping track."

"How else did you think I could afford such a high priced consultant?"

"I guess your partners share in some of these operations might be worth more than $300 a week."

"Reasonable assumption."

"If I understand, you probably have more than one collector. So, if Brewer took care of 25 collections, five a day and then returning to the office, that would be a full days work."

"You catch on pretty quickly."

"Most of this in cash?"

"None of your affairs."

"Gotcha."

"So, you figure Brewer was doing some things on the side?"

"Exactly."

"Any reason he shouldn't try to make a couple extra bucks?"

"Only if he was doing something illegal. Or something that would get him shot."

"He could give your business a bad name."

"I admire your perspicacity. That's why I need an expensive consultant."

"You came to the right place. Not the expensive part. The consulting part."

1 2

"Would you please tell me what's going on?" asked Vogt.

Arthur shrugged his shoulders and said, "What do you mean, Bob?"

"Brewer gets offed, two men confront me in the elevator this morning and want the names of the 'Three Jimmies', and it seems to me everything is coming apart."

"You gave them the names?"

"Either that or I wind up with a big lip and maybe a broken collar bone. What do you think?"

"Hell to get older. A few years back you would have taken them in no time at all. What were they, a couple of cheap hoods?"

"The way they were dressed, I think a big step above cheap. More like they were carrying some heavy hardware and I had no intention of arguing."

"Who sent them?"

"Come on, Thurman. You tell me."

The two men were seated in a quiet section of The Orchid Room, a space reserved for confidential talk. Henry Kriger the manager stopped to make sure everything was all right. "Got enough coffee? Have you decided what you want for lunch? Chef just made some Pepper Pot Soup that he claims is the best in Philadelphia."

"Sounds good, love soul food," answered Arthur. "And how about a cup of Chamomile tea."

"I'll have a Vodka Martini with a twist of lemon. No, make that an olive."

"On the way."

"Early in the day for drinking, isn't it?"

"Not when you've had the kind of morning I have had. Getting braced by a couple of tough guys in an elevator isn't my idea of fun."

"So, how can I help?"

"Tell me what's going on. I know about you and me. We have set up a beautiful business structure. There's one piece missing and maybe we can do that. But, what's this about Brewer?"

Arthur moved his water glass around, thinking about how much to share with Vogt. "Here's what I can tell you for sure. Brewer is meaningless. He was a small time collector. Let's just suspect he had his hand in the cookie jar. That's not nice. So, maybe somebody decided to get his hand out of the cookie jar."

"You telling me that just because he was lifting a couple of bucks somebody decided to get rid of him. Hard to believe."

"I'm just guessing," replied Arthur. "But, what's the difference. He was very small player."

Vogt snorted. "It attracts a lot of attention. Who needs that?"

Arthur shrugged again. "Nothin' to do with me."

"Look, Thurman. We've been together for a long time. Everything is straight up, no nonsense. If we can make the next step there's a lot of money to be made, all of it honest."

"That's what I like to hear. How to make lots of money—honest. So, we have about thirty restaurants lined up. How much you think we can squeeze out of the distributors?"

"Near as I can tell they spend about half-a-mil each. That comes to fifteen mil all told. Let's say we make a deal to funnel purchases to one place. Get a rebate of four points. Comes to six-hundred thousand, no sweat."

"All we got to do is insure the purchases. And we own maybe forty percent of the restaurants, so they gotta do what we say. No need to even tell them about the rebate. Or whatever you want to call it."

"Plus the partners' income from the profit. Could come to at least three-quarters-of-a-mil. Totals out to about one-point-three a year before

46

expenses."

Arthur smiled broadly. The creases in his face receded as happiness overtook worry. "Great to be in a legitimate business. Expenses for accounting and collecting only a hundred and fifty large a year. Not bad."

"Good thing you have a lawyer who works cheap."

Kriger returned, double-checking on two favored guests. Albeit they also were partners in his business. "Another drink, Bob?"

"Think I'll switch to food. After all, it's only one o'clock. How about a Caesar salad with blackened chicken. And, some Melba toast and black coffee. I have to work this afternoon."

"And you, Thurman?"

"One of your spring salads. Oil and vinegar on the side. And another cup of Chamomile tea."

"Who gets the bill today?"

"I do," said Vogt. "Put it on my American Express. I need the points."

"You saving up for a trip?" asked Kriger.

"Yeh. Thinking of flying to Paris for the weekend."

"Not bad."

13

Frane tried to think through his next assignment. At the suggestion of his client they agreed to let the police find the killer of Chips Brewer. "With Sergeant Rogers in charge of the investigation I'm sure we'll soon know who did what," Frane said.

"That's good. Now you can pursue some other avenues," answered Pentram. "Do you understand what we're trying to do? Straight forward, no twists and turns. Just a financial understanding."

"Let me go over this one more time. I'm going to approach a Foodservice Distributor, say Star Foods. Pretty much I'm going to guarantee them about $300,000 worth of business each week. Comes to around $15,000,000 a year. One delivery a week to each restaurant. No sales rep, orders placed according to a regular schedule."

"Yes."

"We, that is you, want four percent commission on the business. That's about what a sales rep would get."

"Not exactly, but close enough."

"Also, the bills would be paid weekly, after the first two orders are delivered."

"Yes."

"What makes you think they will accept without some kind of guarantee? After all, they don't know me from a row of canned tomatoes."

Pentram smiled. "You are a great cop, but I'm not so sure you understand business. Each of the restaurants is a valued customer. To extend them credit for two weeks is not a big deal. Particularly when the money starts to flow after the third week."

"So, how do you make out?"

"As my consultant you are obligated to maintain my confidences. That so?"

"Absolutely."

"Okay. If each restaurant averages $10,000 a week, and the credit terms to me are three weeks, it means I can go to these restaurants and tell them I'm buying an interest in their business for $30,000."

"How does that figure?"

"They pay for their food shipment every week. I take the money, bank it, and then give it to them at the end of the third week. That's my part of being an owner."

"How do you convince them to sell you a piece of the business for thirty grand? And how big a piece?"

"My dear Mr. Frane. You have no idea how convincing I can be."

"Oh."

"Of course, I shall also provide some additional services."

"Like?"

"My accounting people will be keeping the books. Easy matter once we get the computers running."

"So, you're going to be operating all these restaurants."

"Not me. I'm just going to be overseeing what's taking place. Several collectors, such as the now-deceased Mr. Brewer, will make regular visits to secure my fair share of the profits, as well as making sure that the food bills are paid."

"I don't get it," said Frane. "Seems like a lot of work."

"Ah, you have to keep an open mind. I want these businesses to be profitable. The more they make, the more I make. I don't mind sharing in the wealth. In fact, I'm anxious for my partners to make money. Keeps them happy."

"Then, why do they need you?"

"That's a very interesting question. You see, Mr. Frane, too many people are trying to avoid making a profit. My wish is for everyone to do well."

"What do you mean they are trying to avoid making a profit?"

"You're getting quite an education today. That's okay. I think we will have a long relationship, one of deep understanding and appreciation. Look, you read the papers about all these high powered executives and how they spend all their time trying to avoid taxes, cheating the government out of its' due. If they concentrated on just plain making money, they would be way ahead of the game. Sooner or later they get caught up in thinking they are smarter than everybody else."

"Forgive me for saying it, but isn't that what you're trying to do?"

"No, no, no. I am using the money in the best way I know how. All legal, all fair, and all taxable. Would you believe I love to pay taxes?"

"You love to pay taxes?"

"Think of it this way. The more I pay it means the more I have made. No profit, no taxes. More profits, more taxes. It's the American way."

Head reeling, Frane held his hands up as if to fend off any more assaults. The onrush of thinking left him wary and flustered. "There has to be a catch somewhere in here," he said.

"Indeed there is," said Pentram. "In fact it's amazing. When you have lived as long as I, engaged in the kind of activities that I have known in the past, taken the chances, risks, things you don't want to know about, there comes a time when wisdom takes over."

"Wisdom?"

"A realization that making money the honest way works."

1 4

Rose Fable Brewer, widow of Chips Brewer, mother of John Charles Brewer, sat quietly on the flowered couch in her living room. Her face was drawn into a mask that tried to hide the disbelief in her eyes. Once the smiling, dancing, high school cheer leader, she showed signs of constant house work, the necessary cleaning that went on day after day. What else was she to do? Her husband worked for a powerful man in the neighborhood who paid just enough.

When Chips bought the new Cadillac she thought it signaled a change in his luck. After twenty-four years of marriage he spoke of moving on, buying a larger house, taking a vacation. The annual trip to Wildwood for one week in the summer lost its' excitement after the fifth year. Still, it was all they could afford. Now, less than two months after he announced their new lifestyle, he lay dead next to an oversized green garbage container behind Julianis' Restaurant.

"Mrs. Brewer, I'm sorry about your husband," said Greta Rogers.

"Can you tell me, did he have any enemies?"

Hands folded in her lap, Rose Brewer answered, "He had all kinds of enemies."

"What do you mean, all kinds?"

"Everybody was his enemy. He never had a friendly word for anybody. It was always somebody else's fault."

"I'm afraid I don't understand."

Staring straight ahead she said, "He was my husband. When we got married I was just a kid, barely out of high school. He told me how good things would be, that he knew people, had a good job. It took me years to realize what a loser he was. Still, he was mine."

"When you say, 'loser,' what do you mean?"

"His job was nothing. He went around and collected money for one of the neighborhood toughs. An errand boy. That's all he ever was."

"Who did he work for?"

"He never told me by name."

"You mean after more than twenty years together you didn't know who he worked for?"

"I never wanted to know. I always thought it was something not really kosher."

"So, why do you say he had many enemies?"

"Because he was always telling me that when things went wrong it wasn't his fault. It was his boss, or somebody he was trying to collect from. He never took the blame for anything. Life was tough and his was tougher than anybody. A born loser."

"Then, his enemies weren't really people who didn't like him. Just that he blamed the world for his problems."

"You said it, baby. He was always right. They were always wrong. But, I don't think anybody hated him. He just had this hard-on with the world."

"When he told you things were going to be different, did he give any idea what was happening?"

"Yeh. Said he was going to expand his horizons. Do some things for another man, guy from West Philly."

"What kind of things?"

"Same routine, collecting, making deliveries. Like that."

"What was his work schedule? For instance, what time did he go out in the morning? Or, did he work nights?"

"Mostly it was afternoons and nights. He would leave home around noon, go to a restaurant, have some lunch, make a few calls, come home for dinner and then go out till ten, eleven o'clock."

"Doesn't sound like much fun for you."

"After a while you get used to it. I was going to try and get a job, you know maybe in a store, or a beauty parlor. Anything to keep busy. He wouldn't hear it. 'Not my wife,' he used to say. 'I make a living. My wife doesn't have to work.'"

Greta Rogers thought she had heard this all before, at another time in another place. Growing up in Frankford where men worked and women stayed home was the way of life. When she wanted to get a part-time job as a waitress, her father took it as an insult to his manhood. "Better you should do things around the house, help your mother."

The big blow-up came when she announced she was going to college; Philadelphia Community College. It was a new idea in the family; that anyone would go to college, especially a girl. Unheard of. Only after she registered on her own, made arrangements to work after school and pay her own way did her father relent. That was before she revealed her innermost desire; to be a cop.

Looking back, she realized her mistakes. No need to say what you were going to do—just do it.

"Mrs. Brewer, thank you for your help. We'll do everything we can to apprehend your husband's killer. In the meantime, if there is anything you can add to assist us; here is my card. Please call."

"Yeh. I think of anything I'll call." Then she added, "Know anybody wants to buy a slightly used Cadillac?"

15

Frane pulled against the curb and waited. Night had begun to encroach on the day and the early warmth turned to slight chill. He watched as Rogers found a space on the lot next to the Melrose Diner. Leaving his car he walked slowly toward where she was parked. As she lowered the window he said, "Not exactly the Ritz. But, we know the food."

"I thought you said you had a big check coming in and we could spend it anywhere."

He nodded. "Caught. Okay, this is just a beginning. I have two bottles of Cabernet and the video of 'Chicago.' We can go to your place after we eat, have some wine, watch the show. What do you say to that?"

"You're about as exciting as 'Dinner at the diner.'"

"Hey, things could be worse. We could be working."

The Melrose is unique. Maybe the only diner in the country where the booths seat as many as six people; all strangers. That's the rule. Two people take a booth that seats four, two more will be seated with them. Makes for good company and lively conversation. Certainly no place for holding hands and thinking about after-dinner sex.

"Every time we eat here," Rogers said, "we enjoy the food and the atmosphere. It's just one-of-a-kind. Don't forget, let's pick up an apple pie to take with us."

They were signaled to a booth and welcomed, "Have a good dinner."

An elderly couple turned out to be their eating companions. "You folks from around here?" the man asked.

"Not exactly," Frane said. "We just come for fun and talk. How about you?"

"We eat here at least three times a week," the woman answered. "Been coming here for more than twenty years."

"Try the meat loaf," the man added. "It's great with their mashed potatoes. You know, they make them from fresh. None of that canned stuff."

"I didn't know mashed potatoes could come from a can."

"Oh, yeh. You can get the same thing in the supermarket. Just add hot water, a little butter and some salt. Whip it around with a spoon and you got mashed potatoes. But, I been in the kitchen here. They got a great big mixer, really big and they mash whole cooked potatoes. Reminds me of when I worked in the kitchen when I was in the navy."

"Again, with the war stories," the woman said.

"That's okay," Rogers smiled. "Tell me more. I don't know a heck of a lot about cooking. What else about this place?"

Puffed up the man said, "You know they must use fresh apples by the ton. That's their biggest pie. But, in season, blueberries, cherries, and peaches. Make the best pies in town."

"Look," said Frane, "tonight's special is hot dogs and baked beans."

"Take it," the man said. "Where else will you get fresh baked beans?"

"What'dya mean, fresh baked beans?"

"Not canned. Start with the dry beans, soak 'em, cook 'em, add tomato sauce, a couple pieces of ham, and lots of brown sugar. Then they get baked again."

"You sound like an expert," Frane said.

"After twenty years, what did you expect?"

"So, you two cops?" the woman asked.

"That's a strange question," said Rogers.

"Not so strange. Lots of cops eat here. When they're not drinking."

Frane laughed. "Where did that come from?"

"Hey, look out the window, across the street. See that bar. Bet there are a dozen cops in there now."

"Along with another dozen citizens just relaxing at the end of the day."

"What made you think we're cops?" asked Rogers.

"Cause you look like cops."

"Damn," said Frane. "And we thought these disguises were good."

"No kidding. You really cops?"

"I am," said Rogers. "My friend here used to be. But, now he's a consultant."

The woman nudged the man. "Told you so. Minute I saw them. They just look like cops."

The waitress came to the table and asked, "What'll it be, officer?"

Frane and Rogers looked at her, smiled and said, "That obvious?"

"Spot 'em a block away. Try the dogs and beans. They're very good."

With a nod they both answered, "Done."

16

Rogers carried the apple pie.

"Find anything on Brewer?" he asked.

"RC, I'm a little uncomfortable. Not sure how to answer. Or if I should answer at all."

"This is new ground for both of us," he answered. "But, let's be realistic. First of all, you know I'm a confidential person. Second, if I really wanted information I'd go to Bailey. He'd give me all I needed. More important you and I have a relationship goes way back. So, if I'm asking, no way I want to get you in trouble. It was just a casual question. Besides, my client isn't interested any more."

"Tell me who your client is and I'll tell you about Brewer."

"Greta, you know I can't do that. This consulting thing has certain rules, understandings between two people. In this instance I'm committed to secrecy."

"Right. I understand," she scolded. "I tell all and you tell nothing. Doesn't seem quite fair."

The laughs at dinner, the talk with the older couple, even the jibes of the waitress were all suddenly depreciated. *To Rogers it suddenly appeared that getting together was Frane's way of gaining information. The man who had trained her, promoted her, and on many occasions loved her, was now using her.*

"My head is spinning from work," she said. "How about we skip tonight. Here, you take the pie."

Frane stood aside as she got into her car. "What am I going to do with two bottles of wine?"

"Red wine just sits quietly. Keep them on their side, so the cork stays wet."

Rogers wheeled the car towards Broad Street and headed into town. She stayed on Broad Street, turned right on Race Street and then made her way to the Round House. *The last conversation was more than upsetting, it was damaging. She remembered the shooting, when she killed a two-bit robber who had a gun aimed at Frane. It took months with the police psychologist to grapple with taking a life. Even in defense of her partner. They had a lot of history between them.*

This was more than a tiff, this was a full-blown disagreement; a sharp cut that separated them in ways unimaginable. She coasted to a stop, turned off the motor, and rested her head on the steering wheel. "Eight years together, almost day and night, and I blew it. What was the big deal about sharing some stuff with him?"

Frane stood still. He was rebuked and rebuffed at the same time. The apple pie weighed heavy in his outstretched hands. Light from the opening door of the diner caught his attention. The older couple was coming down the steps. He walked toward them, extended the pie and said, "My friend thought you might like to have an apple pie. I think it's still warm."

1 7

"Oh, it's you."

"Surprised?"

"Not many things surprise me anymore."

"I was feeling pretty rotten. Anyhow, you going to invite me in?"

She stood there in bare feet, an ill-fitting T-shirt with a Phillies imprint, red running shorts, and almost no make-up. He realized that between the "h" and the "e" were two unencumbered breasts.

Opening the door wider, she motioned him inside. "See you still have the two bottles of wine."

"Well, we can just set them aside for some future time. I wanted to come around to straighten things out."

"Look, RC, I know these are strange times. Here I am in the midst of my first case and you're still acting like my boss."

"Okay, G. You're right. I was off base. But, that shouldn't be the end of the road. Hell, we have history." *It's hard to say these words; they came out slow, quietly. All the years in Homicide taught me to keep my own council. Matters of the heart never take precedence over matters of murder. Even though I'm no longer in an official position, it's tough being open. Just as it took time to become a hardened detective, it's gonna take time to become a softened man.*

"Think it's safe to open one of those bottles?"

"It may not be safe, but it could help. Don't forget, you owe me."

"I owe you? How's that?"

Again, the words had trouble gathering enough energy to leave his mouth. Finally he blurted, "Dammit. You saved my life."

Rogers laughed heartily. "Sure, I killed the sonovabitch who was going to shoot you. Doesn't that mean you owe me? Man, you got it backassward."

Frane moved closer. He took her by the shoulders, pressed her to his chest and said, "You don't understand. Since you saved my life you have to take care of me. I'm now your responsibility. Try to think of it as a reward for a courageous deed."

She didn't answer. Then, very smoothly she raised her arms holding tight to the t-shirt and lifted it over her head. With a deft motion she pulled the red shorts down and tossed them aside. "If you're my reward, we better get to it."

Later, stretched out in her queen-sized bed they talked softly. "Are you going to open one of those bottles?"

"I'm so relaxed now, not sure I got the strength to get up."

"Well, we had dinner, had a fight, and had some fun. Sounds like a full day. Guess the wine can wait. Anyhow, who are you working for?"

"One client is just a small store. Small meaning privately owned, six or seven employees. Things are missing so he called me in. I'm in the middle of making some security arrangements. Would you believe he doesn't even have an alarm system? Anyhow, there are some things he can do to keep track of his inventory. Like get a computer."

"That's sort of a no-brainer. You get paid for that?"

"Handsomely."

"What else?"

"I have a pretty fair size paper distributor. You know the kind, enormous warehouse, lots of doors. Business grew pretty big and the idea of security never got much attention. There's nothing wrong at the moment, but the owner wants to get ahead of the game."

"And the big one, the one wants to know about Brewer?"

Frane sat up and dangled his legs to the floor. "G, I'll tell you. But, before I do, you have to know I think you're better off not knowing."

"Okay, I'll only listen with one ear."

"Heavy confidential?"

"Whatever you say."

"You won't get sore, no matter who it is?"

"Promise."

The words came out in a whisper. "John Pentram."

She sat straight up and grabbed a piece of sheet as a cover. Deciding no comment was the order of the day she slipped into a pair of panties and a bra. Walked slowly toward the bathroom, turned and said, "You're right. I was better off not knowing."

"Does this make a difference? Between us, I mean."

"Make a difference? You floor me. Just suppose," she paused, "just suppose I have to do something that has to do with Pentram. We know him as an important player on the other side of the table. Means we would be on opposite sides of the table. You think that makes for an enduring relationship?"

"Look, I'm working on a very big deal with him. Very big. But, it's all legal. I'm a consultant carrying out an assignment. Purely legal business."

"Gimmie a clue."

"Confidential?"

"Until I think it's off base."

"Man has an idea about putting together the purchasing power of some restaurants he either owns or maybe he's a partner. Wants to use that purchasing power to buy better. See anything wrong in that?"

Rogers sat on the edge of the bed. "I'm not so good with this business stuff. No, it doesn't sound bad. But, suppose he owns these restaurants because he forcefully showed them who was boss?"

"Like how?"

"C'mon, RC. He has a background of being in the enforcement racket. You hold a gun to somebody's head they'll do whatever you want. Sounds like you're new to this game."

"You know damn well I wouldn't be part of anything illegal. This is just plain smart business. Like buying something in quantity, you get an inside discount. And, follow this, you pay taxes on your income."

She shook her head in amazement.

"All open and above board," he continued. "Too many people involved to try to cheat Uncle. Besides, like the man said, 'More taxes you pay means more money you're making.'"

She frowned in disbelief. "RC, let's cool it for a while. See what happens."

18

The Irish Pub is a good place to get an oversize sandwich and a cold beer. Fries next to the food are curly, something the chef thinks are "cute." They're spicy and add to the need for yet another beer. Preferably something imported that carries a higher profit. A comfortable place even though the captain's chairs are hard.

When the two men in the double-breasted dark suits came through the door they were in contrast to the informal working-class surroundings. No heads turned, but notice was taken. They moved toward a round table where three men were seated, drinking their beers straight from the bottle. One of the suited men pulled an extra chair up to the table and both men sat down.

"Jimmy, Jimmy, Jimmy. Nice to see you boys all together before you left town."

"You know us?"

"Got your names from a friend. But, everybody knows, 'The Three Jimmies.'"

The second suited man said, "After all, your reputation preceded you. Trenton isn't that far away."

"Trenton?" questioned the middle Jimmy. "Where's that?"

The first suit looked at the second suit and said, "Smart, eh?"

"Let's cut to the bottom right off. You three did a friend of ours. In fact, I understand you also did a woman who is also a friend. Maybe not all of you, but at least one of you. So, if you want to make things easy, why not just belly-up, take your punishment and we can all go back to work."

The one called, "Big Jimmy" decided to answer. "We're not looking for any trouble. Why don't you two just shove off before I break your head."

The second suit said to the first suit, "Sounds like a very tough guy. Must come from Trenton. I think they talk that way up there."

"Yeh. It's a tough town. But, this is Philadelphia. Guess they don't know the rules. You know, about peace and quiet. You want to talk to the big guy?"

"Think he might want to step outside with me for a little talk. Sort of get things in perspective?"

"Here's what I think. My Sig Sauer is looking at these two Jimmies. How about you and the big guy step through the back door and have your talk. I'll wait here for you. Take the door out by the toilet. Do be careful, he looks strong."

"What kind of shit is this? We're just passing through and stopped for a bite of lunch. You want trouble, that's my middle name."

"You talk too much, Jimmy. Best thing for you is to sit still with this other Jimmy. Won't take too long."

"You bet it won't," said Big Jimmy. "C'mon you little pissant. I'll even walk first."

"Oh, we can go together. Hold hands if you like," said second suit.

"I'm gonna keep my hands out in the open. Do it Trenton style."

The two men rose and walked slowly toward the rear of the Pub. Big Jimmy opened the door, looked outside, found a backyard where cases of empty beer bottles were stacked waiting for the next delivery. He turned, faced the second suit and backed several steps, hands extended at his side. He figured the extra fifty pounds would help him pulverize the fancy-Dan in the suit.

Second suit stood quietly, arms hanging loosely at his sides. His eyes seemed disconnected, as if he was in a different place. Another strength, one learned in his martial arts classes, took control of his body. He visualized the lessons he had learned. The stiff fingers forged into steel rods protruding from the ends of his hands. The practiced speed as they flashed toward Big Jimmy, reaching just below the rib cage, plunging into the soft flesh before curling upward and grabbing the lower ribs; then with an equally powerful withdrawal, tugging, pulling, and separating them from the other ribs. This could be a fatal blow. Second suit decided that significant damage was all that was necessary. Enough to ruin the career of Big Jimmy who would wish he died. The pain was severe, excruciating; unbelievable.

Looking down at the fallen man, Second Suit stepped back. In less than ten seconds he had reduced the big man to a huge lump of humanity writhing on the ground. One cracked rib hurts like hell. Six cracked ribs are unbearable. Leaning down close to the panting man he asked, "Who pulled the trigger on Chips Brewer?"

Big Jimmy could hardly breath. Inhaling the air he needed to sustain life reached unimaginable levels of agony. The damage sent tremors of relentless pain that brought tears flooding down his cheeks. "Duncan," was all he could mutter.

Moving back into the bar, Second Suit approached the table and said, "I think Big Jimmy wants to see you, Duncan. Curtin, you sit still."

Using their names sent a message that no amount of cover would conceal their identity. "How'd you know who we are?"

"Same way you don't know who we are. Let's go."

With Duncan in the lead the two men returned to the back door. The sight of Big Jimmy curled up on the concrete; face twisted in anguish stunned Jimmy Duncan. He turned to face Second Suit, who smiled slightly and said, "That wasn't nice to shoot Chips."

"I didn't even know the guys' name. Just following orders."

"I know," said Second Suit as he raised his Sig Sauer. The silencer muffled the two shots that tore through his chest.

First Suit said to Curtin, "You get to take care of your friends. And don't forget to tell your boss. He'll want to know what happened. Just tell him the score is settled. Should be peace after this."

"Who you working for?" asked Curtin.

"Your boss will know. He knows how things work. You take out one of ours, we have to repay the compliment."

Suit Two added, "You better see after your friends."

19

Frane pulled into the customer parking area in front of the warehouse. Twenty years of police work taught him to plan what he was going to say. Simple steps, one point at a time, get agreement on small issues before moving to tougher issues.

Chasing bad guys always gave me an inner charge. The excitement of catching a culprit, particularly in homicide, satisfied my need for a challenge.

Never quite thought of it that way. Dealing with honest people is a new kind of challenge. Do they think differently than criminals? How can you tell if they're straight? This is an unusual place to be. And I'm working for a man known for his other-world activities. What the hell am I doing here?

Before getting out of the car, he opened his small black notebook, flipped several pages and came to the notes he had taken during his conference with John Pentram. A list of subjects to be covered. He considered them, tried to follow the logic and then closed the book and headed to the front door.

The telephone operator behind the bulletproof glass looked up. "Can I help you?"

"RC Frane to see Mr. Star."

"Do you have an appointment, Mr. Frane?"

"No."

"Can I tell him what it's about?"

"No."

Put off, she responded, "I'll see."

She swung around and faced away from Frane before touching button number one on the inner-office communication bank. "Mr. Star. A Mr. RC Frane to see you. He said he has no appointment and he won't tell me his business."

She nodded her head. "Yes sir."

Turning to Frane she said, "Take a seat over there. He'll be right out."

Frane had been here before, but on official business. This was just business. He took time to examine the row of pictures that detailed the growth of the company. Star Distributing started out small more than fifty years ago, probably when Star senior founded the company. The four framed shots grew in size even as the company had expanded.

The door opened and Mr. Star appeared. "Good to see you again, Lieutenant. Hope this is pleasure and not another murder."

"One things for sure, Mr. Star. This is not anything official. Maybe you didn't know, but I have retired from police work."

"That's a surprise." Waving him in, he added, "Let's go to my office. Is this a cause for some sort of celebration?"

"Well, yes and no," answered Frane. "Sort of depends on you."

"Sounds ominous."

"Not really, just different." Sitting at the round table Star used for special meetings, Frane said, "Thing is this. I'm really too young to not work. So, I have become a consultant."

"Well, how can I help? You offering your services? What kind of consultant?"

"Let me just say I'm doing a couple of different things. I have been asked by a client to approach a couple of foodservice distributors and present them with a proposition."

Laughing, Star said, "Is this the kind of offer I can't refuse?"

Frane sensed he had started off on the wrong foot. In an almost apologetic manner he said, "Please understand, I don't know a lot about your type of business. I'm here to talk about a couple of business ideas that may prove useful and profitable. If you find what I have to say sounds good, we can take it further and go into more detail."

Star appeared skeptical. Former homicide detectives might be interested in security for the distribution center. Or maybe some form of screening for employees. Or catching people stealing. "Why don't you just tell me what's on your mind and I can direct you to the right person who can give you an answer."

Frane nodded. "My client is putting together a concept he calls The Food Buying Group. This group will initially consist of ten restaurants that buy about four to five million dollars a year. By consolidating their purchases along with a couple of other ideas, he plans to deal with a single company. You know, like Star Distributing."

Still skeptical, Star said, "That's very interesting. Been done before you know. But a couple of million dollars a year isn't very impressive. Are these privately owned restaurants?"

"From what I know, these are private restaurants in the sense that they are not part of a chain. Just a group of like-minded individuals who think they can save money by consolidating their purchases."

Star leaned back in his seat. "As I said, this kind of thing has surfaced in the past. Not necessarily a bad idea, but it doesn't seem to take hold. Maybe if there was more to it the idea might be appealing."

"How would it sound if there were twenty restaurants averaging orders of $5,000 a week? Would that be more appealing?"

"You just upped the ante."

"How about if there were thirty restaurants averaging orders of $10,000 a week?"

Star got up, went to his desk and returned with a calculator. He punched in the numbers and said, "That comes to $15,000,000 a year. Are you saying your client controls that much potential?"

"Mr. Star, I'm sort of new at this business. You know, just delivering some information. What I have been told is that for a restaurant to buy $10,000 a week means they would do about $30,000 a week in business. Is that about right?"

Head nodding, Star said, "That's pretty accurate. With our broad line of merchandise, it might even be more if you add in paper goods, equipment and supplies, and a few other things, like cleaning materials."

"Does this sound good?"

"I'll tell you, Lieutenant, sure it sounds good. But so does peace in the Middle East. Making it work is another story. In the past the people who have agreed to these kinds of deals find all manner of reasons to get out. What makes you think your client can make it work?"

Deciding to avoid this kind of discussion Frane asked, "Are there any other particulars you need to know at the moment?"

"Who is going to be responsible for the bills? Each restaurant on their own?"

"That may require a little negotiation. However, my client said to tell you he would put up one week's bills in advance. However many restaurants are on board, you get a bone fide check for an agreed amount. Three weeks later you begin to get regular weekly checks. So, while you're holding one week's bills in advance, you are only extending credit for two weeks. How does that sound?"

Now Star began to pay close attention. He recognized that his outstanding accounts usually ran around thirty days. Turning money over in fifteen days was very attractive. He looked for the catch. "And what does your client get for all this generosity?"

"Considering he is fronting a lot of dollars and being responsible to see that you are satisfied, he gets four percent."

"What about pricing?"

Frane looked at the notes in his black book. "Based on your costs, the mark-up will be 13 percent."

Controlling himself Star answered, "If I have to pay four percent that leaves nine percent. That's a losing proposition. Our expenses are more than that."

Still trying to imply a lack of understanding, Frane asked, "Well, you would still have the cash discount which I think comes to about one-and-a-half percent."

Star agreed reluctantly.

Continuing, Frane said, "And there are always quantity deals from your suppliers. What does that amount to?"

Grudgingly Star said, "Between one and two points."

"Is the money turnover every two weeks interesting?"

"Yes," he admitted. "But, how about deliveries?"

Realizing he was succeeding, Frane said, "Once we get the volume we're talking about we would limit deliveries to twice a week. Think in terms of a drop of seven or eight thousand followed by a two to three thousand follow up, like at the end of the week."

Star stood, walked to the window, thought for a minute before asking, "When do you have to know? This is all coming at me fast. Lots of things I need to think about."

20

Greta Rogers was having problems with Tony Schindel. As the detective in charge he reported to her. As the Criminalist on the case he felt that he knew more than the Sergeant. Not only that, he was a man.

"Let's clear the air, Tony," she said. "Tell me what you saw, what you think about the crime scene."

"Sure, Sarge," he smiled. "Glad to help you with this case."

"Knock it off," she demanded. "If you don't like what you're doing, just say so and I'll have Captain Bailey transfer you to another case."

"Don't go hoity-toity on me," he said.

Resigned, she asked, "Did you walk the grid?"

"Of course I did. It was a small alley, didn't take long. Up one side, down the next. Very easy scene."

"So?"

Referring to his notes, he answered, "Just two sets of footprints, the vic and the perp. No scuffle, the vic half a step ahead before he gets it."

"How could you tell that?"

"Some of the footprints tended to overlap, like one man was walking

69

behind the other. Then, at a certain point they stop. Perp goes down, lying flat on his face with two bullets in his head. Near blew his head away."

"And the second set of prints?"

"Just turned around and walked away. Reached a car in the lot and that was it."

"Could you tell from the prints if he was tall, short, heavy, skinny, big feet, fancy shoes, something to go on? You know a clue here a clue there."

"Nothing significant."

"Why don't you let me decide what's significant?"

"I'm telling you, nothing to get excited about."

Disgusted she asked, "Tire tracks?"

"Running them through the system. Looks like a big car. Lincoln or a Caddy."

"Anything else?"

"My opinion, the perp held a gun to this guy's back and walked him to his death. Probably had a silencer. Imagine you'll find they had lunch together. ME can tell you that. Easy hit."

"You've been a great help," she added, hardly covering her frustration. Schindel had been around for years, doing a modest job and carrying a big mouth. Lots of talk when it came to what he thought and not much in the way of useful information. Time in position kept him where he was. The idea of referring to him as a Criminalist bothered Rogers. He was a hold-over-hack. There's one in every department. Sometimes more than one.

Adding to her frustration was the reality that she wasn't getting anywhere. Chips Brewer was hit, obviously a planned job. She knew he worked for John Pentram, doing a little collecting work, all presumably on the up-and-up. His wallet was in his pocket, a couple of hundred dollars in cash, and the usual driver's license, Blue Cross along with some credit cards. Peg Wilson checked the charges for the last three months and found nothing out of the ordinary.

I can't seem to think. Used to be when RC was around we could always come up with some fresh ideas. Damn.

21

Philadelphia overflows with history. From the startling 37-foot high statue of William Penn atop the 548-foot tall City Hall to Elfreth Alley, the oldest continuously occupied residential street in the country. In easy walking distance from the Betsy Ross House that is credited as the place where the first American Flag was designed, are the earliest vestiges of religious freedom in the colonies. Every faith remembered by significant houses of worship.

Not the least among these reminders of the past is the City Tavern, where members of the First Continental Congress met and ate and slept in an informal setting. Built in 1772 the original burned in 1834 and was finally demolished in 1854. In 1948 the National Historical Society commissioned a reproduction and it was finally completed in 1976 in time for the Bicentennial Celebration. Still, specialties of the restaurant remain to this day as leading items on the menu. West India Pepperpot Soup, an amalgam of beef, pork, taro roots, and greens is synonymous with the City of Brotherly Love. The ten independent dining areas serve Corn Meal Fried Oysters, Sausage Mélange, a blend of beef, turkey and fried leeks, and Pennsylvania

Dutch Sauerkraut.

"Strange place, this."

Lifting his glass of Merlot as if in a toast, "I like to come here. It gives me a sense that life is short, history is long."

"Still, it's a strange place to discuss business."

"Not so," answered Pentram. "Entirely appropriate when you consider the kinds of business that was discussed here. Don't you find the precedent appealing, knowing that you may be walking in the footsteps of the founders of the country?"

"You really think what we are doing ranks with those people?"

Slowly Pentram rotated the wine glass. His eyes showed a slight glaze as if he was transported to another place. In a lowered voice he reflected, "My father came to this country before World War I. Basically he was a farmer living in the city. So, he learned a trade, cobbling shoes. To say he worked hard says nothing. He married, raised five children with my mother, bought a small house and managed to save a few dollars. His aspirations were limited; putting food on the table was a constant struggle. With it all, it was better than life in the old country. There were times he wanted to go back, just to see what changes had taken place. But, who had the money to pay for such a trip."

"You have confused me, Mr. Pentram. What has that to do with having dinner at The City Tavern?"

"It puts things in context. My father took the initiative to come to this country, which provided me and my brothers and sisters the opportunity to lead a different kind of life. Now it's my chance to help my children go even further." He signaled to the waiter, "Would you bring us a bottle of Mouton Cadet, '94."

"From what you're saying you have a master plan. Give me some idea of what you're after and I'm sure I can offer ways to fulfill your desires."

The waiter arrived, showed the label, cut the foil and twisted the corkscrew into the neck of the bottle. With only a small tug he deftly removed the cork, showed that it was damp, that the bottle had been lying on its side, and then poured a small amount into a fresh glass.

Pentram swirled the wine, tested the bouquet, and then savored just enough to give the wine full rein on his taste buds. With a nod of the head he acknowledged acceptance, even as he motioned to fill the glasses.

Once again, she started, "So, how can I do what you would like to see done?"

"You come from a different environment. That's good. What I want to do is consolidate some of my affairs. You realize that I have a number of business interests. These have changed over the years. Currently, I am building what I think will be the biggest and most profitable of all. And, you will be happy to know, very business-like."

"Does that mean you want to divest yourself of some of the older businesses?"

"Ah, you are good. That's what I was told, Miss Mercado. By the way, I know you do work with Harry Waterhouse in Trenton and Martin Seelman in Camden. Are you at liberty to tell me who else you work with?"

"I'm licensed in New Jersey, Pennsylvania, and Florida. Some of my clients have retired to the south. Seems they want to get out of the cold."

"Isn't it confusing, dealing with different laws in different states?"

"True, but I am 'Of Counsel' to several firms. Means I have access to more geographic areas, and a bit of legal help if needed."

"Does that mean you don't want to tell me who else you work with?"

She smiled, a showing of strong white teeth accented by bright red lips. Her long black hair was brushed back. When she walked into the restaurant he noticed the erect posture carried on long slim legs. "Would you want me to tell my other clients that I work for you?"

This did not call for an answer. Instead he said, "And your fee?"

"In a sense it depends on what needs doing. We can work on an hourly basis, a contract basis, or any other way you care to consider."

"Such as?"

"Mr. Pentram, you are a man of many interests. I too, am a person of many interests. Money in and of itself is not the initial goal. Perhaps, as we go forward I can join with you in some of your ventures."

"Interesting. In almost all of my activities I have been the sole owner. The idea of having a partner never really appealed to me. Let's have some dinner and talk some more."

The table server who had been assigned to their station, his only duty for the evening, came over immediately to announce the specials of the day.

"If you're really hungry, the Turkey Pot Pie is something remarkable."

22

"Pretty fancy."

"Sort of what I had in mind."

"Can we afford this? Is your consulting business going that well?"

"No problem. And, yes, consulting is going well."

Rogers was glad she had changed into her favorite black pantsuit. She wore a white silk blouse, rather high-heel shoes and had stuffed her gun into her black leather shoulder bag. "Don't leave home without it," wedged in her mind.

"It's good to see you in this setting," she said to Frane. "Enough with the take-out Chinese dinners at home. But, this is some classy place."

"I just sort of discovered it," answered Frane. "Interesting, those few steps leading to a red door. If you didn't know this place was here you wouldn't know it was here."

"French, isn't it?"

You could not tell from the décor. The small room they were in had only two tables of four and three tables for two. Other dining rooms at Deux Cheminees were larger. This was intimate dinning at its best. The silver sparkled, each table had fresh flowers, the dark wood reflected the early 19th century, and the massive gold-framed pictures on the walls were a perfect fit for a town house in the center of Philadelphia. Windows looking out on Locust Street gave the impression that an outside world existed that did not interfere with the calm of refined dining.

"Haven't you noticed that French cooking lives in some foreign country? What we have here is a great chef using all the cooking ideas to offer superb eating. The lines are blurred between one style and another."

Now, she laughed. "RC, you have become a piece of work. Where did you pick up all these fancy interpretations? Where did you get all this high-type language? You used to be a straight up-and-down cop." Almost convulsed she added, "What ever happened to the downtown, meat-and-potatoes, pizza-loving, murder-chasing man I once knew? Where did you go wrong?"

A shadow of dismay crossed his face. "I thought this would be a big treat. Would you rather leave and go to McDonald's?"

"Don't be such a jerk," she said. "This is terrific. Let's have a good bottle of wine. They have a great list. Hell, we could eat for a week on what some of this stuff costs."

Properly reprimanded he answered, "White or red? Or, do you want to start with something stronger? We have all night."

"How about we just talk about old times over a glass of Scotch, Blue, if they have it. Then we can get serious."

"Blue?"

"Since you have all this money from consulting that you want to spend on me, why not the best?"

"What's Blue?"

She reached across the small table and touched his hand. "It's a step up from Johnny Walker Red and Black."

Startled, he asked, "Besides, when did you start to drink Scotch?"

"You have been away for a while. I got introduced a couple of days ago. Some of the guys were out for a drop and I tried Scotch. Makes for a wonderful start to a good time. We are going to have a good time, aren't we?"

"It's been strange, getting used to a different life style. At least for me. So, sure, let's go for a good time. I miss you."

Touched by a degree of intimacy that rarely surfaced in the past, she smiled broadly and answered, "I miss you too. Maybe you should reenlist or maybe I should become a consultant."

The waiter wearing a tuxedo interrupted. "Care to hear about the chef's specials for this evening?"

"Not yet. Why don't you bring us two Blue Label Scotches, neat, and a wine list? After a couple of minutes we'll talk about specials."

Turning back to Rogers, he said, "Just to change the subject for a moment, how are things at the Round House?"

Without being too specific Rogers said, "The Captain is still behaving in the normal fashion. Makes some noises, but really is supportive. When you left he insisted I keep Wilson and Thomason, so my life has been okay."

"You going to take the Lieutenant's test?"

"Bailey's pretty good. He's guiding me through some of the steps and he said he would tell me when to make my move. You know, when there might be an opening, how to go about it, what to study. He has been trying real hard. Seems caught up in all this diversity stuff."

"We talked about this once before. You have the makings. Why not go for it. You're a good cop."

"Trouble with being a good cop is it becomes a 24/7 life. I thought tonight we could just talk about, oh, world affairs, how the president is doing, and maybe even S-E-X."

"You're right. I know about all the other stuff. But, that last thing, I need more information. Maybe even some practical experience. Yeh, I could use some of that."

"Does that mean we're not going to have wine with dinner?"

"Just the opposite. This is a great place for relaxed eating and drinking. Portions are the right size and the desserts are incomparable. Just wait till you try their Napoleon."

"It's only been a couple of months and you sure have changed."

"How's this, let's languish over dinner and food, think dirty, and go home and try out that sex stuff."

"I'll try to contain myself."

23

Pentram liked the city. In particular he liked all of South Philadelphia from Market Street to the bend in the Delaware River and west as far as the Schuylkill River. This was where he grew up, went to public school, knew the neighborhood and did his best to stay with what he knew. Walking the streets from his small family home on 17th Street, north on Broad Street often as far as Walnut Street, a far-reaching jaunt that allowed him to remember the "Old Days." It troubled him when parking in the middle of Broad Street was permitted. The increase in cars made it necessary, but to his mind it cut the street in half and changed the wide expanse into nothing more than a glorified parking lot.

Further along, the changes taking place as the Avenue of the Arts developed were impressive. Looming above it all was the new Kimmel Center, an enormous modern structure, standing near but not replacing the Academy of Music. Moving along Pine Street, he looked into the windows of the shops along Antique Row. Four blocks of small stores with inviting artifacts overflowing; all intended to attract collectors. He usually turned left on Ninth Street where the extended borders of the Pennsylvania Hospital dominated and traced his steps for three blocks to Walnut Street and another left past the Wills Eye Hospital. All places locked into his memory, institutions that made the city great.

On this day he turned right on Locust Street, just before reaching Walnut and walked the block-and-a-half to Washington Square, where the Tomb of the Unknown Soldier stands close by the statue of George Washington. This was a favorite place where he met with friends, colleagues, and business acquaintances. By appointment only. John, Jr. was waiting for him on his preferred bench on the southeast corner of the Square.

"Good walk, pop?" the young man asked.

"You should try it. You could use the exercise. Besides, there's no better way to understand and appreciate the city."

"Pop, we been over this a couple dozen times. I like the city, but not like you. In case you forgot, I'm thirty-two-years old. So, I know what's going on."

Thinking out loud, Pentram said, "My father came from the old country, had the guts to pick up and leave so he could raise his family and get away from some of the bad guys. He almost succeeded."

Now the younger Pentram sat quietly. He heard this story many times before he finally realized the best way to deal with it was to sit in silence. Nothing wrong with what his father said, just that the repetition grew whiskers.

"Must be important," said John, Jr. "We don't meet here very often."

"Best to be able to talk in private. This is a wonderful place, especially when the weather is clear. So, you have any idea where our business is headed?"

"Seems to me you've been cutting back. Guess what happened to Chips Brewer really got to you."

"John, you don't remember the bad times. Too much rough stuff, people getting hurt, some killed. Lately I been thinking different. Our investments have been profitable and they're all legal."

"So, you're saying we should just sit back and live off our capital?"

"Let's put it this way. If you never worked another day in your life you would still be in pretty good shape."

"So, are we going to retire?"

Shaking his head, Pentram added, "Absolutely not. Now we have the resources to do some very interesting things and make a whole lot of money. The easy way."

"Like what?"

"First, let me ask you a question. Suppose you had $10 million. And you buy some stocks and bonds, good stuff. And suppose you do the safe thing and you earn four percent. That comes to $400,000 a year. Think you could live pretty good on that much?"

Weighing what he thought was the proper answer, John, Jr. said, "Sure, Pop. I could live pretty good on that much. Nice house, cars, college for John III. Trip to Europe every once in a while. Is that what you mean?"

Smiling, the father said, "You got that right. But, how about investing in something good where the return could be eight percent?"

"Where you going with this, Pop?"

"How about ten percent? How about $30 million at ten percent?"

"You saying we got that much money?"

Gazing off into the horizon, John Pentram said, "I been taking big risks all my life. Getting too old for that. So, now I have come up with a plan that looks like a sure-fire winner with a big pay-off."

"So, what's the plan?"

"How many restaurants you figure there are within a one hundred mile radius?"

The younger man looking confused said, "I have no idea."

"Well, we don't need many. Work up to about thirty, each one doing close to $2 million a year and we're off and running."

"Pop, I don't understand."

"Look, we're talking about $60 million in business which means they're buying between $15 million and $20 million."

"If you say so."

"We're going to sell them what they need."

"What? We're going into the grocery business?"

"Not exactly. We're just going to sell them what they need."

"But, how we going to do that? We don't have all that stuff."

"True, but we do have a company who will do all the work. All we have to do is line up the customers. Thirty seems like a good start. In time it could run up to a hundred."

"You know, Pop, this is all new ground. I don't have any idea what the restaurant business is all about."

"Exactly. And you don't have to know. Your job is going to be to line up the customers. It will take a little time. But, we already have three who are ready to go. Once we get them rolling we'll sit down and see how long it will

79

take to add some more."

John Pentram was building for the future. He recognized that his son was not going to be a doctor or a lawyer or any kind of professional. The child of his dreams barely made it through high school and he then struggled through LaSalle because his father insisted he stay in the city. Living at home was important, traveling to school on the Broad Street Subway was convenient, and the rigors of the institution were intended to concentrate all of John Junior's energies on his studies. Graduation was a major event, the first of its kind in the family.

The Pentram business was marginally legal. Some money lending, which from time to time called for a little enforcement, an aversion to anything to do with drugs, and investing in small businesses all added up to financial strength. How much, only the old man knew. Now, he wanted to build a huge structure. Explaining to his son was the second step. The first had been for RC Frane to prepare Star Distributing.

24

The black Lincoln Town Car was not John Junior's first choice. Bowing to his father's wishes because the family had a relationship with the dealer overrode his desire for a "Beemer." Not that the car wasn't commanding, not that it didn't send a clear message of importance, not that it wasn't recognized as a vehicle driven by a powerful person, just that it wasn't a car for a young man.

When he pulled into the parking lot of Martin's Diner on Rt.130 no one paid much attention. When he sat on a stool at the counter and ordered coffee and a hamburger, no one paid much attention. When he went to pay the check, no one paid much attention. Then he asked for Mr. Gregory.

"Here's the story, Mr. Gregory. You do a lot of business. That means you buy a lot of food and other stuff. Work with us and you will be able to save a lot of money and still get exactly what you want."

"Who do you represent?"

"Well, I'm John Pentram, Jr. Maybe you heard of us. We're located in South Philadelphia, but we got connections all over."

"You sell groceries, like that?"

"No, but we are partnered with a big company and we will get you anything you want. Prices right, quality good."

"Who's your partner?"

"Outfit in Philly named Star. Been around for a long time. Nice people."

"Look, Mr. Pentram. I'm not interested. Star I've heard of. Right now I got six distributors busting their chops to do business with me. I get prices nobody can beat."

"Maybe I didn't explain too clear. We will see that you get all your needs from one source. Guaranteed."

"You know anything about the food business?"

Laughing he replied, "Yeh, I eat out a lot. My wife is a lousy cook."

"So, that makes you an expert." It wasn't a question, it was a challenge, one Gregory had made many times in his thirty years running a diner. Fending off sales reps was something he did often, and well.

Because he was told to stay calm, John Junior backed off. "Look, Mr. Gregory. I figure you spend maybe a million dollars a year for food and supplies. If I can save you one point, that amounts to ten thousand dollars. How can you refuse?"

The older man turned grim. The diner was busy and he simply didn't want to waste time. "Not interested. Have a nice day." He reached for the check and some cash a customer pushed toward him.

Junior waited. As the customer left he returned to Gregory. "How about if I guarantee two points, that would put an extra twenty thou in your pocket. Does that sound better?"

"Can't you see I'm busy? It's lunchtime and I'm taking care of the cash register and overseeing everything. See what I mean when I asked you if you knew anything about the business."

"Okay. When can I come in and see you?"

"You're wasting your time."

"Maybe you're right. But that's what I do. Next time I'll bring in some of my experts and we'll try to convince you."

"You threatening me?"

Junior turned this thought over in his mind. "We do whatever it takes to get your attention."

"You better leave before I call the cops."

"Yeh. That's for now. Next time will be better."

The Lincoln engine purred. All eight cylinders seemed ready to leap into action as soon as he pressed the pedal. The contrast between how fired up he was and how smoothly the car eased into traffic did not last. He jammed his foot down and forced his way into the stream of cars causing raised fingers and angry words that he did not hear. Only when he reached seventy miles an hour did he ease back and concentrate on the road. "I'll show the bastard," he snarled. "Who the hell did he think he was talking to."

25

Peg Wilson said, "You better let me lead."

"Sure," answered Milt Thomason. "Maybe I shouldn't even be here?"

"Nah. You make good back up."

"Think they'll frisk us?"

"No way, man. We the cops. Just want to talk."

"He does know we're coming. You made an appointment."

"You better believe it. You don't just drop in on this man."

The two officers had pulled a non-descript car from the pool to attract as little attention as possible. To fit the occasion, they dressed in street clothes. Wilson had on gray slacks, a tan scoop neck top, and a Navy blue single-breasted jacket. Her shoulder bag included a small notebook, a couple of pens, and a 9mm Sig Sauer. The flap of the bag opened to show her badge. To keep things informal Thomason wore tan slacks and a button-down shirt with tie under a dark blue jacket. The heavy 9mm Glock was seated in a holster under his left arm.

They drove out to West Philly on Walnut Street and eased into the curb just short of 52nd Street. There were two "No Parking" signs in front of the big house. To avoid any problems they left those zones open and slowly walked up the steps.

Before her finger was off the bell the door opened. Waiting to greet them was a man half-again as big as Thomason, shoulders nearly covering the entry. "Welcome," he said. "Please follow me. Mr. Arthur is waiting."

Down the dark hallway, then a turn to the right and they entered the living room. The same room Frane had visited. Large overstuffed chairs, a fireplace for use in the cold winter, Oriental rugs scattered throughout. Thurman Arthur rose from his seat and signaled toward a couch opposite his own chair.

"Will you join me in a tea, or do you prefer coffee?"

"Coffee is fine," answered Wilson.

"Me too," added Thomason.

The big man who led them to the room disappeared and on cue, a maid in full attire rolled in a cart with cups, saucers, tea, coffee, and an assortment of small cakes.

After pouring coffee, Arthur said, "How may I be of service?"

Jumping right in, Wilson said, "You are aware of the shooting of Chips Brewer. We are working on that case."

"Yes."

"Did you know him?"

"Only in the vaguest way."

"Bad question. Did he work for you?"

"Officer, I have a great many people who work for me. Do I know them all? Probably not."

"You mean your organization is so large you don't know all your employees?"

"Exactly."

"Just how many people does that include?"

"This is getting complicated and fairly personal. I own some businesses that are run by people who report to me. They may have ten, fifteen, or more people working in the business. Do I know them all? No."

Thomason was doing most of the note taking. He interjected, "Must be rather difficult to keep track of them all."

"Not my concern. Does your captain know all the officers in the Round House?"

"You make a good point," said Wilson. "I guess the answer is not necessarily. But, he does know or has knowledge of all the Sergeants, Lieutenants, Captains, and on up the line all over the city. So, what you're saying is that Brewer may have worked somewhere in your organization, but you didn't know him well."

Arthur sipped his Chamomile tea. In a very calm voice he said, "When you called you said you wanted to ask a few questions. We seem to be veering off course. Should I have my attorney here?"

"Would that be Mr. Vogt?"

"He is my number one lawyer. Should he be here?"

Wilson tried again; eager to conceal that Arthur intimidated her. His pictures and reputation had been plastered throughout the gym department at West Philadelphia High School where she played basketball. He was a three-letter man, though football was his major sport. At the time there was talk that he might go all the way, maybe even play with the Eagles.

"You see, Mr. Arthur, we're just gathering information. This man Brewer was in the collection business. Running errands for people. Delivering and picking up things. But, he was murdered gangland style. So, anything we can learn about him and what he was doing will help us solve a bad crime."

"Surely you don't think I was involved in that? It's not my style. If he was one of my people who didn't do the right thing, why I'd simply have him fired. No need to murder anybody. That's for gangsters."

Nodding her head, Wilson continued. "You are well known out here. And whatever goes on, you know about things. That's why we're here. Asking your help, say, in pointing us in the right direction."

Arthur was not a man to be swayed by such an obvious appeal to his ego. He reflected on the many lessons learned on the street; too much talk leads to too much disclosure. Still, he recognized that he had the chance to lead the police away from his own world. "My understanding is that you are correct, he was something of an errand person, almost said errand boy. He did collections, whatever. Best guess, he might have been involved in a competing activity. If that were the case, I would have fired him unless it was cleared by his boss."

"So, you're saying it had nothing to do with you or your organization?"

A nod accompanied by a shrug.

"Care to guess what the other business might have been?"

"Could be anything. Not my concern."

Thomason spoke up. "Mr. Arthur, when we came through the front door your man never asked us to identify ourselves. How come?"

With a big smile, "You called for an appointment. Any reason I should suspect you weren't who you said you were?"

"You had us checked out?"

"Can't be too careful in these violent times."

26

It wasn't really a hideaway; it was just a name that survived from times when it was a hideaway. Chuck's Hideaway was a throwback to early prohibition days when rum runners and mobsters spent a lot of time in New Jersey, overlooking shipments, making deliveries, and looking for places to hide bodies.

To carry out the aura of those early days the walls were festooned with pictures of famous criminals, Machine Gun Kelly, Dutch Schultz, John Dillenger, Pretty Boy Floyd, and for fun, Wyatt Earp. A small gun collection of snub-nose revolvers and even a lugar from World War I hung on the wall. Resting on the bar was an imitation machine gun, the one with the round bullet chambers. When you pulled the trigger a flag popped out and said, "I need a drink."

Mercado and Vogt sat in the lounge area before dinner. Two oversize Martinis arrived; Vogt was known and his tastes catered to. A small dish of Russet Potato Chips, dark in color and devoid of bad cholesterol sat next to a similar dish of fancy cashew nuts.

"Just a nibble," he offered.

"Apparently they know you here. Nice place."

"In our line of work it's good to have a quiet place to visit, have a conversation, and enjoy a good meal. This your first time at Chuck's?"

"It always struck me as a little inconvenient to drive over to New Jersey for dinner. Philly has some great restaurants."

"That's an interesting observation. Whenever I travel I seek out the top places. Like a once-in-a-lifetime event. Have you ever been to Chicago?"

"Ah, yes. Were you thinking of Trotters?"

"Now that's a remarkable place. Chuck's doesn't come close. But, it does have a degree of charm."

Roberta Mercado sipped her drink. "Weren't you taking a chance ordering for me?"

"My dear Roberta," he started, "you have no objection to first names? After all, we may well be working together. And, we're both lawyers. Anyhow, I had my secretary call your secretary and confirm that, yes; you do drink an occasional Martini. These are made with Chopin Vodka."

"I would have thought you were more of a Grey Goose man."

Now he smiled, kindred spirits sharing a thought. "When you're ready, we can easily switch."

Raising her glass, she said, "To a fruitful and fulfilling relationship."

The effortless jousting and the casual talk proved as easy as moving the first pawn in a game of chess. The next moves might just be more complex, but for now, a wonderful start.

"Robert, or Bob, I don't know too much about your client, other than the fact that he and you go back a long way. And that you both have a variety of interests."

"That makes us even. Because I don't know very much about your client. I guess that's what we're supposed to be doing. Finding out about each others client and coming up with a plan that both find acceptable."

"Sort of like solving Bosnia, or Chechnya, or the Middle East?"

Before he could answer two more drinks arrived. They downed the last drops in the first and carefully examined the fresh arrivals.

He raised the glass in toast, "We can do better than that."

"I certainly hope so."

"Let's talk about Martinis," he said, "Not to change the subject, but just as a point of reference. These drinks are made with Vodka and a mist of Vermouth. As you know, most Vodka is only 80 Proof. There are times when I like a strong Gin Martini, say 94 Proof; Sapphire or Tanguery Ten. These are lighter by far, as you can tell by the small tingle on your tongue. Gin tends to snap you to attention. You know you have a challenge."

"There's a message lurking in the bottom of my glass. But, I'm not sure what it is."

"Roberta, let's just say this could be the beginning a lengthy and profitable friendship. Not only for our clients, but even perhaps for us."

"Bob, I'm almost glad you don't place a whole lot of emphasis on the sanctity of marriage."

"What do you mean, 'almost'?"

"Just a passing thought. We are a long way from wherever."

"Let's finish these drinks and have dinner. The wine list is quite good for an out of the way place."

As they rose from their seats a table server appeared, captured their half-empty glasses and said, "Please follow me. Your table is ready. I took the liberty of chilling a bottle of Rio Diamante, a very crisp Chardonnay from Argentina."

"Is that the one I had last week?" she asked.

27

Frane used to wonder at some of the more conventional thinking in the department. Keeping dark areas well lit, as defense against the bad guys seemed to make sense. Robbers would be afraid of detection because of strong streetlights. Then there was a major blackout in 2003 across the northeast section of the country and some fifty million people had no electricity. Great environment for criminals. Records for low crime rates were reported. Why?

He thought about this and came to the conclusion that anybody committing a crime needed some light. During earlier blackouts, 1965 and 1977, there was limited looting because they didn't last too long. Besides, it's hard to steal something when you can't see what you're doing, especially when your flashlight identifies where you are working.

Now that he was a full-time consultant, he became more comfortable with new ideas. While he had no one to share these ideas, he became obsessed with a quote from Oliver Wendell Holmes. "Man's mind, once stretched by a new idea, never regains its original dimensions."

This was all the wedge he needed to challenge and question and adopt new ideas. "It's a fiction," he said to himself, "that confidential meetings should take place in hidden places, where no one could observe what was going on." Quite to the contrary, it was much easier to be in a crowd to be unnoticed. That was why he suggested lunch in the midst of the milling mobs at the Gallery at Market East. This great shopping mall with dozens of stores on many levels was always busy. A wonderful place to be ignored.

Captain Bailey agreed.

"How about a sandwich and a beer?"

"I better stick to ice tea. You forget that I'm on duty?"

Smiling, Frane said, "It didn't take long to learn to drink in the middle of the day. But, of course, you're right. We can just squeeze in past the mess of people and find a seat. I think there's room way back."

They inched their way toward the rear, past bargain hunters standing in line waiting for a take-out sandwich. Outside there were tables and chairs waiting for hungry shoppers to pause, eat, and gain strength before assaulting the stores once more.

"How are things, Ed?"

"I won't say we don't miss you, but we're managing to solve a crime or two."

Elbow on the table, hand supporting his head, eyes downcast, Frane replied, "Thank you, Ed. Guess that's one of the nicest things you ever said to me."

Grumbling, Bailey added, "Well, after all those years having you around was getting real comfortable. So, yes, I do miss you."

"You know what I'm doing?"

"Rogers gave me a clue. Some kind of consulting."

"A little bit of security work. You know, advising a couple of places about how best to make their operations a little tighter. You'd be surprised at the need."

"So, you're busy?"

"Some of the stuff is peanuts. But, here and there I manage. I do have one very significant client."

"Is that what you wanted to talk about?"

"The thing is this, I wouldn't want you to learn about this from some outside source. Too much between us for too many years for you to hear about what I'm doing from some other source."

"Serious as all that?"

A table server arrived and they both ordered hamburgers and French fries.

One beer and one ice tea.

"So, what's the big secret?"

"Not so much a secret as a confidential arrangement."

"With?"

"John Pentram."

Bailey slowly blew out a deep breath. When he thought of his own unofficial contacts with Pentram, this seemed like an incursion on private territory. Fifteen years ago, when he was in Blues, he saved John Jr. from drowning when his car skidded off the road and landed in the Schuylkill River. With a little fancy footwork it turned out to be an accident, not drunk driving. Pentram felt an ever-lasting debt to Bailey. And from time to time he offered good advice and information.

Overcoming his personal resentment, Bailey asked, "Just what are you doing for him?"

"First off, you have to know, nothing illegal. Some investigating, finding out about people. The most important thing is, he is trying to establish a new kind of business. He has explained it all to me, and I'm working to get the team in place."

"You realize you're treading on some very dangerous ground. Much as he and I have a particular kind of relationship, that's business. What you're doing, I'm just not sure."

"That's why I wanted to talk with you. What I'm doing is between a client and a consultant. But, you're a special person in my life. Even though I'm out there in the world. So, I think I want to share anything with you that you might want to know."

"You're talking like I'm your rabbi."

"Aren't you?"

The hamburgers were getting cold. The crowd was noisy. The beer was getting warm. The ice tea was getting weak.

For a few painful minutes that covered a lifetime the two men sat in silence. Finally, Bailey stood, dropped a twenty-dollar bill on the table and said, "RC, I'm not really hungry. I think we better delay any further talk along these lines."

28

It was a very peculiar note. It read, "Enjoy the game." Two tickets to the Phillies game were enclosed. On the back was typed, "Make sure to have a hot dog in the middle of the fifth inning."

There was other mail in the box, the usual gas bill, a request for a donation from a charity he never heard of, and this note. Frane knew what the other two envelopes held, that was why he opened this one first. There was no return address; in fact there was no stamp. It had been hand delivered.

He sank onto the couch, hefted his feet on top of the coffee table and stared at the tickets. Two tickets, down behind third base, and a strange message. There was definitely a message, but it wasn't clear what that message was. And then the instruction to have a hot dog in the middle of the fifth inning.

"Somebody gave you the tickets?"

"They were in my mail when I came home last night. What's the matter, you don't want to see the Phillies play?"

"C'mon, RC. I'd love to go the game with you. Just seems kind of crazy two tickets dropped from nowhere. Great seats."

"Maybe I have an unseen admirer out there. Somebody who treasures my charms. Likes the way I cook. Thinks my body is desirable. You know, all those good things. You didn't by any chance send the tickets?"

Frane was still recovering from his meeting with Captain Bailey. The rebuke had been tough to take. *So much history together and it all seemed to melt away in a tumble of words. No chance to explain. No explanation acceptable. Eight years of father-son, mentor-mentee relationship dissolved.*

"I'm sorry," Frane whispered. "Just getting over a bad time."

"Can I help?" asked Rogers.

"Right. I'll be okay. Sure, let's go to the game. Tomorrow night. How about I pick you up early, get a bite to eat and head to the stadium."

"Looks like between home plate and third base, box seats about three rows up. Must cost a fortune. Yeh. No doubt about it. You have a secret admirer. You keeping something from me?"

"Don't be mean."

"Sorry. Tomorrow night."

Phillies fans are a boisterous lot. They love to cheer and they love to boo. Active, vibrant fans, particularly with Larry Bowa in the managers' seat. Every season with a team that was supposed to lead to a pennant, but always misses the mark.

Rogers and Frane both looked around at the crowds and felt as if they were in a fantasy world. So much of their time had been devoted to examining bodies, gathering facts, searching for killers. Here, they were going to have "fun and games."

A man selling peanuts stopped, offered them a bag. Hard to refuse when you're having fun. When he reached to pay the man said, "Compliments of a friend in one of the back rows."

He turned to search the mass of people. No way to see who might be the friend. Inside the bag Frane discovered a note. "Don't forget the hot dog in the middle of the fifth inning."

"What's that?" asked Rogers.

"I'm not sure. Maybe this is where the tickets came from. Somebody wants to meet me. I don't know."

The warm up, the batting practice and the game itself took on an interminable wait. Frane could barely pay attention to the field. Rogers joined in with the yelling when Pat Burrel got a hit. He was having a rough season and every hit counted.

The top of the fifth ended with a pop-up and Frane immediately got up, announced he was going to get a hot dog. "You want one, G?"

"I'll pass she said. Come right back."

Moving up the stairs to the passageway, Frane continued to scan the faces. Nothing was familiar. Getting lost in a crowd is easy. There was only a short line at the stand and he waited expectantly. He felt a presence behind him and turned, looked down at what appeared to be a ten or eleven-year-old boy sporting a Phillies cap. "Man over there gave me a dollar to give you this," he said, thrusting an envelope at Frane.

"Where?"

"Over there, against the rail."

"Point him out."

The youngster looked around. "Guess he left."

"You know him?"

"Nah. He just said, "Give this to that guy, the last one in line. And he handed me a buck.""

Stepping out of the line Frane held the envelope by one edge. He found the Men's room and went in, looked around till he found an empty stall. Once inside he carefully lifted the unsealed envelope and looked inside. A slip of paper and a key. These he dumped into his empty hand, before carefully sliding the envelope into his pocket. Typed on the piece of paper were the words, "International Departure Terminal, Box 34."

He turned the key over, read a coded number and thought for a minute. The message was beginning to make sense.

29

"Can't we wait till the game is over?"

"Greta, something has come up. You can help me now."

"What the heck is so important, that I can't see the rest of the game?"

"I just got a message from my secret admirer. There's something waiting for me at the airport. Look, you want to see the game, I'll run over, pick it up and come back for you."

"It's a mess, trying to link up in this crowd. Okay, I'm coming with you on one condition. You owe me a game."

Rogers looked at the "zeroes" on the scoreboard and had the feeling she was missing a great game. The only way to appreciate a low-hitting, low-scoring game is to be there. Every contest provides the best in the players. Sterling plays just don't show on the TV screen as the gracious movements; as the third baseman rushes a bunt and scoops the ball barehanded to catch the runner short by a step at first base. Or, the race in the outfield to make a running catch and save the pitcher some grief. The sports pages of the Philadelphia Daily News would try to recapture the moments.

Frane pulled into the short-term parking lot; no longer able to flip down his visor to show he was police. Now he paid as an ordinary citizen. Together they walked across the roadway, found the up-escalator and emerged into the International Terminal. The newly redesigned airport housed stores prepared to outfit, satisfy, and please the weary travelers. Everybody is a weary traveler; the waiting is endless.

A fast look around and they spotted the rows of storage compartments. He examined the key, memorized the number and moved rapidly through the flowing crowd. The late flights from Europe had just arrived and bedraggled fliers hurried toward the baggage area. Scanning the faces of those arriving was meaningless. Rather he looked for people who might just be standing around or even those who seemed headed to the gates. A man studying the magazine rack in the store, another sucking an ice cream cone, a woman with two children eating pretzels; none looked suspicious, all looked in place.

He told Rogers to stand at his side and search for anyone who seemed out of place, or who might be watching them. First he went to the end of the row before moving to the designated compartment. The key opened the door. Inside was a briefcase. Lying on top was a note. "Deliver this."

"You sure it's not a bomb?" Rogers asked.

"I'm not sure of anything. Says 'Deliver this'. Who to?"

"Want an opinion?"

"Why not."

"The man you work for."

Not wanting to use his name, Frane said, "You mean the important client?"

"Look, you figured that out all by yourself."

"Damn it, Greta. This is no time for a smart aleck remark. Maybe the thing will blow up if I open it."

"That's the point. You're not supposed to open it."

Reaching in, he pulled the brief case out and said, "Let's get out of here."

"Heavy?"

"There's something in there. But, it doesn't move."

As they walked down the passageway, the woman with the two children offered a nod and a knowing smile. A look that seemed to say, "We know what you're doing and you're doing just fine."

Rogers wasn't happy when Frane dropped her off in front of her apartment building. "Not much of a night, was it?"

"Duty calls," he responded. "We'll add it to the list of what I owe you. Maybe we can do a weekend down the shore. Nice room. Good wine. Play a little craps or roulette."

"You know Frane," using his last name on those rare occasions when she wanted to show big-time displeasure, "that list is pretty long right now."

"I know," he alibied. "Bear with me G."

She turned and walked up the steps to her apartment.

He pulled around the corner, stopped and tapped in a number on his cell phone. Two rings. "You want to see me?"

"Yes. Join me for a drink. City Tavern. Fifteen minutes."

Frane arrived early, asked for a seat in a secluded corner. The late crowd had thinned out and he had the room almost to himself. Knowing that Pentram would want to sit against the wall, he positioned himself along the side of the table that gave him full range of the door. When he arrived, Frane nodded. The brief case sat between them.

"What would you like to drink?"

"After the under cover work of the evening, I think I'd like a glass of good scotch."

"Ah, yes." With a raised finger he attracted a table server. "Two scotches, water on the side. Johnny Walker Black."

"How was the game?" he asked.

"Good, until the middle of the fifth inning."

Looking down at the brief case, he said, "I guess you're wondering what's in there."

Frane waited as the waiter placed the drinks on the table. He took a small sip and enjoyed the flavor, knowing that the next sip would be even better. "It was a toss-up. Could be stuffed with newspaper or maybe something more serious. I chose not to look. Who knows, it might explode when opened."

Pentram frowned. "Open it. But, just take a peek and keep the open end faced to the wall. Wouldn't want everybody to see the contents."

Frane edged his chair back. Laid the brief case on his lap, making sure it was out of sight, even though the room was virtually empty. He flipped the two hasps and the case opened slightly. He lifted the lid a couple of inches.

"Very impressive," he said. "How much?"

"Unless somebody played with it, there should be a hundred thousand dollars."

"Nice round sum. Should I count it?"

"No need. I know because I counted it on the way in."

Frane took another sip of his scotch. "Then, what was the purpose of all the subterfuge, why the ball game, why the compartment at the airport, and most of all, how was I supposed to know it was you?"

Pentram scanned the room. It was late and the last customers had departed. A server stood at attention by the door, waiting to be helpful.

"I hope what I have to say will be taken in the right spirit," Pentram said. "First, the subterfuge is consistent with conducting one's business in a secret manner. Second, the ball game was one possible way to accomplish this. The third should be understood as an excellent drop-off point for information or, in this case money. The answer to your last point is self-evident. We are here, aren't we?"

"What if I had opened the case, seen the money and decided to go to Mexico?"

It was Pentram's term to sip his scotch. "It would have been a clear signal that you weren't to be trusted."

Frane shook his head in disbelief. "A hundred large to make sure I was honest?"

"Small price for a man of your caliber."

30

"So, what's the connection?"

"This is just a long shot," said Rogers. "Guy we found in the storage area behind the Irish Pub is an acknowledged shooter. Part of a team known as, 'The Three Jimmies.'"

"Sounds like they belong on top of an ice cream cone. Where'd they get that title?"

"Three tough guys, all named Jimmy. They free lance around, used by different people when somebody gets out of line. They do all sort of bad things."

"What's the long shot?" continued Bailey. Working with Rogers wasn't easy. It takes time to get into a rhythm with a new detective and this was her first chance in the big ring. Two murders that are related and this one that doesn't quite fit in the mix. He listened patiently while Rogers explained.

"We ran Jimmy Duncan through the system. He and his partners have bad sheets; lots of arrests, but no convictions. Our working theory is that he did Chips Brewer and maybe one of the other Jimmies did McCabe."

"Okay. So you got a theory. What else?"

"We interviewed some of the patrons at the Irish Pub. Here's what we have. Two sharp, double-breasted heavyweights come in, sit down with the three Jimmies and talk quietly. The one they call 'Big Jimmy' goes out back with one of the suits. The suit comes back in less than a minute. Then Duncan goes out back with the other suit, and again the suit comes back in a minute. The two suits leave and the third Jimmy, I think this is Kennedy, goes out back, calls for help."

"What did he find?"

"Big Jimmy has six fractured ribs, half his chest caved in, and he's blubbering like a baby. Must hurt real bad. The second Jimmy is lying there with one through his heart and one in the middle of his forehead."

"Nobody heard the shots?"

"Must have used a silencer. Besides, patrons really didn't want to say much. When the suits came in they were seen as being from another planet. This is not the kind of place where people wear suits. Working man's drinking hole."

"What's the tie-in?"

"We figure The Three Jimmies were brought in to take out Brewer and McCabe. Then somebody wants to respond. All happened very fast."

"What do you mean fast?"

"Brewer takes it one day. Two days later McCabe gets it. Before The Three Jimmies have time to leave town, they get hit. It almost seems that the person responsible for engaging The Three Jimmies tipped off somebody immediately and arranged for the Two Suits to clean up the mess. Maybe the same person was responsible for both teams of hitters."

Bailey drew some squares on the pad resting on his desk. Three bad guys, two more bad guys, three bodies and one crippled Jimmy. *Big-time mess. Now Rogers was thinking they are all part of the same picture.*

"Assuming you're right, what was so important about getting rid of two low-level collectors? And, why get rid of the shooters who did the work? What's the need for all this coverage?"

"Boss," said Rogers, "I just don't know. My guess is that the collectors were doing double duty. Getting paid by one source and doing some extra work for another."

"This is chicken shit," Bailey said. "You don't kill somebody for doing some side work unless there's a big reason. In the business world we might call it a conflict of interest. Now, on the street, it would have to be real bad to want somebody permanently retired. Find out what these first two were collecting. Who did they work for?"

Adjusting herself in the hard chair, Greta Rogers worried about what she was about to say. Purposely playing for time, she flipped through her notebook, scanned a page, and then said, "Brewer and McCabe both went to different kinds of places. Restaurants, cleaning establishments, gift shops; nothing really fancy, just your up-and-down the street small businesses."

"Something more you want to tell me?"

Clearing her throat, Rogers said, "They both worked for John Pentram."

Bailey stood, walked around the desk, turned to look out the window, and then sat down. "John Pentram. Lately he hasn't been in any trouble. My impression is that he has been getting out of loan sharking, numbers, horses, and he never was in drugs. So, what were they collecting?"

"You see, Captain, I thought maybe you could ask him. Of course, I have no problem calling on him. But, it might be better if somebody with your clout went to see him."

"Let's take this a step further. Let's say Pentram is clean. But, two of his people were into something dirty. Who is responsible for ordering the kill? Wouldn't Pentram just fire the collectors? Why kill them? Unless they were collecting for him and not turning in the money? Even that wouldn't call for killing. Not that much money involved. Unless there was that much money involved.

"Gets pretty sticky. Tell you what, Rogers. I'm going to think about this a little bit. See me later in the day. In the meantime, see if you can identify the Two Suits."

"How about Frane?"

"What about him?" snapped Bailey.

"He used to talk with Pentram."

"Frane doesn't work here any more!"

31

"Hey, pop. How does it go?"

"You always ask the same question. What kind of answer are you expecting?"

"Still looking for something positive like, 'I feel pretty good today.' Or, 'Yesterday was great.'"

"Why the hell would I say something like that when life stinks?"

"Things never change, do they?"

"You get to be my age, what d'ya expect."

"Pop, you're only touching seventy. I was reading the insurance tables the other day and they say you got another fifteen to twenty years ahead. Why not enjoy them?"

Frane had been over this ground with his father at least every two weeks for five years. The old man retired at sixty-five and had devoted these past years to complaining—about everything. Last year it was the election. This year it's taxes. Put them together and that takes up the whole visit.

"Brought you a bottle of red wine from Chile."

"What do they know about wine? They ought to stick to fish. You know, sea bass. Heck, I used to take you down the shore to try and catch bass once in a while. Do you remember?"

"Sure do, pop. I was just a little kid, nine or ten. We had some good times together." Usually the ride on Saturday began at six in the morning, reached the beaches in Wildwood before eight and fished till around eleven when the tourists hit the beach and it got too crowded.

"You remember that?"

RC smiled. "Probably the happiest memory of my childhood."

His father worked at the Philadelphia Navy Yard for almost forty years and when he left he was a Master Carpenter. He regretted not having worked on some of the major ships built during World War II because he was too young. RC wanted to take him on a tour of the Battleship New Jersey, the most decorated battleship in the world. Since the Big J was permanently moored on the Camden side of the Delaware and had been converted to a museum, thousands of visitors came for a tour. Still, the old man refused his offers. There seemed no way to satisfy him.

"Anyhow dad, I see the Phillies aren't doing too well."

"They go up and down. Just didn't have the juice to make it this year. Still, that Jim Thome has been a great help. Forty-seven homers. Big year."

"And the Eagles have a bad start. Losing the first two games is no way to open the season."

"Enough with the bad news," his father growled. "Let's talk about important things."

"Sure, pop. World politics? Voting rights? Mayor Street? You name it, we'll talk."

"I'm talking serious. Like two men roaming around the neighborhood asking all kinds of questions."

Frane pulled his chair closer, his attention hooked by this strange outburst. "Two men asking questions? Did they ask you anything? What did they want?"

"I spotted them one day when I was sitting on the porch. They didn't come near me and that's the problem."

"What dya' mean?"

"Look, I'm no dummy. If they were asking all over the neighborhood and they skipped me, must mean they were asking questions about me."

"Why you?" Frane asked skeptically.

"Hey, ever since you retired you stopped being a detective. If you want to know something about somebody, you don't just go and ask them. You talk to their friends, relatives, neighbors."

Nodding agreement, Frane said, "You're right, pop. Can you tell me how they were dressed?"

"Yeh. Like real business people, maybe bankers or something like that."

"Suits or sport jackets?"

"I told you, like bankers."

"Dark suits?"

The old man closed his eyes in disgust. "Yeh, dark suits."

"Single-breasted or double-breasted?"

"That makes a difference?"

"Just think, pop, were they wearing single-breasted or double-breasted suits."

"Boy, are you getting particular. Single-breasted."

"Hats?"

"Gee whiz. You're getting to be a pain in the ass. Yes, they wore hats."

"Here's a tough question. See if you remember. Were the hat brims wide or narrow?"

"Is this really important?"

"Wide or narrow?" Frane repeated.

"Narrow, damn it."

Frane walked into the kitchen, saw that everything was clean and orderly, the sign of a man accustomed to taking care of his tools. He found a corkscrew and wound it into the bottle of wine. The cork was tight and he worked to ease it out, trying not to break any pieces into the bottle. Then, he lifted two glasses from the cabinet and went back into the living room.

"Try a little of this, Pop. It's a cabernet, nice body and lots of flavor."

"Since when did you become a wine expert?"

Deciding it was a waste of time to answer because the question had been repeated every time they were together, Frane said, "Did any of the neighbors tell you what these two guys wanted?"

"What took you so long to ask? Sure, they told. Guys wanted to know what you were doing now that you retired. Who you worked for, how often you came to visit. Shit like that."

"Doesn't sound like much. Even I could come up with better questions."

"Maybe they're not detectives, like you used to be."

"Sounds from your description that they were FBI."

"How'd you figure that out?"

"Clues, Pop."

"Clues? What clues?"

"For one thing they wore single-breasted suits."

"What else?"

"The hats, Pop. Narrow brimmed hats. I should have asked you about their shirts. What kind of shirts were they wearing?"

"You're getting crazy. Like with the wine. They wore white shirts. What does that tell you?"

"Like I said, Pop. FBI."

32

John Lacey always wore a white shirt. It was out of respect for the dress code first established by J. Edgar Hoover. After twenty-six years with the FBI, Lacey still identified with a time that seemed past. Dark, single-breasted suits, hats with narrow brims, and ties that did not attract attention. He even remembered that agents didn't carry guns. Of course, that had changed.

On this particular assignment, he wasn't trying to be invisible. In fact, his orders from Arnold Fisher, chief agent in the Philadelphia area had been explicit. "Don't hide. Make sure the neighbors see you. And make sure that old-man Frane sees you. In other words, we want him to let RC Frane know he is on the screen."

"And you want us to follow him. Make sure he sees us."

"That's right agent. He'll get the message. Simple as that."

As he left his father, still tippling on the wine, RC Frane easily observed the two agents making themselves clearly visible. The message was so obvious, almost beneath the dignity of such a vaunted agency.

It sounded cloak-and-dagger style, only this was more like amateur hour.

Frane called the inside number to Fisher and said, "Usual place, 3:30 today."

He arrived a few minutes early, bought a fresh Philadelphia Soft Pretzel and slathered it with mustard. The salty, doughy pretzel costs $1.50, a treat that was only ten cents when he was growing up. Times change.

Before he finished with the first mouthful, Fisher appeared. "Have one?" he asked.

Watching with disdain, Fisher said, "Not today. Shall we walk? Can you walk and eat at the same time?"

Taking another bite, Frane said, "Arnold, let's get to it. You wanted to see me you could have called. What's on your mind?"

Fisher knew that Frane mistrusted him. Their various encounters when Frane was on the force tended to be cordial. When he suggested a Florida trip to Frane to investigate what became known as the "Shrimp Murders," he even had the department pick up the air fare and then offered to put Rogers and Frane in one of their special apartments down on the Panhandle. It never occurred to him that the two detectives realized the apartment was loaded with tape-recorders.

This and other experiences of a deceptive cooperation between the two agencies kept Frane on his toes. Anything Fisher wanted was suspect. Only now he didn't have to cooperate, he was a consultant.

"Let me tell you what's on my mind," Fisher began. "Ever since you left the Police Department I have been trying to find a way to engage your services."

"Come again."

"You know we sometimes employ outside talent. In police work, I think you call them Confidential Informants, CIs. More commonly known as 'snitches'. We have similar sources, only at a more professional level."

"I see," Frane answered, taking the last bite of pretzel. "Should I imply from what you have said that you want me to be a snitch?"

"Oh, nothing as plebian as that," Fisher explained. "What we need is a high placed consultant who might help us learn some things about citizens in whom we have an interest."

They were slowly approaching the newly constructed National Constitution Center, off Market Street, extending from Fifth Street to Sixth Street. The entire area evoked Colonial history; Independence National Historical Park, The Liberty Bell, U.S. Mint, and Congress Hall. Always impressed with the sight, Frane paused, stood still and gazed in awe.

"It's almost a desecration to have this conversation in this neighborhood," he said to Fisher. "Let's head back to less hallowed ground."

In an accommodating way, Fischer answered, "Of course. Really, what I had in mind was to offer you an assignment. Since we're government, we don't have the kinds of money you might receive from a private client. Still, it's honest work and may lead us to catch some very bad people."

"Why not go to the police? Captain Bailey has worked with you in the past."

"The point is this. You have a client in whom we have a great interest and you're in a position to help us. In other words, you are on the inside track."

"You're that interested in Star Distributing?" Frane smiled. "They don't seem like criminals."

"Come, come, RC. You know I'm not talking about Star. I'm interested in John Pentram."

"Who?"

"RC, I've tried to be upfront with you. Let's cut out the games. Pentram has been doing some things, or knows about certain things going on and since you are so close to him; you could provide us with some useful insights."

"You think I'm working for Pentram?"

Exasperated, Fisher thundered, "I see it's no use talking like a normal human being. I'm interested in catching criminals who are hurting all of us. You want to crap around and play games with me, that's okay. But, let's get one thing straight. If we find you are doing bad things working with Pentram, your ass is up for grabs like any other criminal."

"I gather nothing would give you more pleasure than catching me doing something wrong. Well, sorry you feel that way. There was a time I almost admired you. Thought you were on the up-and-up. But, you have screwed me over so many times, taken credit for work I did in the Department, and treated me and my people like peons that, 'Quite frankly, I don't give a damn.' Gee, I think somebody else said that already."

33

Diners were conceived in the first decade of the last century. All over the country, wherever old railroad cars were lying dormant, cooks who thought they were chefs had them moved to a promising location, tore out the insides, installed a steam table, an oven, and a grille. They added a coffee urn, a toaster, and a deep sink; and the diner was born. The idea was that they would be mobile, able to move if the business declined. When construction of a manufacturing plant began, suddenly a diner would appear on a nearby road.

In their earliest incarnation, a long counter with revolving stools made for all the sitting space. The food was fresh because there was little space for refrigeration. Freezers were unknown. Home fried potatoes would be stacked on one side of the grille, properly seasoned with oil, salt, and paprika. In time, deep fryers were introduced to meet the demand for French Fried Potatoes. Always the food was accompanied by conversation with the cook. Everything was contained within the confines of the former rail car. The regular customers were comfortable because this was a substitute for home.

By adding a kitchen in the rear, the cooking was moved out of sight and that made room for booths where a family could eat. Menus grew; home baked pies became the norm, and table servers who chewed gum and tended to call everyone, "Hon," became part of the environment. Each diner boasted its own unique design and style. In the burgeoning foodservice industry, no one ever considered franchising a diner. Some owners collaborated with their cooks to own a second diner, or even a third. That seemed to be the limit. Diversity was the rule, individuality the objective.

New Jersey was the prominent location for manufacturers of diners. Their designs and models became landmarks visited over and over by nearby residents as well as travelers. What began as an enterprise that could start with a few hundred dollars was now an entrepreneurial challenge frequently reaching a million dollars. Martin's Diner, with its three hundred seats, liquor license, staff of almost two hundred and volume over $4,000,000, was a major target for John Pentram, Jr. That was why he brought Tommy Jenkins, owner of the Uptown Diner with him to help make the sale.

"What do you want me to do?" Jenkins asked.

"I been in to see this guy a couple weeks ago. He gave me a big rush, didn't seem to appreciate what we had in mind. I figure, maybe I didn't explain it right."

"So, you think I can make him understand?"

"Sure. You're involved; you know what the plan is. Makes sense to get some major players together to save some money."

"Yeh, but I been with Mr. Pentram for a long time. He helped me, big time. So, when he says he wants to do something, I know I'm gonna do it."

"You making good money at the Uptown Diner?"

"More than I was making before I joined the Company."

"Things going smooth, you got time to concentrate on cooking and customers?"

"That's the name of the game. I spend the mornings in the kitchen, overseeing the cooks, and then I walk around the diner and greet people. Get to know them."

"Fun?"

"A lot better than standing behind a hot steam table all day."

The ride in the big Lincoln was easy. John, Jr. decided to make the call after lunch, around two in the afternoon. Leave time for a cup of coffee and then get together with Mr. Gregory.

"What do you think will get his attention?" John, Jr. asked.

Jenkins thought about this. "Probably the idea that he will get exactly what he wants, when he wants it, and the prices should be stable."

"Well, suppose our distributor doesn't have the stuff he wants?"

"Then we have to get it for him. Guy in the kitchen used to a certain kind of merchandise is gonna be very unhappy getting some new brand."

As they pulled into the parking lot, John, Jr. said, "It's a good thing you're with me. I don't have any idea what you're talking about."

Mr. Gregory wasn't happy to see young Pentram. During their earlier meeting, it was obvious that they had crossed swords. Jenkins took the lead.

"My name is Tommy Jenkins and I own the Uptown Diner. We got a lot in common. You know, both run big diners."

Showing a touch of interest, Gregory asked, "How big?"

"Oh, not as big as yours. But, last year we ran about two-and-a-half million. Don't forget, we only have a hundred and fifty seats. And no liquor. What do you do?"

Motioning to a far corner of the back dining room, Gregory said, "Let's go where it's quiet. That's a lot of business for your size."

A waitress followed them to a booth and said, "Coffee?"

Gregory said, "Bring us a bottle of Dewar's; three glasses and a pitcher of water."

Since he ran one of the busiest food operations in the state, Gregory decided to take charge of the conversation. "Naturally, we do quite a bit more. When your friend came in a couple of weeks ago, he caught me at a bad time. People are always coming in, trying to get my business. I just don't have time to talk with them. You involved in this scheme of his?"

Jenkins saw the opening. "It's not really a scheme. It's a modern way of doing business. For instance, when we came in, you were taking cash. Maybe it's time to do more important things."

"There's nothing more important than taking cash," Gregory pronounced. "We both know what happens when the boss takes cash."

The server placed the three glasses on the table and started to pour. When she left, Gregory turned to John, Jr. and said, "Why didn't you tell me who your father was?"

Tempted to offer a smart answer, John, Jr. bit his lip. "We got a good business proposition, Mr. Gregory. That's why I brought Tommy with me. You guys got a lot in common. If you want, I can bring some other restaurant people around. They'll tell you how the system works."

"It's true, Mr. Gregory," added Jenkins. "It's like that Pennsylvania Dutch saying. 'All of us are smarter than some of us.'"

Gregory nodded. "I thought that was a Greek proverb."

34

"Is this seat taken?"

Frane looked up at the woman carrying her tray. She was what he thought of as a, "Nice looking woman." Not overly pretty, not too old, dressed in conservative clothes. Just your average human being.

The restaurant at the corner of 19th and Market was one of his favorite spots. Always crowded, plenty of seats and the kind of place where people might join you for lunch because no other seats were open. The food variety was extensive and the salads crisp. Nothing fancy, wide range of sandwiches, soups, and enough salad selections to satisfy. Two long counters arranged in cafeteria style offered a fast moving line in which you placed your order, picked up a drink and looked for a table. Shortly a table server would bring your selection.

Sometimes mocked for his minimal social graces, Frane concentrated on his lunch; hardly looking at the woman. Until she said, "Mr. Frane, or do you prefer Lieutenant?"

He looked up, surprised and answered, "You know me?"

"You'd be surprised how well I know you. For the moment, let's just say

I'm very aware of the fact you are working as a consultant, and with some very interesting people."

"How come you know so much about me and I don't know anything about you?"

She stared at him before answering. "Because in my work I have to know a lot about the people I deal with. Right now you are my major concern."

Feeling safe in the midst of all the traffic; people walking past to place their lunch choices, carrying drinks, talking, he said, "Am I supposed to be impressed?"

She dumped a packet of sugar into her ice tea, stirred the drink and turned her eyes to stare at him again. "Let's just say we have a few things in common, and by the time lunch is over we may have even more things in common."

Adding a bit of levity to what seemed a serious conversation, "If you're looking for a top flight consultant, I'm pretty busy. Maybe I can suggest a name for you."

"You're my man," she answered. "The question is, are you ready for an important piece of work. We feel you have all the skills, knowledge, and expertise for the work. We also think you're basic instincts jive with ours."

Frane put his fork and knife down and stared back at the woman. "Who is the 'We' you keep referring to?"

She slid a card across the table. On the back, hand printed, were the letters, "CIA."

One glance and she pulled the card back and slipped it into her jacket pocket.

He laughed. "Seems like ever since I retired a lot of people are interested in me. I don't suppose you have a name."

"In my work names are not terribly useful. On the other hand, when I have to identify myself to you, think of Muriel."

"How do I know you are real, Muriel?"

"We'll get to that in a minute. My mission today is to sound you out, make sure we're on the same track, and then get into specifics."

"You, and whoever you work for, must think I'm some kind of patsy. In fact, I am highly insulted by your effrontery. You plop down when I'm having a bite of lunch; give me some strange tale and I'm supposed to roll over and play nice. Get with it, sister. I was a cop for a long time. You want to get in touch with me, call the office.

"Matter of fact," he continued, "I think you might be with the Culinary Institute of America. Now that would be good, since I'm deeply involved in

114

the restaurant industry. But, they aren't secretive. They come right out and tell all."

"You think this is some kind of Mickey Mouse game," she snapped. "I'm very real and I have a very real assignment. Maybe you just don't like doing business with a woman."

"Damn. I was just going to enjoy a simple lunch when you arrived. How about we just eat quietly and then go our respective ways."

"Listen, Frane. I know you're a tough guy. I told you I would give you all the proof necessary when the time comes. All I want to do now is outline a way you can help the Company. Not only that, it's important for national security."

"Spare me. I just had this conversation with the FBI. What is it with you people? Can't you do the work yourselves?"

Leaning forward she asked, "What did the FBI want?"

"Nothing much. They wanted me to teach their agents how to tie their shoe laces. You see, they're not allowed to wear loafers to work. May have to run after the bad guys and they have to be sure their shoes won't fly off."

Muriel took a sip of tea. "Do you mind if we get back to business? I have a job to do. I'm supposed to ask for your help. Just as simple as that."

Enjoying himself at this point Frane said, "What do you need? Want me to clear the table? Dump your used plates? Maybe shoot somebody? Take your choice."

"You are some kind of smart ass," she threatened. "I'll just have to tell Washington that you're not the man we thought you were."

"Oh my, that is scary. Why don't you just tell the Station Chief?"

"You arrogant bastard, I am the Station Chief."

Now Frane laughed heartily. "Lady, lady, lady, you are so full of surprises. If only I had known. That changes everything. So, first of all, send me a letter to that effect, and I'll stop by your office and we can have a nice chat."

"You know I can't do that."

"And I'm not about to get involved with somebody who sits at my lunch table and shoots me a bunch of boloney. You must think I just got off the farm. Next thing I know you might try to sell me the Liberty Bell."

She stood, whispered softly, "We'll meet again. On my turf next time."

35

Rittenhouse Square really is one block square, from Locust Street to Walnut Street, from 18th Street to 19th Street. Diagonal walking paths crisscross, meet in the middle where a large circle serves as a central location, and more paths spoke out to the streets. Benches line the pathways and green grass welcomes those who choose to languish in summer warmth while reading novels. In the winter, when the sun is shining, people bundle up and enjoy the country-like quiet in the heart of the city.

Depending on the time of day, early morning and mid-afternoon are near perfect for baby carriages, many guided by the live-in caretakers. Those children not attending private pre-school activities run free, but are always kept in sight. On three sides, high-rise apartment buildings surround the sanctuary, while two upper-class hotels in the corners anchor the park. Both house superb dinning rooms. Along busy Walnut Street there are professional buildings sheathed in marble.

As if guided by a miracle, the sun always seems to shine on Rittenhouse Square. Students mingle with stragglers and an occasional out-of-place person who wondered in by mistake. Business people take time to sit quietly and absorb the unruffled environment before returning to the day's skirmishes.

Roberta Mercado spotted Bob Vogt seated on a bench along the path near Locust Street. He smiled when she asked, "Is this going to be billable time?"

"Somehow or other all my time is billable." Then thinking for a moment, "Other than the time we spend together privately."

She left ample space between them as she sat down. "After you filled me full of Vodka Martinis and wine at Chuck's Hideaway I'd believe almost anything you say."

"That's what I like about lawyers. We can talk freely to each other and not worry about breaking a confidence."

"Well," she answered, "that's not altogether true. It means we can't be called upon to reveal to the outside world what we're talking about. Our world of privileged information is great cover, even here in the open air."

"Ah, you always want to talk business. Okay. It strikes me that we may be able to work out an agreeable territorial arrangement."

Mercado crossed her legs, allowing the slit in her long black skirt to reveal a flash of skin. Vogt didn't miss the move; it reminded him of their last meeting. "Nice shoes," he fumbled.

Stretching her leg out straight, she said, "Yes, they are rather stylish."

"Do you think we would do better at your office? Or mine?"

"Not exactly what I had in mind," she said. "But, let's get started here."

"Tell me, can you speak for Pentram?"

"You know better than that. Nobody speaks for Pentram. Certainly I don't."

"Would you care to say how far you can go?"

"Since you been so upfront with me," she almost laughed, "I'll give you something to chew on. Yes, I do some law. My credentials are top drawer. But, I don't do much. I have other interests which seem to attract a fair number of clients."

"Like what?"

"How come I'm telling all and you're not telling anything."

"Guess you might say we are both in the same boat. Some law, mostly outside activities."

"Clue?"

"Big interest in the foodservice business; restaurants, diners, clubs, wherever food is served. And you?"

"I'm spread around. My forte is the financial side; is it good, how can it be improved, is there money to be made."

"Then we're really not competitors. Only thing is, I concentrate."

Mercado nodded agreement. "Then, there's not really any reason to discuss territories. If I get involved with a restaurant, I'll give you a buzz."

"That sounds good. But, if I move into some other area, how will I know if we're going to bump heads?"

"See, we're already making progress. We're talking like old friends."

"I think we have an initial problem. One of my clients has a big interest in restaurants. I understand Pentram is now getting involved in restaurants. There may be some need to keep these two clients separate. That is, set some fair geographic limits."

"Thurman Arthur is new to this business. Sure, he has some pieces. Pentram has a different business approach. Who knows what he's dealing in?"

Vogt was surprised that Mercado knew about Arthur. "Well, somebody is pulling some rough stuff. That's not good for anybody. Attracts too much attention. If we can straighten out some of the borders, we can avoid conflict."

Now she threw him a curve. "What about Trenton?"

"They know to stay out of Philadelphia."

"And Camden? Seelman is a big shot there. Is he going to be part of the picture?"

Vogt pulled a cigarette from his pocket; offered one to Mercado. She shook her head, "No."

"This whole thing is getting complicated. Too many players; each with a different agenda. What do you suggest?"

"I'll give you an idea. My man has a scheme, no, a method for restaurant people to work together to get better prices, better service, and help in running their business. He has a well-thought out plan. When he presented it to me, I was intrigued. And, it's perfectly legal. Just plain old-fashioned smart business."

"Does that mean he's taking his collectors off the street? After all, two of them were taken down in the last couple of weeks."

"That's an area in which I am not concerned. I was brought in for different reasons; business and law. Those collectors are not on my screen."

Vogt got to his feet. "We have a lot to discuss. How about if we wonder over to The Warwick, have a cocktail and talk some more."

The one block walk to 17th and Locust to another landmark hotel was just enough to tantalize the taste buds.

36

It happened when he was running. The early morning, long before the sun made its appearance, when dim light turned everything grey; shadows became the rule. The streets were always black, asphalt never turned grey. The curbs were easily visible because their three inches of height cast a shadow that became clearly visible even in the faint street light.

Green leaves on trees became dark fluttering splashes. Slight indentations in the roadbed were obvious, helping him to avoid danger as if the surface was spotted with cancer. Objects left in the way, a discarded coffee carton, a wrapper from a candy bar, a cigarette butt took on distinguishable shades that became part of the canvas. It was a revelation that so much was to be learned from the shadows. Frane paid increasing attention to these variations. It wasn't necessary to know the exact shape or form of the object, as long as you knew there was something matchless, something to be avoided, a warning sign.

Jogging was a time when he gave his imagination free reign. The world of shadows took control not only for running, but in other ways. *People are shadows. When you look at them it's important to see these shadows, those variations from what you think you see. There are shadings, slight discrepancies, something that makes them unique.*

From his police work he thought of the many interviews with suspects, how they were all shadows of what he wanted to know. Reading the shadows, alert to their existence, seeking a way to shed light was a challenge. The lesson, he thought, is that you don't have to see things clearly. Knowing that something was out there waiting to trip him up, was all the warning he needed.

Happily, he realized this new insight; the strength of shadows was a valuable tool. It meant he could navigate to the bathroom in the middle of the night without turning on the light switch. He knew to avoid the darker shadows that warned a chair was in the way. Or, that big dark void in front was really a wall. Find another way around. Such was his meandering this early morning as he stopped to rest on one of the benches along Penns Landing.

Across the Delaware River, the now bright sun glanced off the Battleship New Jersey. This famous warship always drew attention, guns now silent, but memories of so many battles still resonating. Then, a shadow fell from behind.

"Good morning, RC. Hope I didn't startle you."

Turning slightly, Frane saw Arnold Fisher, dressed in running gear. "Ready to jog a little?" he asked. "Thought when we were both in shorts with not much to hide we could find some common ground. Last time didn't work out too well."

"I'm on my final minutes," Frane said. "So, let's do it, slowly."

Together they ran south, knowing there would be no streets to cross, just a concrete runway; hard on the knees and back, but easy on the traffic.

"The thing is this," Fisher said in a very conciliatory tone, "I could use your help."

There is a shadow there; not sure not sure where. "What's on your mind?"

"Even though you're off the force, I think you still harbor some feelings about the bad things happening in the city."

"What things in particular?"

"Drugs."

Their pace was easy, maybe ten-minute miles. "Arnold, there are all kinds of drugs floating around. Why the big push now?"

"That's what I wanted to talk to you about. You know that many shipments of food products come into the country in containers. You've seen them aboard trucks, some bigger than others. But, even the small containers carry a lot of weight."

"You think there might be some containers full of drugs?"

"Consider the possibility. A container might easily be able to bring in a couple of tons without being noticed. Let's just say one ton of heroin. Imagine what that would sell for on the street."

"You're talking a whole lot of money," answered Frane. "Time it gets stepped-on once or twice; you're talking mega-bucks."

"Sort of gets your attention."

"In the old days, yes, it would be of interest. But, my time was usually spent with homicide. So, I don't see what you want from me."

"Good point," Fisher added. "Did you read about those two collectors who were murdered? The one behind Julianis' Restaurant and the McCabe woman up near Columbia Avenue? As you said, in the old days they would be yours."

Frane shrugged.

"Also, and this is very interesting, a strong-arm killer was murdered out back of the Irish Pub. And next to him was another strong-arm guy with his rib cage smashed all out of shape."

"What's the point?" asked Frane.

"The two runners worked for John Pentram. They apparently were taken out by these two tough guys. Who took care of them is up for grabs."

"Arnold, you started out talking about drugs. Is there a connection?"

"We think there is."

Hiding his own shadow, Frane said, "Who's covering the murders?"

"I think your friend, Rogers."

"See, since I'm out of action, I don't know what's going on. Glad you brought me up to date."

They jogged without speaking for a half-a-block. "RC, I said we need your help. You know I don't usually come asking. And this is the second time."

"Got to admit you are persistent. Okay, tell me what you want and then we'll see." Frane thought, here comes a flow of departmental verbiage, shadows in disguise. Easy to detect, if you know they're coming.

"We think Pentram is involved in something very, very big. He has people all over town collecting. We think they're collecting drug money. Now, we know he has his fingers in a lot of restaurants. Container of heroin, restaurants throw off a lot of cash, we've seen some characters hanging around, transactions taking place. Have to believe he is the mastermind. You work for him. What can you tell me?"

"How does the heroin get from the container to all these restaurants?"

"We're working on that. We figured with you being in touch with the man, you might be able to give us a clue."

Frane stopped and walked, warming down. "What do you know about the distribution of food? Where does this supposed container come from? How does it get through customs? Where does it go? Who handles it? How do they convert it to street product? How do they distribute it? Who buys it? On and on. You're talking about a very large organization. Particularly when you're talking a ton of skag."

"Once again, I have to say, that's what we thought you might help us with. You have outlined the problems. What we need from you is some way to get into the system. Find a way where we can start. So far it's been pretty tight."

"Let's get real, Arnold. I'm a consultant. What I do is perfectly legal, and I might add, imaginative. You are asking me to do some undercover work for you that might cause me to reveal secrets about a client. Since I am a law-abiding citizen, I think there may be ways I can offer some counsel. So, here is a suggestion. Hire me to do some work for you. Send me a letter confirming the kinds of things you want done and your agreement that my time is valued at $10,000 a month for a year."

"You know I can't do that," Fisher said, gasping at the demand.

"Why not?"

"I don't have that kind of authority. Oh, a few bucks here and there, but you're talking $120,000 a year."

"I'm not asking for bennies. I'll pay my own taxes."

"And a letter absolving you of any misdeeds. Wow."

"This is life in the fast lane. I'd squeeze your requests in-between my work with other clients. You just don't understand how valuable I can be to your thought process. Let me give you an example. To mount the kind of operation where you would be selling $20 million worth of junk would take a major organization. Ask your own people to design a flow-chart for the distribution."

"Dammit, Frane. You know I have all that information. What I need is some inside help. Sending you a letter is out of the question. No way."

Frane took a deep breath. "Gee, and I was looking forward to working with you."

37

Life after all those years with the Philadelphia Police Force was certainly a change for Frane. Here it was almost 10 o'clock in the morning, following a long run, an encounter with Fisher of the FBI, a leisurely breakfast, time to read the morning paper, and now off to work. This was only partially true, because he hadn't decided exactly what to do this day. There were several options, visit Star and iron out some details, call Pentram for instructions, or stop in to see his two small clients, the ones with security problems.

He took time to admire the blue sky, adjusted his suit jacket and felt uncomfortable because there was no gun under his arm as he started toward his car. There were no shadows because the sun exposed all the obstacles. Until he reached the corner where two men in dark blue suits joined him, one on each side.

"Good morning, Mr. Frane."

The three men stood silently before Frane responded. "If you say so."

"We were asked to invite you to visit with Ms Abate at her office."

He thought, if they are from Muriel Abate, they probably know more about Judo and Karate than I do. If they aren't that is a different story. "How do I know you're for real?"

"Will a badge do it?"

"Try something else. Badges are easy to copy."

The second man joined in. "Look, we know you're a tough guy. We're not trying anything funny. Ms Abate wants to talk with you. Pretty serious stuff. How about I ride with you in your car while my partner follows in a company car."

"That means if I behave I get to drive myself home?"

"Absolutely. You know the routine. We're just doing what we're told to do. Following orders."

With a small shake of the head Frane observed, "Where have I heard that before."

The two cars headed south on the Schuylkill Express, took the exit for Central Philadelphia and turned right on 4th Street to Chestnut Street, then left to a small office building near the corner. A slightly hidden parking lot had space for only six cars, very private.

Frane scanned the entrance and spotted the security devices. No doubt pictures of his arrival would become part of the CIA archives. There was no reception desk, strangers didn't just drop in, they came by invitation. Somewhere an agent sat in front of a screen observing all who entered. This was an inner sanctum.

At the end of a long hallway the door stood open, waiting for him. Muriel Abate sat behind a desk with few papers and three telephones. "Thanks for coming down," she said.

"My pleasure," answered Frane. "I was just planning a visit when your two emissaries arrived. We talked over old-times, usual chit-chat. And here I am."

"Please make yourself comfortable. Coffee? Tea?"

"No thanks, I had a power breakfast this morning."

"Oh. Where?"

"You'd never guess. At home."

"I'll have that to look forward to. But, you're not really that retired. You are working."

"Just enough to get by."

From her top desk drawer she drew a sheet of paper. "According to our information you keep pretty busy." She slid the paper across the desk.

Alarms went off in his head. Here were some shadows coming his way.

What you see is not what you get. Without touching the paper, he leaned forward and saw that it was an hour-by-hour report of his activities over the past three days.

"Don't you want to study our work?" she asked.

There it was, he thought. Touch the paper and they have your fingerprints. Not that they were hard to get, but on this piece of paper, who knows? "I could have saved you the trouble. Why didn't you just ask where I had been? You know how cooperative I can be. You even have our lunch meeting detailed."

"We also have you handing over a brief case full of money to John Pentram."

"You know how much was in that brief case?"

Abate smiled. "I'll bet you just want to tell me."

"Miss Abate, or is it Mrs.? Can we get down to business? I have some important things to do today."

"Can I assume this conversation is confidential?"

"If you wish. Make any assumption that satisfies."

"It's a matter of national security. So, if you don't agree to confidentiality, then this meeting never took place."

Frane rose, stood behind his chair and said, "You have stated the rules of engagement. If you want to talk, I'm here. Otherwise, I'm out of here. What's your pleasure?"

"You are one piss-cutter," she muttered. "I'll tell you what I need to know. Simple. Pentram may be involved in some subversive activity. We need a line into him. Will you help?"

"Spy on a client? That's not very nice."

"For your country."

Frane pursed his lips in deep concentration. "Will you pay me for my time? And how about a letter saying that I am working for you?"

"Sounds like a step in the right direction. But, you know I can't give you that kind of letter. This is CIA business. We trust one another."

Ah, a cloud of secrecy has created more shadows. It's like running into a wall. It must be time to shed some light on what is becoming a nightmare within a nightmare. Reaching into his jacket pocket, he drew out a black notebook. On a blank page, he printed a telephone number.

"When you're a consultant, there are times it's necessary to clear with other clients before taking on a new assignment. I'm going to ask you to call this number and explain what we have been talking about and see if you can get approval for me to work with you." He held up the number, showed it to

Abate, then tore off the edge of the page, crumbled that paper, and shoved it into his mouth.

"It doesn't taste very good," he mumbled.

"You son-of-a-bitch! You know I can't call that number."

38

Rogers met with Captain Bailey. "Here's where we are, boss." She knew he liked her way of addressing him when they were alone. In a more public setting, his title was appropriate.

"Witnesses have identified two of the men who escorted Brewer out of the restaurant. One of them was the dead man in the storage area of the Irish Pub. The other was this big guy whose ribs looked like a jig saw puzzle. He was barely moving, writhing on the floor next to his friend when we got there. The third man was gone. We only know that he was there because several of the patrons at the bar described him."

"Any connection with the McCabe woman?"

"Method was the same, bullets match, but no gun, yet."

"Witnesses?"

"None that we have uncovered. Seems both McCabe and Brewer were collectors for Pentram. All pretty legal. He is partners in all kinds of places. So, each week he sends around to collect his share of the profits."

"Suppose there are losses?"

"No way. Pentram has a system where he keeps the books. Controls expenses and sees to it that there is a profit every week. Private enterprise at its best."

"I guess you're going to tell me he pays all his taxes."

"It seems that's part of his routine. Nobody at IRS will talk to me. But, if he is legit, there's every reason to believe he's straight."

Bailey leaned back in his worn leather chair. "Amazing. When bad guys discover they can make money legally, they do it right."

"We're still looking for motive. Why would anybody want to knock off these two small time characters?"

"Two reasons," Bailey offered. "First, because they're unimportant it doesn't attract a whole lot of attention. Second and more important, it sends a message to Pentram. May have nothing to do with the people or their work. Could sure be telling Pentram something."

"Does that mean you send in two very professional killers to respond?"

"Exactly. You hit me, I gotta hit back. Any news on them?"

"Nothing yet. We're pretty sure they were imported."

Bailey waved her off. As she rose to leave. "Guess I'm not cynical enough."

"You'll get there. Takes time."

The message on her answering machine was simple and direct. "Dinner with Andros tonight. Pick you up at six."

Not exactly a love note. Still, a good meal is hard to turn down.

At six on the dot, she stood on the white stone steps of her apartment building. Every property on the block had five scrubbed white steps, worn from constant cleaning. It is part of the culture, row houses; some dating back a hundred years, all cared for in similar fashion. A stiff brush and a bucket of soapy water every week to keep the steps sparkling.

Frane double parked the Burgundy Chevy as Rogers came around to the middle of the street and slid into the front seat. When he first bought this car she teased him about its color; red, cherry, crimson, even scarlet. She contended that a cop shouldn't drive a car that was so easy to spot if you're tailing a suspect. He claimed that, "Lieutenants don't tail suspects."

"What's the occasion?" she asked.

"Nothing, really. Just wanted to see you, have a good dinner, maybe a glass of wine, interesting talk with Andros. He always has a story to tell."

"Which propelled you: me, wine, dinner, or Andros?"

As they pulled into traffic he said, "Isn't just being together enough reason?"

"What a charmer you're getting to be."

"Hey, I've had a couple of rough days. Thought it was time to relax and just enjoy being with you. Especially as how we don't work together, I kind of miss seeing you."

She nudged him in the ribs. "Be careful how you drive."

The Sand Box had become their favorite restaurant and Leonides Andros, the owner, had become a favorite person. They first met when the chef at the Captain's Table was found under eight boxes of shrimp—in the freezer. As the case unfolded, Thelma Andros, his daughter was murdered along with a couple of others. The old man behaved in the best stoic manner, true to his Greek background. When the most promising suspect disappeared, Rogers and Frane suspected Andros might have taken justice into his own hands. An absence of any real evidence and the lack of a body, led nowhere. What disturbed them was the disappearance of the old-fashioned diving apparatus that was on display in the restaurant. It would have made for a perfect shroud, one easily resting at the bottom of the Delaware River.

As they entered the restaurant, Andros materialized from the kitchen. "My dear friends, this is a welcome surprise. It's been weeks since last we dined. I have the perfect setting; come this way."

They followed to a secluded table where three place settings were already in position. "Were you expecting us?" Rogers asked.

"In a way, yes. The truth is, this table is always ready for special people. I hope you brought a healthy appetite with you."

By the time they were seated a table server arrived with three glasses, a bottle of Ouzo, and a pitcher of chilled water. "Just to set the mood," Andros said. "Next, tell me what kind of day you have had, and I'll suggest something to make it seem worth the while."

"You first," said Frane to Rogers.

She lifted the glass of Ouzo in a mock toast and said, "It was really a pretty good day, had an excellent meeting with Captain Bailey, learned a few things and found this delightful message on my answering machine. Almost a command performance to have dinner."

"Wish I had some nice days like that," added Frane. "I was accosted by two very professional men who escorted me to a meeting where demands were made on my soul."

Andros laughed. "It's good to hear police people have souls."

"It's been some time since we talked. You may not have heard I have retired from the department. So, my new work doesn't carry the same kind of perks and the two escorts were very persuasive."

"Gangsters?"

"As a matter of fact, government men."

"And now you want to know how to deal with them?"

"On target. From both of you." He drained the glass of Ouzo. "Can we have a real drink now?"

39

Fortified with an extra dry Martini, Frane began. "This gets complicated and I'm not sure why. Let me get your opinions. My client wants to put together a group of restaurants, have them all buy from a single distributor, and get price considerations that will make everybody happy. I can go into details, if you want. But, my question is, does this make sense?"

Rogers spoke first. "I can see where there might be some problems, even though I'm not a business person. Still, it makes sense in the big picture, joining together gives them muscle. What's wrong with that?"

Turning to Andros, Frane sought his view. "She is right; beside the problems of putting it all together could be difficult. The idea sounds reasonable. But, you said there were other things; I think you said it gets complicated."

Back to Rogers, he pointed and said, "There are a couple of murders that seem to get in the way. Don't know how they relate to the whole picture."

"Can I interrupt," Andros said. "This sounds like serious talk. So, I'd like to suggest a somewhat less serious dinner. Something easy, a 16-ounce New York Sirloin Strip, or, we have fresh Red Snapper, broiled, just a touch of

131

olive oil. Maybe start with a small Greek salad, just so you'll know where you are. And a bottle of Yellow Tail Chardonnay."

"Yellow Tail?"

"It's an Australian wine, very pleasant."

Frane and Rogers exchanged glances. "One steak rare and one Snapper. And you?"

"Ah, choice of the house, baby calves liver sautéed Greek style. Guaranteed to increase your cholesterol level."

Draining his glass, Frane interjected, "I think gin has the opposite effect, changes the bad cholesterol to good." Their private table server got the message and was off to get him a refill.

"So far," Andros said, "you haven't told us why your day was so difficult."

"Since I'm with some of my favorite people, I'll try to spell it out without divulging any names. This assumes that my problem goes no further."

Both Andros and Rogers offered small nods of agreement.

"Anyhow, I am doing some consulting with a very powerful man. Certain agencies are interested in his activities. They both have approached me separately, to do some, shall we say, spying on him."

"Agencies?"

"What kind of spying?"

After taking a deep breath he answered, "FBI and CIA."

Dinner arrived, just in time. The steak was rare, as ordered, the Red Snapper tinged with a light coat and topped with three shrimp, and the calves liver remarkable in a variety of Greek seasoning. The wine was mildly chilled and sipped gently did justice to the food.

"Let me guess," said Rogers. "The CIA thinks he is a foreign agent and the FBI thinks he's bringing drugs into the country."

"You really think that's what they want?" asked Andros.

"The question is, should I be doing their work? Am I right, that my client is entitled to my confidence? One of them used the words, 'National security'. Where is my first obligation?"

Andros said, "Let me tell you a short story. On my island, that is the island where I lived, there were German soldiers. You remember World War II? I was only a little boy, maybe six or seven, but I knew the story of one of our neighbors. There were two sons, one was a loyalist, the other favored the German occupation. They both knew how the other felt. What were they to do?"

"You mean they were on the horns of the dilemma. Each should blow the whistle on the other. Brothers! Wow. So, what did they do?"

"Thinking back, I'd like to say the loyalist told the underground about his brother. But, it didn't work that way. He wound up in jail. Unfortunately, I don't know the end of the story."

Rogers said, "That sounds like the end."

"I see your point," said Frane. "The brother who was not only certain he was right, but sided with those in power had no problem deciding what to do. The loyalist brother was equally certain, but with little power."

"Does this help?" asked Andros.

Frane put down the heavy steak knife and reached for the bottle of wine. He poured a full glass, drank deeply. On top of the Ouzo and Gin, he knew he would have to ask Rogers to drive home.

"Good story. Good point. Still doesn't really get to the nub of things. Does national security come ahead of my responsibility to my client? That's sounds pretty easy. Drugs aren't very important; we've been fighting that one for years."

"How sure are you about national security? Who were you talking to? Just what did they want you to find out?"

"Let me bumble around with those questions later. For the moment, I told them both to go pound sand. Thing is, how did they even know I was involved? One of them was having me followed. Can you imagine that, following a former police lieutenant?"

"Sounds like you're a pretty significant player in their game."

"What do you think is the link with the murders?"

Rogers volunteered, "There are really three murders. We're pretty certain the third was the killer of the other two. We're still trying to find the person who did number three. But, I don't see how they get in the way of making your decision."

"Suppose," said Frane, "just suppose the first two victims knew something that the feds were interested in. They come to me because they think my client is the key to a major crime. That's where the national security stuff fits in."

"How?" asked Andros.

Rogers observed, "It could be they were carrying messages. Maybe the collections routine was just that, a routine to throw everybody off balance. Maybe they were the bad guys and that's why they had to be taken out."

"You want my advice?" asked Andros.

"Like to hear it. No guarantee I'll take it."

"You can't work for both. Choose one of the agencies and see what they want. If it gets too sticky, walk away."

Frane smiled. "You don't walk away from the FBI."

"How about the CIA?

"They make the FBI look like pussy cats."

40

Frane liked the idea of telling Rogers and Andros about his problem. It gave him a chance to keep them in the circle, in case he needed some confirmation about what he was doing. His life since leaving the force had taken on operational intricacies far in excess of dealing with the political bureaucracies that infested the Round House. Against his better judgment, he began keeping a diary, names, dates, and pertinent conversations. It meant storing at least one copy in a safe deposit box. Even this was a new experience.

In his years working through the system, Frane learned when to speak out, where the power resided, whose ass had to be kissed, and how to survive. Not that the police department was different, just that it too was an organization and had all the characteristics and anomalies of large groups, people stumbling over one another trying to get to the top, cutting throats when deemed necessary, and in general being careful of whose toes were smashed.

His head was full of all these hazy thoughts following a night of heavy eating and heavier drinking. The Remy Martin Cognac that appeared toward the end of the meal was too good to miss. It also meant jogging an extra couple of miles this morning in an attempt to prepare for the day. He never noticed the runner closing the space between them. Until he realized the pounding in his head was accompanied by the thump of running feet.

"You're good."

The voice seemed to boom out. With a little turn, Frane realized the man behind him was one of his two escorts from yesterday.

"Don't tell me you're going to take me to your Mistress again."

"You're confused. She's not my mistress. More like my master."

"Okay. So, this is just you and me. Friends."

"Not exactly, but close. I admired the way you ate the evidence. Good thing she knew the number."

"You know the number?"

"That's a tough question. At my pay-grade I'm not supposed to know that number."

"But?"

"Let's just say, I'm acquainted with it."

"That's pretty interesting. Problem is; you've been trained in this cat-and-mouse game. I'm just a beginner. I'm having trouble trying to find out who to trust."

"Constant problem in our business."

"That why they call you, 'Spooks?'"

"Nah. That goes back to the Cold War. This is now. We're just out there doing the best we can."

"Okay. Enough of this love making. What's on your mind?"

The two men pounded the pavement in unison; not too fast, not too slow. "Is it alright if I ask your name?"

"Why not pick a name you're comfortable with, then when you want me I'll know exactly who's calling."

"Does that mean I get a phone number?"

"One time use only."

Frane felt he was trapped in a fragmented world, one replete with twists and turns. In an attempt to add his own touch, he answered, "How does Marmaduke sound?"

With a laugh, he said, "One name is as good as another." Reaching out, he handed Frane a card with a phone number. "One time only. And use an out of the way pay phone."

"Does your boss know anything about this?"

"Of course."

Thinking better of the answer, he went on. "Who is your boss?"

"No comment."

"When do you want me to call?"

Now, Marmaduke stopped running. He barely touched Franes' arm. "When you uncover or confirm what you were sent to discover."

"And what was that?"

"Coy doesn't seem to be your style. Let's just say we're both on the same side."

Frane realized that running shorts and sweaty shirts didn't allow for concealing the miniature tape recorder he usually carried. After his meeting with Muriel Abate only the day before, he decided to make at least seven copies to be held in confidence by seven different people.

"Tell you what, Marmaduke; we should spend a few minutes together in some less public place. Sort of get our objectives lined up. Make sure we're talking the same language."

"My dear RC," he intoned. "We are lined up. What you're working on and what I'm working on are one and the same. Find out where Pentram stands."

"He's just trying to make a living. This business proposition has great potential. What else do you have in mind?"

"Back to being coy? That wasn't your assignment."

"Assignment? What the hell are you talking about?"

"Okay, Frane. If that's the way you want to play." With a burst of energy, he turned and retraced his running steps, this time at his usual marathon pace.

41

Maintaining a non-committal expression took effort. The first words out of his mouth sent a silent alarm, like the one you don't hear when the system is broached on entering an armed house. You know it's there, but there is no sound. Not like the clanging of fire engines, which meant there was trouble up ahead. Or, the undulating horn aboard ship that indicates sinking is a distinct possibility. Or even the flashing light in the rear view mirror when the police are about to pull you over.

Greta Rogers heeded the warning when the man said, "Good morning, Sergeant Rogers. They call me Marmaduke." In his mind this was a wonderful opening gambit, it immediately identified him and was sure to open the door to further conversation.

She stopped, stood by her car, scanned the street to ascertain there were people walking, some to work, others to shopping. She took some comfort that no one seemed to be paying much attention to this well-dressed man talking to her. They were alone in the center of the city. She was well acquainted with Franes' use of the moniker, "Marmaduke" to identify people who were not to be trusted. When leaving an interrogation room he was known to say, "This Marmaduke is for you."

With a very straight face she asked, "What can I do for you, Marmaduke?"

"Now that's what I call a wonderful start," he oozed. "However, the question really is, what can I do for you?"

She pressed her lips together, deep in thought. "How about you tell me what's on your mind. Then we can decide who is the do-er and who is the do-ee."

"Fair enough. Can we start with the thought that I was one of the team who brought your friend to headquarters? Following that, we have jogged together and we seemed to get on pretty well. Since you are involved in work that touches on his, I thought it would be useful for us to talk."

This is an unusual game. Let's take it further. This is just for fun. "What you're saying seems to make sense. However, I'm on my way to the office and I really don't have time right now. Give me your phone number and we can arrange to meet somewhere." Digging into her bag, she drew out a business card. "Here's where I can be reached. Can I have your card?"

"Gee, I'm fresh out of cards. But, I'll call. Unless we can make a definite appointment now. Say lunch at the Sheraton. It's a nice place, convenient and we can hang out in the lobby if we are there for long."

She made a face, took out an appointment book, ran her finger down the page, and answered, "That won't work. How about next week sometime?"

"I'm at your disposal, only sooner is better than later. Maybe this evening, after work?"

Referring to her appointment book again, she responded, "I'll put you down for seven tonight. You know Smith and Wollensky, at the Rittenhouse?"

"That's good," he responded. "Plenty of people."

With a wave of the hand, she started to open the car door. "See you there."

"Hold on a minute," he smiled. "I have something that might prove useful."

Halfway through the open door, she got out and asked, "Now what?"

"Just something so you'll know I'm interested in you. That is, in you and your work. Nothing personal." He paused while she frowned. "Those two hot-shots you're looking for, try Trenton."

"I don't have an inkling of what you're talking about."

"Come now, Greta. The two shooters who took down the two Jimmies. You're looking for them. I'm just trying to help. What's the problem?"

"You seem to know quite a little about what I do." Now playing innocent she asked, "You said you took my friend to headquarters. What does that mean?"

"Sounds like you're beginning to have some confidence in me. What it means is that my boss wanted to see Frane. So, an associate and I invited him to join us for a ride to her office."

"You work for a woman?"

Looking around to ascertain they were not within hearing distance of people passing by, he leaned forward and lightly said, "She's the head of the local CIA station. I'm sure you understand what that means."

Suppressing a smile, her face took on a look of anxiety mingled with surprise. "What did he do? Is the CIA after him for something?"

Standing tall, he said, "These are the kinds of things I want to discuss with you. Until tonight, remember what I said about those two in Trenton. But, be very careful. They are good—-and deadly."

She watched as he walked toward Nineteenth Street and turned the corner. Then she slipped behind the wheel of her Jeep and sat quietly, reviewing the conversation. A plan immediately formed. One that she decided to share with Captain Bailey.

42

"Are you sure he was CIA?"

"I'm not sure of anything, Captain. When I gave him my business card and asked for his, he said he didn't have any with him. That's strange."

Bailey stood, walked slowly around the office, stopped at the long table piled high with various reports, thumbed through some of the pages and took time to stare out the window.

"Rogers, there is something going on that is very eerie. Strange doesn't even begin to define what you have told me."

"How's that boss?"

Moving to his desk chair, he sat down heavily and leaned forward, his most intimidating posture. Rogers had noticed in the past that when he was angry, or when he wanted to make a serious point this was his pose. She couldn't determine his mood at this time.

"Let's get this straight, Sergeant. Man stops you in the middle of the street, gives you this cock-and-bull story, and tells you he's CIA. He also tells you he and his partner picked up Frane and took him to see the Station Chief, a woman. Then he wants to meet you. Oh, he also tells you the two shooters you're looking for come from Trenton."

"That sums it up pretty well. But, why eerie?"

"First, let me ask you something. Did you know that two men braced Frane and took him downtown to the CIA office?"

"No. This was the first I heard about that."

"You have a date to meet this guy?"

"Tonight at seven, at Smith and Wollensky."

Standing again, Bailey once more moved to the window. Without turning he asked, "Did you know the CIA isn't supposed to operate in the country?"

Taken aback, Rogers answered, "Well, I know they're a bunch of spooks, spies, call them what you will. What do you mean; they aren't supposed to operate in the country?"

"Just that. Sure, home base is in Langley, big, impressive and tough as hell to get into. But, they're supposed to do the international policing while the FBI takes care of things domestically."

"If I hear you right, you seem to think he may not be CIA, maybe some other agency."

"Or, a bad guy."

Rogers slumped in her chair. *I don't like being pursued. I'm supposed to be doing the pursuing, chasing murderers, killers and the like. Seeing that they got caught and sent away. Lies are part of interviewing suspects and even witnesses. People prefer to hide the truth when there's nothing to be gained. Marmaduke wanted to talk with me, interview me; I'm being stalked, followed and treated like a criminal.*

"Chief, I'm not sure how to deal with this. What do you think is going on?"

"Here's my read. This guy, whoever he is, thinks you're some kind of patsy. So, meet him tonight. We'll get the techies to wire you and we'll have two plain clothes dicks follow this guy. What did you say you call him, Marmaduke?"

"Yeh, Frane gave him that name. Usually we refer to lying suspects that way. So, the signal from Frane was clear. This bird is a nogoodnik."

Bailey laughed. "Right out of 'Guys and Dolls'."

Rogers had never worn a wire before. It wasn't uncomfortable, physically. Captain Bailey told her it would be a good experience, that she would gain a feeling about using this technique with witnesses who were asked to trap culprits; she would be able to alert them to the stomach flutters that go with subterfuge. Embarked on this adventure, the flutters jumped around in her stomach with abandon. As she walked toward the restaurant, the idea of having a sandwich or a drink brought a sour taste surging upward. She paused for a minute, surveyed the park, and regained control.

Smith & Wollensky is part of a chain of steak houses. The Grille is on the first level of The Rittenhouse Hotel on the west side of Rittenhouse Square.

Marmaduke was standing at the bar when she entered. He raised a hand in recognition and guided her to a booth. "I was waiting for you before ordering. What will you have to drink?"

Scanning the room, searching for the two detectives who were tailing her, Rogers answered, "Think I'll have a cup of chamomile tea."

"Pretty tame for a Homicide Sergeant."

"You seem to think I'm some kind of hot-shot-shoot-em-up cop."

"Hey, everybody knows how you saved Franes' life, taking down a bad guy. That's big-time. Gives you a lot of points on the board."

"Listen, Marmaduke. Let's get on with it. What's on your mind?"

When the table server appeared, he ordered. "Scotch rocks for me and chamomile tea for the lady."

Leaning forward he almost whispered, "There are some bad things going down. Maybe illegal arms shipments, maybe dope. We're not altogether sure. What we need is an inside track to discover what's going on."

"Tell me," she responded. "How did you come to know about the two suits from Trenton? Where do they fit in?"

Hands open, palms up, he said, "You know I can't reveal my sources. Let's just say we had some inside information about the Three Jimmies and then about the Two Suits. That's why I passed that data along to you, for the benefit of your investigation."

Rogers began to feel better. A few sips of tea went a long way toward calming a churning stomach. "And in return, what do you want?"

Marmaduke smoothed his tie, took a swallow of scotch, reached into his coat pocket and drew out a card. "Here is how to get in touch with me. It's an answering service, but they will know where I am every minute of the day. Or night. What we really need is an entree into the workings of Star Distributing."

Feigning ignorance Rogers said, "I don't understand. What has that got to do with me? And, what does it have to do with illegal weapons?"

"Ah, here's the track, as we see it. You and Frane are close. He is working for John Pentram. By the way, did you know that?"

She nodded, yes.

"Well, Pentram has a big business deal that includes Star. If we can become part of the equation, we will be able to discover how the guns are coming into the country."

Now Rogers leaned forward. "You said a few minutes ago you were interested in illegal arms, maybe drugs. Now, you're talking about guns. Big difference."

"Just that I didn't want to be too specific," he alibied. "The important thing is for our team to become part of the Pentram team, so we can have access to Star."

"And you think I can get Frane to make it happen?"

"Exactly. You are good."

Again, she nodded. "So, what do I get out of this mess?"

"Well, one Jimmy is dead, another is in very bad shape in the hospital, and the third is available to you whenever you ask. And, we'll even give you the Two Suits."

"But, suppose I can't convince Frane to make you part of the Pentram team?"

"Well, at least you will have solved three murders. We'll just hope you can give us what we need."

"And, if I don't want to play?"

Smiling broadly, he said, "There are more where the Two Suits came from."

43

"You gentlemen know RC Frane. I think he has met with each of you when he was gathering some information for me."

Both Arthur and Waterhouse acknowledged his presence. Simultaneously they signaled for a private moment with Pentram. When Frane closed the door, the mood in the suite turned. "What's he doing here? What do we need with a cop?"

Unaccustomed to being questioned, Pentram spoke quietly. "Former Lieutenant Frane is now retired. I felt that someone with his capabilities would add to my program. He now serves me as a consultant."

"That all sounds real nice," Arthur injected. "But, once a cop, always a cop. Besides, he was homicide."

"You know, John, times have changed. Last thing we need is a homicide cop hanging around."

Pentram reacted to the use of his first name with a stern response. "This program is mine. I conceived of the idea and then invited you both to join because there is enough for everyone. Frane works for me." Then in a more conciliatory tone, "I have been in business for a long time. You should respect my knowledge and understanding. When I converted Pentram Enterprises into a more, shall we say, professional activity, it produced far more profits and far less grief. Shooting from the lip is less deadly than shooting from the hip."

Continuing what had become a small lecture he added, "To paraphrase, 'When I was a child, I played as a child. Now that I am a man, I have put aside my childish playthings.' If you want to work with me to create something that will send streams of money our way, good. If not, we can end this meeting now and go our separate ways."

Waterhouse spoke. "I'm from Trenton. In fact, I pretty much run Trenton. I'm not used to taking orders."

Arthur continued. "We've been getting along pretty good in Philadelphia. I have my area, you have yours."

Pointing a finger at Waterhouse, Pentram observed, "You don't run Trenton. You control a small piece, with muscle." Turning to Arthur, "And you have your piece of Philadelphia because I allowed it to happen. If you doubt what I have said, think back to when you were both in short pants and I was the power. Do you think you survived without my influence?"

A race for clout surged through the room as the three combatants faced each other in a show of strength. An invisible puff of steam seemed to rise above Arthur's head as he fought to control his temper. Waterhouse made a silent decision to keep his mouth shut. He flicked at a piece of lint on his sleeve.

Pentram relaxed, knowing that this minor uprising was not a major revolt. Simply a necessary transition; like crossing a small stream to get to the other side where dry land beckoned. He raised his hand, signaling for Arthur to open the bottle of champagne that had been chilling. The struggle was over.

There were four flutes sitting on a silver tray. "Harry, why don't you invite Mr. Frane to join us." It was not a question, more of a directive delivered in a very soft voice.

The trip down the Atlantic City Expressway to the casino began when Frane met Pentram at Julianis'. "Where we headed, Mr. Pentram?"

"We have a suite reserved for a private meeting. You know the casino. I believe you have visited there with your friend in the past."

The son of a bitch knows everything. "No problem," he answered. "Can I ask if we're meeting anyone?"

"Yes you can, because I will need your help in smoothing the waters. This project you're working on is very big. We don't have the resources to do all the possible things. So, my plan is to enlist some others in a wonderful opportunity to make a lot of money, easy."

"You think I can make some kind of difference?"

"What I think is this. They will probably object to your being involved. In fact, you know the two men we will be meeting; Thurman Arthur and Harry Waterhouse."

"Mr. Pentram, I am on board as your consultant. So far, the work has been fairly easy and it seems legal. But, these two characters may not be ready for prime-time honesty. What's your take?"

Pentram seemed to retreat into himself, searching for the right words. "RC, we have only been working together for a couple of weeks. Prior to that, we tended to be on opposite sides of the desk. In this brief period of time, I think we have established a fair and open relationship. Considering that you are a consultant and prepared to hold a confidence, I intend to share more and more information. You have correctly perceived that what I am embarked upon is a legitimate business. It has some twists and turns, but you certainly realize that my honor and integrity are significant factors. Now, today we will meet with two very difficult men who have each built their own small empires. You know and I know that when I was a younger man, I too built an empire."

The Expressway was almost empty at this time of day and Frane only exceeded the speed limit by five miles an hour. Still, seventy miles an hour is fast. "So far I'm with you. Yes, I do believe what you are putting together is legit. And, yes, I'm part of the picture. That's why I find it strange that you are bringing in these two men."

In a very serious tone, Pentram explained. "Two things. First, I am not invincible. Under the best of circumstances, we all die in due course. At my age, this is a very serious subject. Believe me, it stands heavily."

"And the second?"

"Ah, this is an area in which I may have to pull rank and say, when it is time for you to know, you will be the first to learn. At that time, I will need you more than ever. First, we set up a business to take care of my family. My son needs direction and help. If it happens that I am not available, I hope you will fill some of the void."

As they pulled away from the Egg Harbor Toll Booth, Frane thought, *In one sense it's an honor. In another, I wonder if I know what I have gotten into.*

Once Frane reentered the suite, the glasses were filled. Pentram proposed a toast. "Gentlemen, we are going on a remarkable venture. In front of us is the opportunity to build a national organization, dedicated to making money honorably." Raising the glass, he toasted, "Fortuna."

44

Ronald Star spent hours with his financial vice president, Gary Exton. Together they pored over projections of how additional business of $15 to $30 million a year would impact their business structure. Their main concern was how to make a net profit when the margins of gross profit would be narrowed.

"It still costs us the same to do business," said Exton.

"I don't think so," answered Star. "The warehouse remains the same; heat, light, general overhead don't change. We'll need more trucks, more drivers, and even some more warehouse people. The three big things are, we don't need salespeople, deliveries will be concentrated, and collections will be half of what we experience today."

Exton nodded. "Yeah, and that should help the purchasing department."

"There are other benefits," added Star. "If this deal comes through it will jump us into the $100 million club. Not too many independents doing that much business. Get more respect and better prices. What I want you to do is run a series of pro formas using different increments. Say 15, 20, and 25. See what they look like. Because of the guaranteed order size, you can figure about $4 million a year to a truck. So, at 15 that means we need maybe four more trucks. Probably not that many, because we can become more efficient with our regular fleet. Take a look-see."

"Is our data processing system able to handle all this?"

"She's next on my list. I'm meeting with Hope and Frane in about fifteen minutes."

Star took ten minutes to consider the future. *If my early thoughts on this opportunity take hold, there's a chance to add close to half-a-million dollars to the bottom line. It'll take a lot of maneuvering, but the best part is the money will be on the table. Just have to run a better business. What's wrong with that?*

Hope Rutan knocked on the door just minutes before the receptionist announced Frane's arrival. "Come in, RC. Say hello to Hope Rutan our Vice President of Information Systems. She is an ace. Hope, this is a man I have known for a little time and he has brought us this fascinating proposition."

Her handshake was strong. She stood almost as tall as Frane, dressed in casual business attire, including comfortable low shoes, and wore very little make-up. "Nice to meet you, Mr. Frane. I guess we're going to be working together."

"With a name like 'Hope' we can't help but succeed. I'm a little more at ease with 'RC'."

Star inserted, "Okay. Now that we all know one another, let's figure out how to make this thing work."

"Tell me what you need."

"Let's say we bring in thirty new customers. They will each have some specific items they need. They'll order by computer, expect zero outages, and deliveries will be within a very set time limit. Payment of bills and other money matters we have pretty much lined up."

"How many deliveries a week? And what size?"

"Since these are individual restaurants there will be some variation. We think an early delivery, say Mondays and Tuesdays, an order ranging somewhere around $8,000. Then later in the week, maybe Thursday or Friday, possibly Saturday if that works, a follow-up order for two or three thousand."

Rutan was taking notes. "So, what's the problem?"

Star asked, "Do we have enough computer for this much added business?"

"We're talking about sixty orders a week. We're processing over 70,000 orders a year. Another 3,000 won't even raise a sweat."

"See," Star said. "I told you she was an ace."

"I'm a little new at this. Hope, can you describe how it works?"

"We'll put a computer in each restaurant, write a separate order form for each one, and link them to our main frame. Also, we'll create a usage report; break down food cost per serving, profit per item based on selling price, and almost anything else you want."

Star smiled.

"Let me see if I have this straight. Each restaurant will place their order. They will know what they ordered for the prior two or three weeks, prices and a whole lot of other stuff. Once they put that on the computer, and tap the 'send' icon, the order goes to the delivery department and then the warehouse takes over."

Rutan added, "It's basically what happens. Little more complicated than that, and we have to do a lot of things to make it happen. But, you have the right idea. Once we put it together, it should work like a charm. How does that sound, Mr. Star?"

"You said we would put computers in each restaurant?"

"Not really. Terminals. A direct link to our mainframe."

"Cost?"

"Considering the volume of business, peanuts. Oh, there is another wrinkle we can develop. When this thing gets going, we may be able to get the restaurants to keep track of their own inventory and then the ordering becomes routine. Every time somebody takes a case of something, it gets fed into the computer and the order writes itself. You have independent restaurants who will get this involved?"

"Our idea is for everybody to run a more efficient operation," Frane said. "We might get into some heavy bookkeeping, stuff like that."

"How are you going to get them to accept what you're saying?"

"Good point. We have several people selling the idea. They can be very persuasive."

"Anything else, RC? In fact, can't we tie into the cash register, Hope?"

"That's where we can go, if they let us."

"Sounds good to me. Thank you for the explanation, Hope. As we get closer, you and I will work together. That is, I'll sort of stand around while everybody does the work."

Rising to leave, she laughed, "You sound like a great executive."

"It's the thing I do best," he said as she headed for the door.

Star pointed to the coffee machine. "Pour you a cup?"

"Not today, thanks. I have to get along. Just one more thing. We had anticipated aiming for thirty restaurants. Met with some of our other colleagues last week. We may want to raise our aim to fifty."

Star fought for control. *I can't believe this.* "We'll handle the whole shooting match."

45

The note read, "Penns Landing. 30 minutes. M."

Frane stood next to his burgundy Chevy, where the piece of paper had been secured under the windshield wiper. *If he left the message, it means he followed me here. He must have an idea of when I would leave the building.* Carefully, he wrapped the note in his handkerchief. No telling what might be revealed in a fingerprint check.

Dozens of cars were neatly parked in designated spaces. He strolled to the end of the building, where another parking area held at least ten tractor trailers waiting to be unloaded. A normal day in the food industry.

Reaching to turn the ignition key, he paused. *I wonder if there is a bomb under the hood of the car.* A sudden drop of perspiration crept down his arm pit. He twisted the key and the motor stirred. Slowly he backed out and headed toward I-95 North that was only five minutes from Penns Landing.

Meeting Marmaduke was getting to be a habit. Frane knew what he wanted, a way to get at Pentram. *It's a toss-up. Either he wants what he thinks Pentram used to have or he wants a piece of what he thinks Pentram is about to have.*

He pulled into the curved entry to the Hyatt, motioned to the door man and handed him two dollars. "I'll be back in fifteen minutes. Keep an eye on the car."

As he strolled along the concrete walkway, he spotted Marmaduke a block away. A few visitors were headed toward the Battleship Olympia. Virtually no traffic at this time of day. Within ten feet of reaching Marmaduke, Frane held up his hand and said, "Just stand there and tell me what's on your mind."

Feigning surprise, Marmaduke answered, "My goodness, RC. Don't you trust me?"

"The long answer is 'Yes'. The short answer is, 'No'."

"Well, I'm truly sorry to hear that. Oh, maybe we were a little heavy handed last time we met. But, really, there are things we have in common. And Ms Abate wants to get to know you better. Maybe work something out that will prove mutually beneficial."

"How about if we start by telling me your name?"

"That's not really important. You know in our work, it's better to remain nameless. That way you can always deny knowing me. See, you don't know my name so there's no way you can identify me. Makes our negotiations more secure."

Looking at his watch Frane responded, "I have an appointment in ten minutes. Let's get this over with."

Stepping forward, Marmaduke gestured in a friendly fashion.

"Stop right there," Frane demanded. "One more move and I'll shoot your balls off."

"What are you going to use, a water pistol?"

With a quick gesture, Frane pulled a 9mm Sig Sauer from his belt and aimed it at Marmadukes' crotch. "Want to find out?"

"You haven't got the nerve."

With that, Frane edged the gun to the side and fired. The silencer covered the noise, as the bullet churned the ground near Marmaduke's foot. "Now, just step back four paces and keep your mouth shut."

The silent shot caused a trickle of urine to sneak through his shorts and stain his trousers. He did as told.

"What did you want to see me about?"

Biting back his shame, Marmaduke said, "Ms Abate wants to meet with you."

"She set the time and place last time. Now, it's my turn. You tell her I'll be having lunch at the cafeteria in two hours."

"That's all."

"Unless you want to test my nerve again." He added, "You walk away as fast as you can, now!"

Frane took time to make several phone calls. One from a pay phone, two from his cell phone. Allowing time for Greta Rogers and Peg Wilson to connect, he sat in his car thinking. *I used to have a desk and an office where I could retreat to consider what to do next. Now, I have a car that serves as my office.*

Slowly, he eased the car into traffic and turned onto Walnut Street for the trip to the cafeteria where Abate had first accosted him. When he reached Nineteenth Street, he found a lot and parked. Still early, he walked along Market Street until he found a vendor. "Hot dog with mustard and relish," he said.

The paper-wrapped, long hot dog dripped. He held it away from his body as he bit off a large chunk. Relish slide down his chin and he wiped vigorously with a hand-full of paper napkins. The street vendor looked his way and smiled. "Taste good?"

"Absolutely delicious. Good for the cholesterol too."

"Hey, they're low-fat dogs."

"Yeh. And the Phillies will win the pennant this year."

He shoved the rest of the roll into his mouth, wiped again, and headed for the delivery entrance to the cafeteria.

Standing to the left of the door that led to the dining area, he scanned the room, spotted Rogers on one side and Wilson sitting at a table, sipping ice tea. Though he was no longer a cop, his former team members were still available when he called on them. Rogers knew Marmaduke, so she paid attention as new customers arrived. Frane caught her eye and raised his hand when Abate came through the door and headed for the line to get coffee. Frane moved behind her and said, "I'll be happy to buy you a cup. Straight or cream?"

"You're early," she said.

"Didn't want to miss you. By the way, where are your boys?"

"Oh, they're around. You know, don't leave home without them."

Frane indicated a table against the wall and they sat down. "So, what do you want? Last time in your office you were kinda pissed-off."

Regaining her composure, Abate said, "Different day, different setting. Let's get to it. We think Pentram is dirty. You're next to him. We want in."

Frane lifted his coffee cup as he said, "I'm not sure what the hell you're talking about."

"Why don't you cut the bullshit! He's either pushing dope or bringing in guns and the like. We need somebody on the inside to get the details. You're the logical one."

"When it comes to bullshit, you are the top of the mound. You're not what you say you are, so if you want to do business, level with me."

"Damn it, Frane, don't you know better than to mess with the CIA?"

Frane stood. "I told you last time, Pentram is clean. You want something, tell me and I'll see what I can do. Till then, I'll see you around."

"Wait," she said. "What's coming into the country in those containers of food? How about you set up a meet with Pentram and we talk."

"Your office still in the same place?"

"No, we move around a lot. I'll have one of my people reach you. When and where?"

Frane took out a business card, turned it over and wrote the number for one of his cell phones. "Call me."

46

Cracked ribs hurt and finally, heal by themselves. Little can overcome the sheer agony of breathing, moving, lying, standing, and just living. Jimmy Duncan was in far worse shape. His entire rib cage had been pulled out of position and that rearranged his chest. One solution was to remain immobilized. It didn't really help, but it held pain to a reasonable amount aided by a constant drip of strong narcotics. Rogers winced as she watched him breath; but not enough to stop the questions from flowing.

"Mr. Duncan, you come from Trenton. Is that right?"

"What'dya want from me?" he burbled.

"Just some information about how you got hurt."

Turning his head to face her caused a rift of suffering to shoot across his chest into his left arm. "I got nothin' to say."

"Let me tell you what we know. One Jimmy is dead. Another Jimmy is under wraps. And you are lying here in a bed of real hurt." With that, she jiggled the bed slightly.

He tried to shout, but it came out as a whimper. "You damn cops get away with a lot of crap. I'll get you, bitch."

"Oh, sorry," she smiled. "I sure didn't mean any harm." Then she jiggled the bed again.

"I'll get you," his voice a hoarse whisper.

"It's going to take you weeks to get back in shape. In the meantime, I'm going to practice my karate. So, when you're ready, we can have at it. Of course, that doesn't count how many years you're going to spend in the box. On the other hand, you might want to answer a few questions. Could save you some time away."

All he could manage was a grunt.

"Who set you up for this job?"

"What job?"

Again, she jiggled the bed. "The two people who went down, Brewer and McCabe. Bet you didn't even know her name."

"You're not allowed to try and scare me. I want a lawyer."

In her sweetest tone Rogers said, "Mr. Duncan. It's just you and me having a private talk. No witnesses. No nothing. Just the two of us. All I'm asking is some help so we can get to the top of the list. Like, who hired you?"

He struggled to look around the hospital room. It was empty. He watched as she held the nurses buzzer out of reach. Nobody knew what she was doing. If she kept jiggling the bed, he would be aching a lot more than he could stand. "Off the record?"

"As long as we can find the big man."

"Yeh. We come from Trenton. Big boss there gave us this job. Said, these two low-life collectors were skimming. You know, you just don't do that."

"But, they were working for a local man."

"That was before they found out there was more to be made doing a couple of things for Trenton."

"Now, that makes sense. Trenton couldn't let on to Philadelphia that they had infiltrated the area. So, how many other collectors are doing double duty?"

"We only had the assignment to get these two."

"Any idea who the two suits are? They did a number on you and your pal Jimmy Curtin just ain't no more."

"I been thinking about that. Best I can come up with is they're from way out of town. But, why take us down? We was just doing our job."

Rogers took another tack. "Seems like heavy duty punishment for taking a little cash. How come?"

"Not our call. Boss wants somebody done, we do it."

"Then, who ordered the hit on you?"

Duncan tried to shift his position. The drugs didn't help and his face turned from jaundiced yellow to gray. "How can I know that?"

"Don't suppose it was your Trenton contact?"

"You crazy? He gave us the sign, why would he want us out of the way?"

"Think about it. A day after you did the job, two hot-shots from a distance take you out. How did they know who you were? Didn't know there were any psychics in the underworld."

Rogers stood, walked around the bed, and looked down at Duncan. "There's some strange things going on with this case. These two killings don't make sense. Unless Mr. Waterhouse was firing a shot across the bow; trying to get Mr. Pentrams' attention. How does that sound to you?"

"We still off the record?"

"Would I lie to you, Mr. Duncan?" *Hard to believe these guys are so dumb. Lying is their way of life and he asks me if I'm lying.*

"Truth is, we just got the assignment. You really think he wanted us out of the way? We're the 'Three Jimmies'. We got a reputation. He takes us out, others might feel pretty bad about that."

"Want a piece of advice?"

His eyes opened wide, help from an unexpected place, the police. "I don't think so."

"Anyhow, let me tell you a couple of things. One, Jimmy Curtin is gone. You're in real bad shape. In addition, you and Jimmy Kennedy are both going away for a while. So, it hardly seems likely that anybody is going to worry about who did what to whom. Quite frankly, your ass is in a sling. You want to make things easier, good idea to square with me, take your rap, and maybe the DA will cut you a break for being honest."

"If you weren't a woman…What'dya want?"

"I'm going to arrange for Ms DeLeon to come see you with a stenographer. Take a full statement; give us some dope on Waterhouse. Maybe she can work out a deal."

She stopped at the door and waved. "Have a nice day."

In the hall, she paused to turn off the small tape recorder in her pocket. *It can't be used for evidence, but it helps if I forget anything. Just keep it to myself.* She snorted, "Would I lie to you? Ha."

47

"Ah, Mr. Kennedy. How are you this morning?"

Rogers was feeling very satisfied. Solving the case of the two murders seemed within her grasp. Kennedy was sure to cooperate. Either that or he could take the rap himself. She seated herself at the steel table, motioned to Peg Wilson and asked Kennedy if he wanted a cup of coffee.

"You got nothing on me," he demanded.

Opening a file folder, Rogers began. "Mr. Kennedy, the reputation of the Three Jimmies is well known. But, let's set that aside for a moment. As of right now, there are only Two Jimmies. You know what happened to Curtin. And Duncan is in the hospital, suffering mightily. There is some room for negotiating. What you need to know is that we are informed about Waterhouse. We think he also brought in the two suits who did you all some damage. So, what would you like to tell me?"

"We being recorded?"

"No, this is an informal interview. Just the three of us. We get the right answers from you we'll make it official. You know, read you your rights, see that you have an attorney and alert the DA's office."

"I got nothing to say. Just get me my mouthpiece and I want out of here."

"Before we do that, I feel compelled to alert you to the idea that one of the two Jimmies is going to take a big fall. The other will hear some sweet words from Ms DeLeon."

"Who she?"

"She's the ADA who will prosecute the case. You talk nice to her, could save you quite a few years."

"I got nothing to say."

"One last time, tell me about the relationship with Trenton and we can go from there. Say nothing, and Ms DeLeon will talk with Jimmy Duncan. One way or the other, makes no never mind to me. Just wanted to give you a shot."

"What did Duncan say?"

Looking over at Peg Wilson, she said, "Should we share some of this with him, Peg?"

"Guy deserves some consideration," Wilson answered. "He give you a lift, you oughta give him a break."

"I'll give you the dope, Kennedy. We know Waterhouse hired you to take out McCabe and Brewer. We think he might have called in some outside help to get rid of the Three Jimmies. Doesn't seem right. What do you think?"

"You know all that stuff, so what do you want from me?"

"Just confirmation."

"I need my lawyer."

"Give me a minute," Rogers said. She headed toward the door and the one-way window. DeLeon and Captain Bailey were waiting.

"Can you make this stick?" DeLeon asked.

"His partner is in the hospital, just waiting to tell you everything you need to know."

"You sure?"

"All you have to do is jiggle his bed a little."

Bailey chimed in, "What kind of talk is that, Rogers?"

With a shrug of the shoulders she said, "Think of it as rocking him to sleep. Does wonders for his memory."

"Officer Wilson, read him his rights and cuff him."

"What's the charge?" Kennedy snarled.

"Two murders, all the way. Don't forget, I asked you to cooperate. Maybe your lawyer will advise you that's a good thing to do."

48

Rogers liked the Food Court on the lower level of the Park Hyatt at the Bellevue. Stretched across three sides were offerings to satisfy every taste. This night she decided on a special pizza with a thick, but airy crust. Her selection included mushrooms, caramelized onions, and heavy on the cheese. *Tends to melt in my mouth no matter what toppings I choose.* Two slices and a bottle of water made for an unusual meal.

On the way out, she picked up an over-sized chocolate chip cookie, a fitting desert for munching on the walk home, a stroll on Walnut Street that was quiet, stores closed, foot traffic light. She spotted Marmaduke coming her way. Even from a distance, she could see a smile on his face.

"Good evening, Sergeant. Nice to see you again."

"Now what?" she demanded.

"Is that any way to greet an old friend?"

"I don't know about old, but I sure as hell know about friend."

He scratched his chin, let the smile fade, and said, "Let's put it this way. My boss wants to chat with you. So, I have asked my two associates to help escort you."

From nowhere the Two Suits were suddenly at her side. Each gently nudged an elbow and they continued walking toward Fifteenth Street. Trapped, she exploded, "You creeps kidnapping a police officer. You must be nuts!"

"Now, now," laughed Marmaduke. "This isn't a kidnapping. In fact, it's an invitation to talk. Don't forget, in our work, there is no such thing as kidnapping."

"Just what is your thing?"

"Something like yours. We gather information, analyze the data, and take action when indicated."

"What's all that got to do with kidnapping?"

"This is not a kidnapping. We're just going to escort you to our office and have a quiet conversation."

"You give up on street corner talks?"

"What we have in mind requires a somewhat different setting."

Without effort, the Suit on her right ran his hand across the small of her back, searching for a gun. The Suit on the left slid his hand into her shoulder bag and came up with her Sig Sauer. "Nice piece."

"Better be careful with that," she said. "It might go off and shoot you in the foot."

"Lady, have no fears. I have lots of experience with guns."

"We haven't been formally introduced. So can the 'Lady' crap. Sergeant will do."

"My, aren't we testy tonight."

A black Taurus parked next to a fire hydrant was waiting for them as they turned onto Sixteenth Street.

"You're subject to a big fine for illegal parking."

Marmaduke answered, "I think we could persuade you to get the ticket fixed."

The two Suits sat on either side of Rogers as Marmaduke pulled away from the curb. "This is only a short ride. See, no blindfold, none of that nonsense. Just a couple of people going to have a talk, might even call it a friendly talk."

Rogers sat quietly, paying attention to where they were going. It was only a short ride to a small apartment building on Pine Street, just off Ninth Street. Marmaduke led the way along a darkened first floor hall to a rear apartment.

A three-part rap on the door followed by a two-part rap and the door lock clicked open.

The room was spare. A large sofa that looked like a reject from the Salvation Army, a card table, three hard wood chairs and a counter with a coffee maker and half-a-dozen mugs. Seated behind the card table, Muriel Abate held court.

"Nice of you to join us, Sergeant," she smiled. "Sorry to have to inconvenience you. This shouldn't take long."

"You are?" asked Rogers.

Still smiling, "For all you need to know at this time, I'm Muriel Abate, Station Chief for the Philadelphia area."

"Very impressive. I'm a member of the Philadelphia Police Force. Do you think it's a smart thing to kidnap a cop?"

"Come, come, Sergeant. We have just invited you for a chat. Really. So, let's see if we can't conclude our work fast. We need some information from your friend, RC Frane."

"He's a convivial guy. Why not ask him?"

Abate scowled. "To the point. He isn't too keen on telling us what we need. And, we don't have a lot of time. You know, national security has no bounds."

"So I've been told."

"What we want is quite simple." She pushed a cell phone forward on the card table. "We want you to call Frane, tell him to meet; I think you call him 'Marmaduke'."

"Why would I do that," snarled Rogers.

"Your incentive to do what I ask is that you will be able to report to your office at 8 a.m. tomorrow. In fact, we'll even drop you off and return your gun. What could be easier than that?"

"Suppose Frane won't agree?"

"Oh, he'll agree. The meet will be at the usual place. He and Marmaduke often run together. Did you know that?"

"And if he says, no?"

"That is a contingency we shall address after you explain that you and I are talking calmly and quietly." She shoved the phone forward. "Make the call!"

"What do you want from Frane?"

"He has some information we need. This is simply a technique for encouraging him to cooperate. Nobody gets hurt, we find out what we need to know, and then, we may just disappear and go on to our next assignment."

Stalling for time, Rogers asked, "Are these the Two Suits who hit the Three Jimmies?"

"Changing the subject only wastes time. Make the call, tell Frane about the meet, and we can all go home and watch TV."

"And you get to hold me hostage until he gives you what you want."

"Um, that's about the size of it."

"Sounds like kidnapping to me."

"Sergeant, let's not quibble. If you don't make the call, I will."

"Be my guest."

49

"Is this going to be a problem, Mr. Andros?"

"Let me repeat your instructions. Sometime between 7 a.m. and 8 a.m. you want me to see to it that the back door of the restaurant is open. And, you want me to make sure nobody is around and nobody enters the restaurant. Is that correct?"

"Yes. I have to interview someone and it's top secret. So, make sure nobody comes in until, oh, ten o'clock should be fine. I think that's all the time I'll need."

"Okay. The answer to your question is, this is not a problem. I'll be sitting in my car at the far end of the parking lot. You need me, just yell. If not, I'll stick around to see you're not disturbed."

Frane reached Penns Landing at 5:30 a.m. The appointment with Marmaduke was for six. There was a little chill in the air as he slipped out of his running suit down to shorts and a T-shirt. He assumed that was to prove he wasn't armed. The .22 stashed beneath his supporter hardly made a bulge. I can always tell him I'm well endowed.

He left the car and decided to take a short run to keep warm; maybe a half-mile down and a half-mile back, ending in front of the Battleship Olympia. It was close to their last encounter, when he fired a round into the bushes to prove to Marmaduke that he meant business. Today would be a different game. The call from Muriel Abate and the voice of Greta Rogers claiming she had been kidnapped put him on high alert.

The one mile jog was just enough to start his blood pumping. Now, he slowed and walked back and forth the length of the Olympia. Three times before Marmaduke made his appearance.

They stood several feet apart, both men in running shorts. Marmaduke spoke first. "You see, I told you I just wanted to talk." Lifting his arms outward, demonstrating he was unarmed.

Frane was not impressed. "What's on your mind?"

"You know we want a piece of Pentrams' operation."

"Is that why you kidnapped Sergeant Rogers?"

"We didn't really kidnap her. Just invited her to visit for a little while; until we could persuade you to work with us."

"Where is she now?"

"You know better than to ask that. As soon as we conclude our business, she'll be dropped off at headquarters."

"How are you going to let Abate know the deal is done?"

"You didn't think I was coming here alone, did you?"

"I see. Well, how does this sound," answered Frane. "There is a man with a high-powered rifle aimed at your left knee cap. So, you have two choices. One, turn around slowly and keep your hands above your head. Or, he shoots now and we talk later. Oh, and one other thing, the Two Suits have been immobilized. For the record, we used a stun gun."

Daylight was beginning to take hold. Shafts of sunlight sneaked through the early mist that hangs over the Delaware River.

"How do I know you're telling the truth?" demanded Marmaduke. "I think you're full of crap."

"Don't move," Frane said. "I'm going to raise my left arm and a shot will be fired. That instruction will lower the aim at your knee to your foot. Are you ready?"

"You're bluffing!"

"Just tell me when you are ready for me to raise my left arm."

"Nobody shoots that well."

"Are you ready?"

Silence.

"Okay, turn around, place your hands behind your back. Don't make any kind of motion."

Frane raised his right arm; the agreed-to signal. From their position behind the concrete abutments that served as benches, Peg Wilson and Milt Thomason appeared. Taking hold of Marmaduke by his arms, they secured his wrists with plastic handcuffs.

"I have just one question," Frane commanded. "Where is Sergeant Rogers being held?"

"You know I'm not going to tell you that," answered Marmaduke. "It could cost me heavy."

"Let's go," said Frane.

Wilson and Thomason led Marmaduke to the burgundy Caprice. The three sat in the rear as Frane slipped into a warm up jacket and started the car. The roads were clear, early traffic had not yet begun. The trip to the Sand Box took eighteen minutes, exactly as planned. Leonides Andros was standing by the open back door.

"There's a chair waiting, just where you said," he told Frane. Then he walked to the end of the lot where his own car was waiting.

The two officers led Marmaduke into the restaurant. "Alright," Frane said, "you can wait for me outside."

The perspiration from his run had dried and Marmaduke sat quietly, waiting.

"Once more, where is Sergeant Rogers being held?"

"Nuts to you."

Frane opened the door to the walk-in freezer. Then he pushed Marmaduke to his feet and forced him into the small room.

"Are you crazy?"

Frane slammed the door shut and slipped a screwdriver through the bolt hole, securing the door. *Exactly as planned; Andros carried out his part to perfection. Now for a cup of coffee.*

50

"Listen up, you two. I'm not the boss any more, but we all have an interest in Sergeant Rogers. So, I'm asking you again, are you with me?"

"What about the Two Suits?" asked Wilson.

"They're yours. When we get Rogers, she'll tell how they kidnapped her. That should get them lots of jail time."

"But, didn't they do the shooting of the Jimmies?"

"There's plenty of time to investigate that. For now, we still have a job to do. How many more 'interested' cops have you got lined up?"

"We've been digging pretty deep. On the QT, Captain Bailey has given us an unofficial blessing. So, whatever we need, we got."

Thomason said, "Lieutenant, that was some story you concocted about the sharpshooter. You got balls."

Frane looked dead serious. "I did what I had to do. No sonovabitch is going to kidnap a cop. Besides, that dumb bastard didn't even know he was being taped."

"So, where is Marmaduke?"

"I left him inside to cool off. Another five minutes and I think he'll tell us

169

whatever we want to know."

Frane poured a fresh cup of coffee. Checked his watch; almost seven o'clock. Marmaduke had been "cooling off" for close to twelve minutes. Cautiously, he removed the screwdriver and slowly opened the freezer door. When Marmaduke heard the first click of the latch, he rushed at the door, head bent low, right shoulder set to force his way out. He had no understanding of the effect of ten degree temperature on his almost naked body. Hands cuffed behind him, the notion that he was a linebacker might have been in his mind. His body didn't receive the same message.

Frane stepped aside, opened the door fully, and as Marmaduke came through the opening, he slammed the door catching his face, smashing his jaw, and pummeling him against the door jamb. He fell in a heap.

Standing astride Marmaduke, Frane asked, "Where are they holding Sergeant Rogers?"

Stunned, head pounding, and cold, he snarled, "I'll get you for this."

Frane grabbed his manacled hands and dragged him back into the freezer. "Let me know when you're ready to answer my question. I'm just going to have a cup of hot coffee. Of course, I won't be able to hear you, so I'll just take a rest and stop back, oh, let's say ten minutes."

"You dirty bastard. When this is over, I'll see that you get yours."

"Before I leave, do you want to tell me where Sergeant Rogers is being held?"

"Go to hell!"

Frane stepped out of the freezer, secured the door once more and sat down to have coffee.

I wonder how long it takes a body to freeze? Probably a pretty long time. Just thinking about it makes me cold. Sitting in a freezer, in running shorts and a jersey, where the temperature is about ten degrees. Guess you don't freeze, but you sure get cold. Think I'll give him a break, open the door in five minutes.

Children are taught as part of growing up that, "A watched tea kettle doesn't boil." Watching for the steam to pour forth takes time and the wait is interminable. At least it seems interminable. Deciding when frostbite sets in, or how bad it might be, or whether it will have a lasting effect is more complex. Maybe sitting or lying in a freezer just gives you a cold, sneezing, or a post-nasal drip. Frane had to judge these complex possibilities. After five minutes he repeated the opening of the door.

Two lines of tears ran down Marmadukes' face, one from each eye. They had not yet frozen in place, but close to it. His dark eyebrows showed touches of white, a touch of frosting. The blue of his lips was just beginning to show and what had been a sweaty t-shirt, formed hard against his body.

"Crawl out," Frane commanded.

"I can't, give me a hand."

"Crawl out," he commanded again. *No way am I going to go in after him. He's big and strong, and dangerous.*

"Help me, you bastard."

"If you want out, crawl out."

Gasping, Marmaduke struggled to raise his head and position his knees. Hands still trapped in the cuffs, he worked his way toward the freezer door. By pressing his chin against the cold concrete floor, he inched forward. Frane backed up as he finally got out of the icy tomb.

Standing well clear, Frane asked gently, "Are you ready to tell me where Sergeant Rogers is being held?"

Marmaduke felt his body become acclimated to the warmth of the kitchen. "Okay. You win this time, but this isn't over."

"First, give me detailed directions. Then, I guess you were to call Abate. Is that correct?"

"Yes."

Lying on his side while Frane wrote down all the directions, Marmaduke began to feel better. He knew he wasn't about to die.

"I think what we'll do," added Frane, "is put you back in the box until we find Rogers. When she's free, then we'll see."

The tears had melted and now freely ran down his cheeks. Fresh tears joined them. The thought of another half hour or more in the freezer was more than he could contemplate. "Dammit, I told you what you need to know. Get me a cup of coffee."

Frane went to the back door and signaled to Wilson and Thomason. "Take him downtown and book him for kidnapping."

51

"We'll take over from here," said Captain Bailey.

"No way," answered Frane. "I've got a big investment in this operation."

"There's no time for discussion. I let you go this far because of your concern. Now, I have a SWAT team and a couple of dozen blues ready to go. You can sit in the car and watch."

"What kind of crap is that, George? I did this whole thing."

"You forget that you're a civilian. Anybody finds out I let you run this and my ass is in a sling."

"How about you got three guys for kidnapping a cop, plus two who did Pentrams' runners, and two who did the original shooters. That's a big score for you. Don't I get consideration for all that?"

"This isn't over yet, we still have to find Rogers. So, let's go and we'll see when we get there."

Six police cars moved quietly through the streets, no sirens, but red lights flashing, forcing cars off to the side. It took more than fifteen minutes to reach the center of the city. Along the way, Bailey blurted instructions, told the sharp shooters where to locate themselves, ordered a team to the rear of the apartment building, and radioed ahead to a string of other cars to isolate the neighborhood, and stop traffic. Early morning walkers on the way to offices were routed at least two blocks away from their destination and cars were detoured. When they arrived, the area was deserted.

Six officers in full body armor, one with a battering ram, assembled for last minute instructions.

"Best we know," said Bailey, "is that Rogers is alone with this other woman. She may have another man or two helping. You know the routine. A knock on the door, announce who you are, give it no more than ten seconds and then break the door down."

"No bull horn? No asking to come out with your hands up?"

"You told me everything we have to know. This is no time to negotiate." Taking a deep breath, he gave the order, "Let's do it!"

Silently, they moved forward, mounted the five steps to the front door and cautiously pushed it open. The hall was dark, a single fixture on the wall added little light. Three of the officers moved down the hall to the far side of apartment 2. The others quickly followed. The lead sergeant knocked heavily on the door and demanded, "Police. Open up."

From inside a muffled voice. He signaled to the officer with the ram, and the door was pounded open with one blow. In a rush, five officers forced their way into the room. Guns drawn, flashlights probing, they scanned the room before spreading into the bedroom and the bathroom. All empty, except for Sergeant Greta Rogers, tied to a chair; a loose gag circling her head.

52

"Guess you were hungry. It's past breakfast time. Did they feed you last night?"

"She offered a soda or a coffee. I turned her down. Bitch."

"Thinks she's a tough cookie. Especially when she has a couple of strong-arms to do the heavy work. Give you a bad time?"

"Not really," Rogers answered, "what she wanted, or maybe still wants, is for you to help her with Pentram."

"Sorry you got involved in this mess. I'm not sure what she wants. Just saying Pentram, doesn't work. Claims to be CIA, but that's bull."

"So, where are we?"

Frane remained thoughtful as he poked at the scrambled eggs on his plate. "Well, you have three murders solved. That's good. They sure interfered with something more important."

"How's that?"

"The two runners were not important to whatever is happening. The third one, was a hired shooter. Then you have the Two Suits who were brought in to take care of the Jimmies. All this killing seems to be getting in the way of the real investigation. But, I'll be dammed if I know what we supposed to be investigating."

"Hold on, RC. You're retired now so, this is my case. With the killings out of the way, I'm out of the game. You're not supposed to be investigating anything. Remember, you turned in your badge."

They were seated in the main dining room at the Doubletree Hotel on Broad Street. The three block walk from where she had been held captive gave Rogers a chance to stretch her legs and gather in some fresh breathing. Captain Bailey told her to go home, grab a few hours of sleep and then come back to the Round House to write out a full report of her kidnapping.

"Signal for some more coffee," she said. "I don't know why, but suddenly I have an appetite. Nice place. Glad you have this new work and we can afford fifteen dollar breakfasts."

"Yeh, well, does this take care of some of the things I owe you?"

"Not quite," she laughed. "So, tell me, how did you find out where they were holding me?"

Pushing his plate to the edge of the table, Frane answered, "You don't appreciate how convincing I can be."

"You convinced Marmaduke to tell you?"

"I was going to say persuasive, but there's a middle ground between persuading somebody and being convincing."

"This gets better all the time. How were you convincing?"

"You don't really want to go there," he said.

"Did you hurt him? Beat up on that poor bastard?"

"Never raised a finger. Only thing I did was ask him where they were holding you."

"Play that again. You simply asked him where I was and he told you?"

Nodding his head, Frane told her, "Actually I asked him four times before he was convinced."

The table server came with more coffee and a small tray of Danish pastries. "Compliments of the chef, says he like cops."

"Not me," laughed Frane. "This here woman is the cop."

"Whatever. Signal if you want more coffee."

"Let's come back to this story," Rogers said. "You just asked Marmaduke four times and he told you the whole story."

Thoughtfully, Frane responded. "Actually that was pretty much all I said to him. Of course, it took place over a period of time."

"Why do I get the feeling you don't really want to tell me what happened."

"GG, I'm telling you. I got a call to meet him at our usual running place, down at Penns Landing. After a couple of minutes, Wilson and Thomason came out of hiding and cuffed him. From that moment on, I only asked him those four times where you were. You just don't appreciate how convincing I was in my questioning."

"I see. So, my two officers were with you. Guess I'll have to ask them."

"That sounds reasonable." *Since they were outside waiting while Marmaduke was cooling his kester, guess she won't learn very much. Better that way.*

From their table next to the railing, there was a clear view of the lower level of the hotel and through the windows facing Broad Street. He squinted at the woman signaling to him, even as the table server returned and said, "There's a message for you Lieutenant Frane."

"I know what it is. That woman down there wants to talk to me."

"I knew you were a cop, probably a detective. She called up and said to give you a message."

"That the woman?" he asked, nodding toward Muriel Abate.

Agreeing, the table server said, "Here it is. We need to talk. Phone booth at the corner of 15th and Locust. Ten minutes."

When he glanced down at the window, she was gone.

53

Phone booths are a thing out of the past. In the United States, they have been replaced by egg-shaped kiosks with sound proof siding so you can stand in the middle of traffic and seem undisturbed. In England, where stark red telephone booths seemed to be a landmark, they have been removed. In one instance, about twenty have been tilted, leaning against one another, and offered as a work of art; London at its finest.

When Frane arrived, he found the line to the phone torn from its inner-workings. All neighborhoods are still subject to vandalism. He no sooner stuck his head in the pod then he noticed a piece of paper with a number printed clearly. "Call!" was the other message.

She must have just left this here. Maybe jumped in her car and she's waiting for me.

Rogers took a cab to her apartment. Walking the seven blocks home past the very spot where she had been kidnapped was to be avoided. He promised to call her as soon as he found out what Abate wanted.

Stepping away from the kiosk, he pulled the cell phone from the zippered pocket in his running jacket. As he walked toward Pine Street, he punched in the numbers Abate had left. After one ring, she answered.

"We have to meet."

"Why?"

"There are still things to discuss."

"How about the Round House? That's a good place for kidnappers. In fact, I think there are a couple of your friends down there. You could all have a happy reunion."

"We have things to discuss, Frane. "Big things. Now, I suggest some place nice and comfortable, maybe where we can have a drink and talk like grown ups."

This woman is blowing through the wrong end of the horn. I know she's dangerous; she's also rocking on one foot. "Now that sounds real nice. Where do you suggest?"

"How about McDonald's on Broad Street?"

"I just had breakfast."

"Okay. Keep walking. Wait for me on the corner of Broad and Pine. I'll pick you up." The phone went dead.

54

Frane called his apartment. The answering machine clicked on. "Sorry, I'm not here at this time. Leave a name and number after the beep and I'll call back as soon as I can." He didn't hang up.

The black Ford Taurus pulled next to the curb. "Why Muriel Abate, how nice of you to pick me up."

"Get in the car Frane. There's a lot of traffic here. We can find a quiet place and talk."

"You're not trying to kidnap me the way your boys did with Sergeant Rogers?"

"Oh, come on. I'm driving. What do you expect me to do, speed across the Ben Franklin Bridge and make off with you?"

"Before I get in the car, do you have a gun?"

"No, that's not my style. Besides, CIAs don't carry guns when they're in the country."

"So, Marmaduke and his playmates aren't CIA?"

"We call them, 'Contractors.' Hire outside help when we need them."

"How's that listed in the phone book, 'Gun for Hire? Threats, murders, kidnapping our specialty. We do your dirty work.'"

"Will you just get in the car. We're tying up traffic."

As he slid into the front seat backwards, he reached into his crotch where the .22 was resting. Turning to Abate, he leveled the gun and asked, "Where we going?"

"Put that thing away before somebody gets hurt."

"Drive down to 11ᵗʰ Street and park. That's only a minute away and that should give you plenty of time to construct a story."

She pulled forward, drove to Locust Street and then right three blocks to 11ᵗʰ, turned right and pulled in next to a fire hydrant. "If we get a ticket, you're going to take care of it."

"You still want to talk with Pentram?"

"My job is to make something happen. I don't have to talk to him, you can do that. What I want is his cooperation now, and in the future. We're talking some pretty high level security issues."

"Sounds very important," Frane said.

"When you talk security, you better believe it's important."

"Give me a couple of clues about what you want and then I'll make a decision."

"Doesn't work that way," said Abate. "First, I need your guarantee of secrecy. You sign on with me you're in another world."

"What do you mean, 'Sign on?'"

She started to reach for her pocket book. Frane brought the gun into firing position.

"Take it easy," she admonished. "Just want to get the papers out."

With that, she pulled two sheets of folded paper with official imprints on each page. "Here, take a glance and then you can sign them."

Frane took the two pages, folded them and slipped them into his pocket. "I'll read them when I get home."

"Sign them," she demanded.

"Do you really have that low an opinion of me? You expect me to sign some papers I've never seen and then we're off to the races." He reached for the door handle to leave the car.

"Wait a minute. If you aren't going to sign them, give them back."

"Ms Abate, I'm going to try this one last time. What do you want from me?"

"You are one big time SOB," she started. "We need two things from Pentram. One, a large slice of his action. Two, access to the containers he will be using to supply his inventory."

"Now, why in the world should he give you a piece of his new business?"

"Let's just say it's a measure of his loyalty to his government."

"You can do better than that."

Shaking her head, Abate continued. "Everybody knows the Fed is cutting every budget in sight. Well, we're suffering from a lack of funds in our department. I can't go into detail, but you can understand that to carry out our mission we need money. Since we can't shoehorn it out of the budget, we have to find other sources. Being partners in a legitimate business makes sense."

"Oh, I am so impressed with what you have said. Sure, you need lots of money to hire contractors to kidnap people. Now that I understand your crushing needs, I'm sure Mr. Pentram will be happy to share his largess with you."

"Don't be a smartass, Frane. Our work is very serious and borders on the critical. With all those crazy terrorists running around the world, we have to do something to stop them."

"So, out of the goodness of his heart and desire to help his country and a strong desire to stop terrorism in the world, Pentram will supply you with money."

"Now you've got it."

This woman is more than twisted, she's beyond Planet 16 on her way into orbit. "And this second thing, his containers of food from abroad?"

"I'm sharing these things with you, even though you haven't signed up yet. From time to time, we may want to bring certain products into the country so we can earn some more money. Once the financing is in place, we will be able to operate with impunity. Now, you can see the importance of our work."

"Indeed."

"Well?"

"Let me think about this for a day or two. Will the cell number you left for me still work?"

"Glad to hear you're getting with the program. The cell phone is gone. I'll call you."

55

Roberta Mercado was a free spirit, in a number of ways. There were times when she dressed in severe lawyer attire; tailored suits, silk blouses, medium heels and a simple piece of jewelry. Her tall, shapely body was barely hidden behind such prescribed attire. On those less formal occasions when she met with Bob Vogt, slacks, loafers, and a more enticing sweater seemed appropriate.

He, on the other hand, had no trouble slipping into clothes similar to those worn on the golf course. Colorful slacks, subdued shirt and a thin sweater, Cashmere, of course.

"This is almost better than working," he smiled. "A day of relaxation, simple lunch, good drinks. What else could we wish for?"

"Glad that isn't a multiple choice question. I might want to add a few caveats."

"Tell me your wildest wish and we'll make it happen."

Retreating into serious thinking, she said, "I'm not sure if I want this deal to get solved and therefore over; or should it go on for a long time. When you work by the hour, long is better than short."

"If you want to talk business, I'll take out my tape recorder and we can go on the clock."

"Just like to have some idea of where we're headed. What do you think?"

Vogt signaled the table server. "Do you have Johnny Walker Blue?"

"Of course, sir. We also have some Glenfiddich 15. What's your pleasure?"

Mercado spoke up. "Why not order two of each. We can taste one, then the other before we get down to serious drinking. Always better to make a final decision once you have all possible information. After all, drinking is just an extension of living." Turning to the waiting table server she asked, "Is there anything else you might suggest?"

"Seems to me, that you two really know about good drinking. Unless you want to try something other than scotch. But, if it's scotch, those two are top drawer."

"Okay," Vogt said, "two of each and we'll see where that takes us."

Talking about high-line drinking added to the general tranquil tone of the luncheon. Both knew that a combination of convivial small talk mingled with excellent whiskey would lead to both fast and slow love-making.

"A little business first," she said. "What do you think are the chances for success?"

Vogt reached for a cashew, popped it into his mouth before answering. "I don't know very much about Pentram and his big plan. But, my client and a few interested parties would find a joint venture very appealing. Without giving away the store, we already have several food operations that could easily be convinced to participate."

The drinks arrived with instructions. "I placed the Blue to the left and the Glenfiddich to the right. Also, a bottle of Evian to refresh your palate."

As the table server departed, Vogt said, "There is nothing as pleasing as the treatment in a fine restaurant."

"Well, if you have several food operations and we have more than that, we're ready to go. We thought to call them the 'Food Buying Group.'"

"How many do you think we need to make this profitable?"

"That's the beauty of the plan. FBG will be profitable from the get-go. There is need for some up-front money, but it's all protected. The actual dollars of profit will be small at the outset, but as we add members, there is no limit."

Introducing a note of skepticism, Vogt asked, "Outside of the idea of having a big group, what's the real need of the two organizations coming

B. ROBERT ANDERSON

together?"

Mercado sipped the Glenfiddich. "Interesting, smoky taste. Very interesting." She paused to examine the light brown liquid in the crystal tumbler. "Here is the idea. Twenty restaurants are more powerful than ten. Forty are more powerful than twenty. And on and on. Let your imagination run wild. Two cities are bigger than one. Four cities are bigger than two. Got the point?"

"Roberta, you are amazing. I can't decide whether I admire your brain more than your body. Or the other way around."

"Later we can try that, 'other way around.'"

Shaking his head, he picked up his tumbler of Johnny Walker Blue, held it up to the light, admired what he saw, rolled a drop on his tongue; then, swirled a mouthful before letting it run down his throat. Examining the glass once more, he whispered, "Sheer delight."

"Shall I go on?"

"Ah, business. Yes. Tell me, how much cash might be required? Initially?"

"Each restaurant would require $10,000 up front. That would only be for a short period of time. So, if you start with five, that's $50,000. The good part is, that within three weeks the money would be moving so fast that further cash investment might not be required. And, if we leave the money with the Group, that is, don't take any profits for several months, the whole project would become self-sufficient. How does that grab you?"

Vogt examined his tumbler of Glenfiddich. He repeated the examination procedure, and ultimately swallowed a mouthful. "Hard to decide which is better. I suppose it all depends on your individual desires at the moment. Probably not a good idea to switch back and forth."

I wonder if I'm going to have any trouble dealing with this guy. He likes his liquor, maybe more than he should. Still, a deal is a deal. "So, it sounds like we are making progress. Let's shift gears. Did you see that small motel just before we turned into the Club? Well, it has a lot more charm than you might expect for a backwater place deep in the heart of South Jersey."

"Just a couple more points. Any thought been given to taking the whole operation public?"

"Every reason to believe that is an avenue to explore."

"Suppose this guy from Star Distributing gets ideas of his own?"

From nowhere the waiter reappeared. "Shall we do it again?"

"Let's stay with the Blue," Vogt suggested. "One more, then we may have

184

to leave."

They sat silently while the table was cleared and two fresh tumblers of Johnny Walker Blue sat in front of them. "Charge my account. And add a twenty for your great service."

Raising her glass, Mercado admonished, "If there is any trouble with Star, our two clients should be able to convince him to stay with the basic plan."

"Convince. Persuade. Influence. Yes, I think that's a can-do."

56

Greta Rogers leaned against the car door, keeping distant from Frane. He was driving slowly up north Broad Street, headed for the Sand Box. Leonides Andros promised him a quiet corner booth where the two could have a serious, and undisturbed conversation. *It's time I shared some information. Things are getting so complicated I don't know who I trust anymore. Strange, that Andros probably avenged his daughters' murder and he now tends to be one of my most valued friends. And Greta is still a rock.*

Several years earlier, Frane was the lead detective tracking down the murderer of Chef Robert Dorrit. Along the way, body parts kept popping up in cases of frozen shrimp. The last murder was the drug-drinking death of Thelma Andros. Still unresolved was the disappearance of Jack Parsell and the ancient diving suit that once decorated the Sand Box restaurant. Frane suspected that Parsell was wearing the diving suit and now resided at the bottom of the Delaware River. When quizzed on the fate of the weighted diving suit, Andros merely shrugged.

"So, tell me, Greta, are you getting over being kidnapped?"

"Spare me your concern," she blurted. "My ass was in a sling and then you come along for the big rescue. How the hell did I get involved in this mess?"

Frane retreated, sensing that the best answer was silence. There was no explanation. That was why he wanted to have a quiet dinner and a serious talk. "Let's wait till we get to the Sand Box and I'll try to respond to your questions. As much as I can."

They rode in silence for the rest of the trip.

The Sand Box was a restaurant of varied tastes; superior seafood, the usual steaks and roasts, and profoundly Greek. Usually, Andros would have the chef prepare something special, along with lessons in how to, "Drink Greek."

"Follow me," Leonides Andros said. "We have a special booth in the back, and your favorite server has already chilled a bottle of wine and a bottle of water. That's just in case you want to mix a little water with Ouzo." Smiling, he added, "It's safer that way."

Rogers admitted, "You are still a great host. If only you were a couple of years younger."

"Ah, but I am younger—in the head. It's the body that seems to grow older each day."

"Are you two done with the love-patter? We have some important things to discuss."

"Make yourself comfortable. I have to seat a few more people and then my time belongs to you."

The table server poured three glasses of Ouzo and three glasses of Henri de Villamont Chardonnay. "Mr. Andros said he wants your opinion on the wine. He says it has just the right métier for a light dinner."

"Métier?" said Frane. "What ever happened to just plain old-fashioned wine?"

"You're right, Lieutenant. But, it took me two hours and two bottles of Villamont to appreciate the tender aroma and delicate body of this rare vintage."

Exhaling loudly, he replied, "I surrender, and don't call me lieutenant. I'm retired."

With an exaggerated bow, he left the table.

Rogers took a swallow of Ouzo. "I needed that. Now, what's on your mind?"

"Let's wait a minute till Andros comes back. I want to tell you both something at the same time. He doesn't know about your being kidnapped. If you want to tell him, that's up to you. How it all came about, I really don't know."

"Of course you know. Abate wants you to do something and she figured she could get to you through me."

"Well, yes, that's the size of it."

"But, you played it like I was a stranger, just another poor slob who got taken."

"What did you want me to do?"

"I don't know. I just thought there was more between us than another case."

He reached across the table before she could draw her hand back. "GG, you have no idea how much you mean to me. Not only that, I owe you big time. When you shot that bastard who had me covered you saved my life. Abate wasn't going to hurt you. She's some kind of weirdo. Maybe you'll understand before the night is over."

Andros returned to the table. "This dinner struck me as something important. Not really a time for adventures in eating. That's why I had the chef roast a whole Chilean Sea Bass so we could share. Some sautéed spinach with plenty of garlic, and a few browned potatoes. But, first, a little salad."

They raised the wine glasses in toast.

"To good food."

"To friendship."

"To understanding."

"I did my part," said Andros.

"I'm here to show I care," said Rogers.

"And I wanted us to be together to try to explain a rather complicated affair. Are you both ready?"

"Shoot," said Rogers.

"Not exactly the right word," Frane suggested. Taking a long drink of Ouzo he continued, "This conversation is top secret and I mean that. It begins and ends here. What I need is your perspective so I can make my next move."

Seeking to add a touch of humor, Andros asked, "Is it sexy?"

"Oh, it's sexy alright. I was tapped by a very important upper-level security person to carry out a mission. The assignment was fairly simple, get next to John Pentram." Turning to face Rogers he added in an apologetic tone, "I know you were upset, Greta. But, it was of the utmost importance that I remain as they say, undercover."

"So, why are you telling us now?"

"Truth of the matter is, the mission has veered off course and I need some outside thinking. That's why what we're talking about is very secret."

Andros chimed in. "I don't know much about this man, Pentram. Except that in the past I have heard his name linked with, shall we say, nefarious schemes."

"Those days are gone. He has discovered it's easier to make money the old-fashioned way. So, he put together a great business idea. When he found out I was 'retired', he got in touch and now I'm his consultant."

"So, what's the big deal?" Rogers asked. "How come I was kidnapped? What's the big secret?"

Andros showed surprise. "You were kidnapped?"

"Just for an afternoon and a night. My friend here arranged for my rescue."

Directing his question to Frane, he said, "How could you let that happen?"

"First, and here it gets really confidential, I want each of you to have a tape of a conversation I had with Abate."

Andros appeared lost. "Abate?"

"She's a dangerous woman backed up with some heavy-duty toughs who wants a piece of Pentram. Keep these tapes, listen to them if you wish, but make sure they're safe. In case anything happens to me."

"And second?"

Shaking his head, Frane said, "It's a matter of national security."

57

Using national security as a cover doesn't make sense. Still, that's what I was told and that's what makes this whole project so difficult to explain. These are two of my best friends, people who I trust. How can I explain something I don't understand myself.

"Here's a piece that's really top secret. Are you ready?"

"Where do we go to take the oath?" asked Rogers, a tinge of disbelief in what might be forthcoming.

Andros shrugged.

"My resignation from the police department is a sham. I'm really temporarily assigned."

"You're what?"

"I'm still a cop. Only you two and a couple of others know that. I'm working on uncovering something I'm not sure about. It's very confusing."

"Play this again," she said. "You haven't really resigned? Does Bailey know?"

"No, he doesn't. In fact, when I told him I was working with Pentram, he walked out on me, left me with an uneaten lunch. He's really pissed.

190

Remember, Greta, how angry you were when I told you. He was even worse. Maybe in time he'll understand."

"So, why are you telling us all this stuff?" asked Andros.

"Because I trust you and I need you to argue with me, tell me what I'm doing wrong."

Andros held up his calloused hands in defense. "Should I be hearing all this? What do I know about undercover work? I'm just an old restaurant man."

Disregarding their comments, Frane continued. "There are times I think I'm working for the FBI. Other times it's the CIA. The head of Police Intelligence is the main man. I report to all three on different aspects of what I'm supposed to be investigating."

"This I can talk about," Andros said.

"How come?"

"Doesn't take much to know that you can't report to three different bosses. Suppose in the restaurant business the second cook reported to the first cook and to the manager and to the owner. How long would that last?"

"Good point. I guess I really know that. So, you're saying I should clarify who is my real boss and what he wants from me."

"Damn right you ought to know this stuff, RC," Rogers almost yelled. "Chain of command."

"I'm listening to both of you," Frane responded. "Here's the rub. When you work 'underground' you have lots of freedom. You don't report in every couple of hours. You're out there floating around, so you have to think for yourself. The rules change."

"Gimmie an example."

"Easy. When I wanted to find out from this Marmaduke character where you were being held Greta, I did some things that don't pass muster."

"Was he the man you brought to the restaurant the other morning? What was that all about?"

"Let's just say I needed a quiet place to interrogate him."

"Wait a minute," Rogers interjected. "You brought him to the restaurant to interrogate him? Why here?"

Andros shrugged.

"Don't forget, we're talking confidentially. I brought him here because he needed time to cool off. In less time than you can imagine he told me exactly what I needed to know. After that, it only took an hour or so for Captain Bailey to get his people in line. They did a very good job. He gave me the address where you were being held."

"Rather forth-coming of him. You strong-arm him?"

Almost laughing, Frane answered, "Greta, you just don't appreciate how influential I can be. How about I just cooled him off and he sang."

"Just the two of you?"

"That's all it took."

"Back to the three people you report to. What the heck are they trying to find out?"

"The CIA think Abate is masquerading as one of their own. The FBI thinks she is set on smuggling guns into the country. Police Intel wants to find out if Pentram is clean."

"You got proof you're working for all three?"

"No."

"No?"

"No."

Andros poured wine for all. Raising his glass he said, "We have us a real bad situation."

"Where'd you get the 'us'?" asked Rogers. Then she added, "Anybody trying to figure this out would figure you couldn't have gotten into such a mess by yourself."

"Another good point," said Frane. "That's exactly why I wanted to get together with you two. Spread the blame."

"Terrific. Just what I need to get a promotion, get involved in a three-way mess."

"There is a good side."

"Tell us."

"Pentram has a grand plan, all legal, that ought to make a lot of money for a lot of people. This Abate woman is crazy. She may be planning a terrorist attack for all I know. What I do know is that she wants a piece of Pentrams' game. He doesn't know this because I haven't told him. The CIA wants to roll up this whole group. Right now, Greta, you have Marmaduke and the two suits in custody with enough on them to clear the deck. You also have two of the three Jimmies."

"What about the two collectors that were shot?"

Frane swallowed hard. "This is tough." He turned to Andros to explain. "Pentram had two people collecting from some of his 'clients.' They each called on maybe twenty or twenty-five places a week and picked up a fair amount of cash. This wasn't protection money. He invested in all kinds of small businesses, gave them money for a piece of the action. Then he arranged to collect his share of the profits. Once he got this really rolling, he made a lot of money, all clean. And, he paid taxes on them."

Andros interjected, "So they got killed for the money."

"This is what makes it tough. They got killed because somebody was sending a message. You might say, 'Death got in the way.'"

"You mean they got in the way so they had to go."

"Exactly. Just because they were there, they were murdered."

"And the kidnapping? What the heck did I have to do to be kidnapped?"

"GG, I'm sorry for that. It had nothing to do with me. The two murders, forgive me, were a side issue. They were carried out to upset the apple cart. The main event was trying to get to Pentram. Show him what he was up against."

"What about the Three Jimmies?" she asked.

"Who are they? I'm lost," said Andros.

"Welcome to the party," added Frane.

Rogers offered an explanation. "Here's the way it worked. Apparently, this Abate woman hired three goons to take out the two collectors. On the sly, she also hired two really bad guys to get rid of the three goons. Then, and this is the best part, she had me kidnapped."

"GG," Frane moaned, "I had no way of knowing she was going to pull that kind of stunt. Don't you think I would have told you, warned you, protected you?"

Once again, Andros raised a calloused hand. "Now I know my role." To Rogers, "He did some really serious things to see that you were saved. Someday, maybe he'll tell you how he 'convinced' this Marmaduke character to tell him where you were." To Frane, "This woman means more to you than just working together. Even I can see that."

He signaled to the table server. "There's a special bottle in the small refrigerator in my office. I was saving it for a special occasion. I think now is the time to share. Please bring it with a bucket of ice and three champagne glasses."

"How come?" asked Frane.

"Why, it's to celebrate my becoming a detective."

58

In his role as a consultant, RC Frane found meeting for lunch was a requirement. Mindful of an expanding belt size, he changed eating habits to include light salads, black coffee, and crackers instead of bread. This enforced regimen coupled with early morning jogging of at least three miles was supposed to hold down cholesterol, weight, blood pressure and everything else he could think of. Until John Pentram suggested they meet at the Four Seasons.

After struggling to find a parking spot, he finally pulled into the entry way and offered his car to valet service. The charm of the hotel, located on Logan Circle at the edge of the Benjamin Franklin Parkway was reinforced by the stirring lobby. He stood still and counted the number of couches and easy chairs until he lost patience; there were so many. Slowly, he found his way to the Fountain Restaurant, took an overstuffed arm chair and decided to enjoy the surroundings while waiting for Pentram.

"Good of you to meet me," he greeted Frane.

Accepting the gracious manner, Frane smiled as he said, "Your every wish is my command."

Nodding, the older man answered, "That's a nice way to put it. Still, we are now associated in several different ways. Also, I was happy to hear that you rescued Miss Rogers."

"How did you know about that?"

"My dear Frane, I know about many things. Shall we have lunch?"

The headwaiter checked off his reservation list without asking for a name. A slight nod to Pentram ascertained he was a known patron. "Right this way, gentlemen." He led them to a table set away from the main stream of traffic. "May I order a drink? A glass of Mondavi Chardonnay; something light to start lunch."

Pentram smiled. Frane added, "Sounds good." (*So much for dieting.*)

Seizing the moment, Frane asked, "Is this considered billable time or did you just want the pleasure of my company?"

"Ah, you have become a quick study, Lieutenant. Since we have such a loose financial arrangement, I don't keep track of time. Remember, you told me you would be available twenty-four-seven. Today is simply a time to play catch-up, a sharing of what has taken place. So, tell me about Star."

"The news is positive. But, before we get to that, how did you know about Sergeant Rogers' kidnapping?"

"You know better than to ask that question. I have many sources, some good, some modest, none quite as good as you."

"I take it that means you don't intend to answer me."

The table server arrived, placed two tall white wine glasses half-filled with Chardonnay on the table, and asked, "Would you like to hear the specials of the day?"

"After a moment, in the meantime, we'll study the menu."

Lifting the glass in a minor toast, he asked, "What is the positive news?"

Frane reached for his small notepad, flipped a couple of pages and answered, "Hope Rutan, the woman in charge of the Information Systems at Star is off and running. She knows more about what you want than I. However, when I checked with her she said the data she received from the first three clients is in the system and currently being tested. Each restaurant has received a special computer linked to the main frame at Star. In the first run, she had to further link the input to the warehouse and also the purchasing department. She is arranging for automatic reordering of products they have specified."

"I gather they are working out any discrepancies in the process."

"Exactly. What she told me is that after the initial trials she'll be able to set up future clients very rapidly. Seeing that inventory levels are able to meet demands will take a little time."

"It sounds as if we are right on schedule. Now, let me tell you about John, Jr. He has six more clients lined up, ready to go. And he is working on five more." Laughing, "We're going to start making money almost from the starting line. How do you feel about that?"

Frane agreed, "That sounds fine. But, my contribution doesn't cover making a profit. In fact, I'm not altogether sure what my contribution is supposed to be."

"You underestimate your importance. When you go to see people like Star, or even the potential clients, you speak for me. You carry my message. That's not something I take lightly. Neither should you."

Why do I have the feeling I'm being taken to the wood shed? He's lecturing me as if I were a child. Running errands is far less than my life in the police department. Even though it pays better. Maybe it's time for him to meet my other 'bosses'.

"Have you ever eaten here?"

"This is my first visit. What would you recommend?"

"Since we have been working together, sharing a meal has taken on a new dimension. We're enjoying the pleasure of eating in some very interesting places. Just examine the décor, the setting, the floral arrangements; things that make a statement, time for serious talk along with tranquil dining."

"Guess I never realized how poetic you are. Think I'll just have a hamburger."

"Perfect choice. When I come here for lunch, it's one of my favorite meals. But, we'll have to switch to red wine. Goes better with meat."

"Let's get one piece of business out of the way," Frane said. "What do you know about this Abate woman?"

Pentram twisted the stem of his wine glass. Then, raised it to his lips, took a small sip and said, "I would say she is a challenging personality."

"Any thoughts about the two collectors who were shot? After all, you enlisted my services when Brewer went down."

Frane detected a whirring of thoughts behind Pentrams' immobile expression. "We can't allow those unfortunate events to deter our efforts."

59

Interstate 95 extends from northernmost Maine to the southern tip of Florida. Once you cross from Pennsylvania to Delaware, traffic seems to expand and oversize tractor trailers dominate the two right-hand lanes. With the installation of E-Z Pass, cars and trucks skim through the toll booths that require a slower speed but guarantee a faster trip.

Frane picked up Pentram at his home later in the afternoon. It was a short distance to I-95 and just over an hour to reach the Maryland House restaurant. The parking lot is so large that it never fills. On a busy summer day, the cars extend the distance of a football field to the front door. As many as ten travel buses have space reserved near the entry so patrons can pour in to reach five different eating opportunities, not to mention several free-standing kiosks, countless coin operated machines and a full-fledged store loaded with magazines, trinkets, toys, and a variety of packaged cookies, crackers, soft drinks, and loads of candy and nuts.

The two men paused at a stand selling sun glasses and watches. Casually reviewing the crowds, they moved toward a restaurant that offered a buffet of cold and hot food, plus a salad bar. In addition, there was regular table service.

"Not our usual choice of food," Pentram said. "Is this the treat you promised me? One day the Four Seasons, the next eating with the masses."

"Good for the soul," promised Frane. "Reminds me of my former life."

Joking, Pentram added, "Glad I was able to save you from a life of making your food selection from a group of pictures on the menu."

A sign read, "Please wait to be seated."

A woman with an identifying plastic ID card dangling around her neck led them to a table. Frane said, "I think we'd prefer to sit over there."

The tall, grey-haired man appeared and gestured that they should take the seats facing the wall while he would sit with his back to the wall, allowing him to scan the rest of the room. He knew them, they did not know him. Only by some furtive reference. "Fish."

Before they could exchange greetings, a table server appeared and announced, "The buffet is $8.95 and that includes soup, salad and a choice of some hot items. Or, $5.95 for just soup and salad."

Pentram squinted. "I'd like a cup of Earl Grey tea, please."

The gray-haired man looked equally pained. "Just a black coffee."

Frane asked for a glass of water.

Left to themselves, off in a corner, the grey-haired man said, "This is the first time we meet face-to-face. Also, it's the first time you are aware that you are both working for us."

Frane decided this was the time to remember a quote from Will Rogers. "Never miss a chance to keep quiet."

Pentram spoke seriously, "Is that why you directed me to engage Lieutenant Frane?"

Maintaining a stolid expression, Fish answered, "It is not important at this time for you to know all those details. You are both men committed to a very high cause. In some instances, the less you know the better."

"How did you come to select us?"

"In Franes' case, it was easy. His entire life is contained in police records. We had all the background possible. For you, Mr. Pentram, it took a little digging. The most important fact is that you are committed. Your early history revealed nothing that would deter us from working together. Surely, you are aware that in our work we often make peace with former enemies. In your case, that was hardly necessary."

"I passed muster?"

"Believe me, if you didn't, we wouldn't be talking today. Shall we have a bite of lunch?"

"I'm going to walk around the buffet set-up," Frane announced. "See if I can control myself."

Pentram offered that he wasn't used to eating cafeteria style.

Fish added that he too, would wait for table service.

When the drinks arrived the two men ordered tuna fish sandwiches. Frane returned carrying a cup of soup. "This will keep me honest."

"What I need to know first, is, what do you think of this Abate woman?"

"Here's for sure, she's something of a flake," Frane said. "Dangerous. Not clear what she's after. Of course, her main boys are safely under lock and key. Does she have anybody else out there?"

"I haven't had any contact with her," Pentram said. "Who is she, exactly?"

Fish said, "What I can tell you is she was a part of the agency. Now, she is something of a renegade. Yes, she is dangerous. Over the years she has had a lot of experience, some overseas, some wet."

Pentram frowned. "What's does 'wet' mean?"

Once again, Frane decided silence was his best friend.

The arrival of the food interrupted any response. The sandwiches, overloaded with a stack of deep brown French fried potatoes looked like too much to eat. Both men nibbled carefully, afraid to admit that they really were tasty.

"That word is one we use to identify any activity that might be considered, illegal."

Pentram said, "I can think of all manner of activity that might be considered illegal. Does your definition include murder?"

In a very dignified response he replied, "There's not much more that I can add. Your assumptions are allowed to run wild. I won't confirm anything. Now, my next question is, what do you think Abate is after?"

Frane wiped his mouth with the paper napkin. "Over and over she has told me she wants to be part of Mr. Pentrams' business and with the profits. She also seems to think that he will be importing things from abroad and wants access to the shipping containers."

Pentram took a small mouthful of tuna, after extracting it from between the two slices of white bread. "I haven't met or communicated with this woman. Frane has told me a couple of things. How she would get into a container and then arrange to remove something is hard for me to understand. I have no contact with containers. If, as, and when Star brings in product in that manner, I probably will have no knowledge. As far as sharing in my business venture; that hardly seems possible."

"What do you think, Mr. Fish?"

Lips pursed, he answered, "We're not sure where she's headed. As I said before, she is dangerous, so be careful. I suspect she is going to approach you with some kind of deal. You two will have to decide what you think it means. Which brings me to the reason for this meeting. We wanted you both to know you are working together. Therefore, when you have something substantive, keep me informed."

"And if you have something substantive?" asked Frane.

The grey-haired man smiled.

60

"Why don't you go to a lawyer?"

"You are a lawyer."

"I mean a real lawyer."

"I thought you were a real lawyer."

"RC, you're getting to be a pain in the butt. Just because I have a degree and I have been working as an Assistant District Attorney, what makes you I can deal with your law problems?"

"My, my, Chris, you're getting frisky as hell. Spend more time with us police types and you'll be talking like a real person."

"I just put in for transfer to a different department, where I can deal with people who are interested in things other than murder."

"No way that Chris DeLeon will leave homicide. Yeh, I can just see you dealing with divorces and retirement plans and two-bit burglars. How exciting."

"Those people need my help. Working with you, catching killers is not exactly my idea of fun and games."

"Sure it is, you know you love figuring out how people kill people and then try to escape. Think of the challenge, outfoxing those bad characters. Beats the hell out of asking questions in a court room; unless you know the answers.

"Tell me, RC. Is that why you invited me to have a hot dog and sit on a concrete slab on Market Street?"

"That's what I like about you, Chris. Get right to the heart of things, talk business. Okay. I need some advice and it's top-drawer confidential. You're the most honest lawyer I know."

Right hand crossing to touch where her heart beat beneath her left breast, DeLeon answered, "You have touched me deeply. Let's cut the garbage. I have to go to work."

The sun beamed brightly on this side of the street, not yet blocked by City Hall. Office workers flowed in and around them, so Frane motioned to a less busy spot where they had some privacy.

"I'll try to be brief. You know I retired from the police department. Then, I went into private consulting. One of my major clients is John Pentram."

"Wait a minute. Are you sure you want to tell me all this? After all, I am part of the DAs' office. If you are cavorting with suspicious characters, that's your problem."

Disregarding what she said, Frane continued. "Along the way I was braced by some strong arms who answer to a woman by the name of Abate. She wanted information and a piece of John Pentram. That's when it got complicated."

DeLeon shook her head.

"Anyhow, through some contacts I have with other law enforcement agencies I found myself working for some high-level people."

Nodding she said, "High-level law enforcement? Care to stipulate."

"That's where you come in. My understanding with them is verbal. I'm out there all by myself, answering to so many people, I need legal advice."

"Nothing in writing?"

"That's it. But, if something goes wrong I may be the fall guy. Feel like I'm already down waiting for somebody to slip a knife between my ribs."

"Why don't you get something in writing, saying who you're working for, how much they pay you, check stubs, anything to prove you're not a solo."

"That's good. You want me to tell the CIA to give me permission to act for them in the continental states when their job is anywhere, but the continental United States."

"Don't be so dramatic. The CIA! Are they paying you?"

"Sure I can trust you? Ah, yeah, I can trust you." Taking a deep breath he said, "I think John Pentram is working for them, and I'm working for him, so yeah, they're paying me."

DeLeon took a sip from the bottle of water. "I guess he won't give you a letter of recommendation."

"That's what I'm asking you. How do I get to be safe?"

"You forgot something. Like, how do you know you're working for the CIA?"

"Just yesterday, Pentram and I took a ride down I-95 and met with this guy."

"Name?"

"No names were necessary. I observed two body guards keeping an eye on us."

"Show you his credentials?"

"Well, no. The phone call I got setting up the meet was clear. Don't ask, just answer."

"You want my honest assessment?"

"I told you I was counting on you because you're honest."

"I'm going to pretend this conversation never took place."

"Figures."

"You're not wearing a wire?"

"Would I do that to a nice girl like you?"

"Girl?"

"Okay, woman."

She rose, crumpled the paper from her hot dog, looked to see who might be in hearing distance, and said, "A three-month vacation far away seems in order, say Alaska, Greenland, or better yet, Outer Mongolia."

61

US Air has excellent flights to Norfolk, Virginia; a good hour from Philadelphia and then a short drive to the beach. Contiguous to one of the largest concentrations of military activity; the beach is a haven of relaxation and superior cocktails. The grey-haired man displayed an uncommon collection of fine scotch and distinguished gin. Not to mention several memorable wines.

"I have a bottle of Chopin in the freezer." Pleased with himself, he added, "Of course vodka is best served when remarkably chilled. Try a cracker with a dab of sour cream topped with a few chopped onions and a drop of caviar. Then the drink will titillate your palate."

"How will I get back to the airport?" Abate asked.

"No problem. One of my people will be happy to return you and the car. Unless you find it necessary to spend the night here."

"That being the case, I'll be happy to join you. Are you certain this is better than a beer at the Pub?"

"Now that you are a free-lance, you are certainly entitled to more than beer at the Pub. You'll just have to learn about some of the finer things in life."

There is a modest degree of pleasure in dealing with those at the lower end of the scale. It even amuses me to observe them seeking to outsmart those of us with superior backgrounds and knowledge.

"Do you want to hear what I have accomplished?"

Taking a cracker and nudging a bit of caviar with the horn spoon, he answered, "That's why you're here." Slipping the tidbit into his mouth he asked, "Do you prefer red, white, or black caviar?"

Seeking to regain some ground, Muriel Abate said, "After all the time I spent in Russia, I have almost reached my fill of caviar. After all, eggs, as they say, are still eggs."

"Well spoken," he responded. "Well spoken."

They sat unperturbed on the upper deck of his beach house, overlooking the vast expanse of beach and water. Sparkles of sharp sunlight flashed off the ripples of the otherwise smooth Chesapeake Bay. A striped awning protected them from the sun, and a small breeze insured their comfort.

She's anxious to talk. At least one more drink and the words will go deeper. This woman is like a tinder box, flights of fancy coupled with periods of sheer evil. "How was the trip down?"

"Dull. Norfolk is a nice town, but not to be compared with some of the major capitals I have worked in. What do you find so appealing here?"

"You have expressed it well. After the excitement of Madrid, Paris, Berlin, and of course Washington, this is exotic in its peace and quiet. In the winter, I like to bundle up and sit here with a hot drink; coffee properly laced, and just watch the ocean meeting with the bay. When you have seen the things we have seen, there comes a need for reflection."

Stifling a laugh, Abate observed, "Not exactly what we have been working on these past few months."

Nodding, he lifted the vodka bottle from the ice bucket and refilled the two glasses. "Still, a little lull in the midst of fierce activity can prove refreshing. Anyhow, on to the news. What have you to report?"

"I need permission to go directly to Pentram. This guy, Frane, keeps getting in the way. I have approached him, offered help, treated him rough, and even took his girl friend into temporary custody. He won't tell Pentram that we want a piece of the action."

"Have you considered eliminating him?"

"Is that an option?"

Without answering the question, the grey-haired man said, "What are your plans if Pentram won't join us? Do you have any other ideas on how to develop an income stream along with the opportunity to utilize some of the shipping benefits, using foreign-based containers? Maybe it's time to separate the two ideas."

"The beauty of doing Pentram is that we accomplish both objectives at once. Going two ways, means twice the human resources. As it is, three of our people are in jail. It took me a lot of trouble to get away from those Philadelphia cops."

"Is your office safe?"

"No. We had Frane 'visit' us once and I'm sure he knows where we're located. Right now, we're in the process of moving to a different space. Can you tell me anything more about Frane?"

"There's not a whole lot to tell. I don't know the man myself, just information that has accumulated from other sources."

"To tell the truth, I even tried sex on him."

One more drink and she'll tell me more than I need to know. "Sex? You offered him sex and he refused. Must be a man of strong convictions. Are you sure he's all man?"

A slight slur covered her answer. "He was married. And, he's doing his thing with that Sergeant Rogers. That was when we held her in custody. He did a super job finding where we were holding her. One of my top people spilled to him. Not quite sure of how he was able to break him."

"Might be a good idea to find out how he did it. May be something you could use yourself."

Abate slipped her shoes off and stretched her long legs. "You never realize how that vodka creeps up on you. Really painless."

"Chopin is not terribly strong, only 80 Proof. If you want to see the difference, I have some Tanquery Ten Gin that's 94 Proof. Now, that's a drink to deal with." *I wonder if she plans to tell me something I don't already know. Her experience with the agency has been extensive, shame she has lost it. It's possible the time has come for her to retire, permanently.*

"How long have we worked together, Muriel?"

As her head dipped forward she said, "I'm only 44. I guess around 20 years. All my career." Turning her head to stare into his eyes, she asked, "Think it's time to go?"

With a double nod, he signaled to the man standing just inside the door. "Please see that Ms Abate gets to the airport. Have one of the other men follow you so you can return her car."

62

It's time to make things happen. The question is, where to dig first. Abate is somewhere in hiding, Pentram is constantly available, the three murderers are under control, Rogers has them in her sights, Fish is a big-time actor, probably with the CIA, and I am in the middle of this entire mess. This retirement business is not exactly peaceful.

There was one avenue still open, so Frane decided to visit again with Star. A number of restaurants had come on board, and apparently, there was progress. Checking in with Star was a mixture of seeing how the system was working and verifying that incoming merchandise didn't also contain some form of contraband. Earlier experience chasing drug shipments mingled with frozen shrimp made him keenly aware that anything goes.

"Lieutenant, good to see you."

"Used to be lieutenant, just plain RC now. Or if you insist, good old fashioned mister."

"Take a seat. What can I do for you?"

"How are things going? How many restaurants have signed on?"

"Thought you would know all about that from Mr. Pentram."

Hard to be a detective when you have to pussyfoot around the questions. "I've been away for a little bit. Wanted to get ahead of the game before the next meeting with my client. So, how's it going?"

Star eased back from the table. "Care for a cup of good coffee?"

"Sure. It's always time for coffee."

He moved to the sideboard where a fresh pot of coffee stood waiting, poured two mugs before asking, "Sugar? Cream?"

"Straight's fine."

"When you first approached me with this deal, I was concerned. It just seemed too good. You know, the numbers worked, the money came in as you said it would, more restaurants came on-board. I'm still looking for the catch. Is that why you're here?"

If he's looking for the catch, or the wrinkle, so am I. "You see, Mr. Star, I come out of law enforcement. I'm trained to look for what doesn't make sense, something out of place. In this deal, I thought you could tell me how the pieces fit together. Maybe even tell me what pieces don't fit."

"Truth be known, RC, the whole deal is a natural. Keep in mind, we have thought about just such a technique for smoothing out our business, making it grow in a painless fashion. But, we have never had the horses to drag the customers to the starting line. When you came along it was like a dream come true."

"So, how many restaurants are on-board?"

"At last count, 13. Do you know how much business that means?"

"Probably comes close to $7 million a year."

"Maybe a little better. And, it helped us improve our total operation. Just an all around good deal for us. And, I assume for Mr. Pentram."

"Tell me, are you getting many containers from abroad?"

"Oh, sure. If you want, I can get you an exact count. Of course, we always got containers, both from aboard and domestically. But, the number has gone up slightly. If there has been any big increase, it's because we can consolidate more products in the same shipments. Just works better."

"How do you know what's inside a container?"

"That's no problem. Every shipment comes with a bill of lading, a complete description of the contents. We check that against our purchase order and when the container is unloaded, everything is counted. Normal business procedure."

"How do you know what's in each case?"

"Well, we deal with reputable companies," Star answered in a surprised tone. "People we know. If they say a case has six cans of tomatoes, or four gallons of stuffed olives of a certain size, or kumquats from Asia, we accept their word. We also have our own testing kitchen, to ascertain that the quality we ordered is the quality we're getting. I'm not sure I understand your question."

"Suppose, and this is a wild shot, but just suppose a container also had a couple of cases of gold coins?"

Star sipped his coffee. "Too many hands touch the shipments for that to happen. Let's go back to the origin. We order a certain number of cases. Send a purchase order, it goes to the shipping department of the packer, a bill of lading is produced, goes to the warehouse, gets loaded into a container, the container is sealed, loaded on a ship, comes across the water, gets unloaded, placed on a truck, reaches our warehouse where it is unloaded, then opened, and the merchandise is placed in our warehouse."

"So, you're satisfied that since the container is sealed, that everything is okay?"

"I just don't see how anything could interfere. This system has been working for years. Everybody uses the same procedure. Once the container is sealed, it's sealed till it reaches us."

Frane nodded. *Amateurs. The system is full of holes. Amazing. Do all these companies lack imagination?*

"Sounds pretty good. And, as you say, everybody is using the same system."

63

Since the meeting was to be sensitive, Pentram suggested the office of the Arizona Diner. His offer was more of an order than a question. After all, Frane worked for him. The Arizona was a new member of the Food Buying Group and still in need of further reinforcement.

"Did John, Jr. explore the future with you Mr. Howell?" Pentram asked the owner of the Arizona.

"Basically, I like where we are and I think I know where we're going," answered Howell. "We've only been involved for a couple of weeks, but I can feel the changes already."

"That's good to hear. By the way, this is RC Frane, he is one of my consultants."

Howell nodded as he shook hands. "Good to know you Mr. Frane."

"My business associates usually call me 'RC'," Frane said. "Glad to hear things are going well."

"Just a thought for you to keep in mind, Mr. Howell. The organization is growing a little faster than we anticipated. That means we may be ready for a really big step before the year is out."

"What's that?"

"Incorporating before going public. Any idea what that might mean to you personally?"

Howell was startled. "You mean putting all the restaurants and diners into a single company? then taking the whole thing public. What you're saying, Mr. Pentram is that my investment translated into stock before going public could make me rich. Didn't know you had that in mind."

"You have said that succinctly. Good. Now, we'd like to borrow your office for a few minutes. RC and I have a few issues to discuss."

"I'll send in a pot of coffee. Do you want anything to go with? Pastry from our bake shop?"

"Coffee sounds good. Thank you."

The office was small; barely room for several file cabinets, a desk and arm chair, and two armless chairs. The men sat and waited for the coffee.

"What do you think of our progress, RC?"

"Last I heard there were 13 restaurants on-board."

"More important than that, the early participants are now buying at a rate in excess of a $1 million a year. And we have upped our target to 50 clients."

"To me that sounds like a lot of dollars. But, is it enough to become a public company?"

Pentram beamed. "Of course, you're right. It's not such a big deal. When you think in terms of 20 cities, it begins to get interesting. Since you are my consultant, I don't mind sharing some confidential thinking with you. We could easily add some vertical integration and possibly stretch back and get into packing specific products for our client-audience. The possibilities are significant. Imagine, control of the outlets and control of the distribution system, and then, control of some manufacturing."

These security problems are way out of my class. Unless I find some people to work with me. I could build an organization with retired cops. Not bad. "It seems that you might want to hire a consultant to deal with these major ideas. Where do I fit in?"

The coffee arrived, so the conversation took a pause. "Just black for me."

"You asked for this meeting," Pentram said. "We can discuss the future some other time. As long as you know, you are my man."

"When we first got together you said you wanted honest, tough opinions."

"That's still the case."

"Okay. I took it upon myself to visit with Star. He filled me in on the procedures used for shipments, particularly those coming in containers."

"My understanding is that the freight rate and purchasing convenience makes that the best way to go. Are you questioning the validity of that idea?"

"Not at all," Frane protested. "What I am questioning is the fact that there are so many loop-holes in the system that fraud, theft, and smuggling can be a real big problem."

"Smuggling?"

"Let's take a step-by-step walk through what happens. A packer packs up to a thousand cases of merchandise. We assume that each and every case is filled with what we ordered. This product is placed in a container. We assume nothing else goes into the container. Then, this container is sealed and loaded on a tractor trailer that goes to a ship or a long train ride. We assume nobody opens the container and places something we don't know about inside. Once on board the ship or train, we have again lost control. Off it comes onto another tractor trailer that is headed toward Stars' warehouse. Again, we assume nobody stops the tractor and opens the container. Now, it's on the dock and one or two of Stars' people open the container and off-load the product. Question? Is there something else in that container that the warehouse slips aside for later delivery?"

"You really think something could go wrong, even though the container is locked and sealed?"

"Mr. Pentram, a locked container is like a lock on your brief case. How safe is that?"

Pentram slowly replaced his coffee cup on the edge of the desk. Then he stood, took two steps back, and leaned over his chair. "Are you borrowing trouble, RC?"

"This is not borrowing. This is a devoted consultant alerting his client, forewarning his client to the vagaries of human nature. Mr. Pentram, you know most of what I'm saying. The question is, 'Are you aware of these possibilities?' In which case I will resign the account right now. If you are not aware, then I'm here to tell you I need to bring in a lot more talent to protect the operation."

64

"You're serious."

"Look, what happened wasn't personal. I'd like a chance to make it up to you."

Rogers leaned back in her chair and stared at the ceiling. Head back, she closed her eyes and struggled to retain her composure. *This is unreal. I'd say bizarre, but that wouldn't be strong enough. She must be dealing from the bottom of the deck. For sure, she's not normal.*

"Maybe it does make sense. How do I know this isn't going to be a repeat of our last meeting?"

"You didn't get hurt. We just needed you to make a point with Frane. Well, we have found another way and it doesn't concern you. So, in all good conscience, I want to find a way to say, there's no hard feelings."

"My dear Ms Abate, how could I ever have bad feelings about being held prisoner for all those hours?" The words spoken softly hardly concealed the sodden sarcasm.

"Don't be like that. We're both professionals. I'd really like to be friends, get the chance to explain my position. You know, respect for each other and what we do."

With great control, Rogers now rested her head in her right hand as she bent forward on the arm of her chair. *Maybe I can capture her and keep her prisoner, just the way she did to me. A chance resembling poetic justice. She got away from the Fibbies.*

"To make sure this is all open and above board, let's meet in a very public place. I suggest the cafeteria at the new Constitution Center. Seems like a perfect place to renew acquaintances. We can even walk around and discover how the laws of the country developed."

"Hey, that sounds great. I'll be at the front entrance in two hours."

"I'll be there," answered Rogers. "No funny stuff."

Captain Bailey insisted. "This is my baby. I'm going to deploy people all over the place. A couple in the garage, a couple at the elevator, two out front, and three more inside. Plus, some more mingling with the crowds. We'll catch this weirdo. In my city, you just don't kidnap a cop. It's not nice."

When she called Frane, he advised, "You can't trust her. She lies. You know, just like a common criminal. Probably a whole lot better. My guess is that she'll be there way ahead of time, casing the faces and making sure the scene is clear. Maybe I'll see you there."

"This isn't your case, RC. I called because I know you would want to know. This is pure police work. Include yourself out."

"Sure, GG. Whatever you say."

From his position in the kitchen of the cafeteria, Frane was able to spot Abate. Today she was wearing casual clothes, sharply creased denim trousers, tight sweater that showed her figure, and a loose jacket big enough to conceal a .22 caliber revolver. She was ready, sipping a coffee, when Frane slid into the chair next to her and grabbed her right wrist.

"If I remember correctly, you are right-handed, so reaching for the gun is quite a problem. Forgive me," he added, stretching across and brushing his hand over her left breast while he lifted the revolver from her inside pocket.

"Damn you, Frane. What are you doing here? I'm just having a coffee."

"Sure you are. Now, why don't you tell me what's going on. Who do you really work for? What's your relationship with Fish?"

"Fish? I only eat them on Thursdays at the Striped Bass."

"Wish I could afford those high-priced restaurants. But, let's talk about the man, Fish. You know, the one you went to visit in Norfolk."

"Let go of my wrist. I can't drink coffee with my left hand."

"Sorry. I didn't mean to interrupt your drink."

He knew what was going to happen. A sudden splashing of the hot drink, aimed at his face. No trick is too dirty.

Leaning close he recaptured her wrist and clamped hard with his thumb on the vein. A burst of pain ran through her arm and momentarily rendered her useless as the shock concentrated all her attention. She reached across with her left hand and tried to dislodge his grip.

"You're hurting me," she cried.

"Why would I want to hurt you? You're such a sweetheart. Tell me about Fish!"

"I don't know anybody named Fish. Damn it, let go."

"Don't say I didn't give you a chance. Here comes Rogers, and here I go."

Quickly, he left the table and disappeared into the kitchen.

"Wasn't that Frane who just ran off?" Rogers asked.

"Yeh, said he dropped by to have a coffee. Want to sit down for a couple of minutes?"

Rogers sat across the table and said, "What's on your mind?"

"Like I said, just a chance to say I'm sorry we had to hold you. Since we're both sort of in law enforcement, thought it would be better if we started over again."

"Just out of curiosity, what do you mean by 'law enforcement'?"

Shrugging away a direct answer, Abate responded, "You know. We're both trying to catch some bad guys."

"Sounds reasonable."

Three of Bailey's men arrived, one on each side of Abate and one facing her.

"Tell you what," Rogers added. "How about if we conduct our meeting around the corner, say at the Round House. We have some comfortable rooms, and we can even tape our conversation. My three associates will be happy to escort you there. Oh, do you think we have to pat you down?"

65

"You know this is a big waste of time," Abate said.

Rogers nodded. "It's what I do. Talk to people, see what I can learn. I don't make the rules. Just try to carry them out."

"Then this isn't an arrest?"

"Of course not. Just you and me having a conversation. If it gets too serious we can turn on the tape recorder."

"Who's watching on the other side of the window? Or, did you think I didn't know others were listening to our conversation?"

"Hey, anybody ever saw a cop show on TV knows about the fake windows. The thing is this. You kidnapped me, held me overnight, and then walked away when my friends arrived. Don't you know it's not civil to kidnap a cop?"

Abate started to stand.

"Sit down or I'll have to restrain you. Now, just sit and talk."

"What do you want to know that I can tell you? Most of what I know is secret. You know damn well I can't talk. As soon as I can reach my people I'll be out of here."

Rogers stood, turned toward the door as she said, "Don't go away."

Just outside the door, Bailey demanded, "Why are you screwing around with this nut case? Kidnapping is a big time offense. Lock her up."

"That's what I plan to do Captain. But, there's some other stuff we ought to find out. Besides, kidnapping is Federal and that's how come the Feds let her walk. Maybe she really is what she thinks she is. Once I make an arrest, she'll clam up and want a lawyer. This way, maybe I can get some dope on what the hell is going on."

"Okay. What'dya want from me?"

"Think you could verify if she was ever with the CIA?"

"Tough call. They don't usually want to say anything about anything. Maybe DeLeon can help us."

"Kidnapping is federal. Should we contact the FBI?"

Bailey grunted. "It's what we're supposed to do. You try talking to her first."

Back in the interrogation room, Rogers decided on a straight forward approach. "Look, Muriel, if you really want to help, why not tell me what's going on. Why do you need to get into Pentram's pants? He's trying to run a business and you want a piece of the action. Why?"

Stretching her long legs under the table, Abate asked, "Guess you don't allow smoking in here?"

"I'd be glad to let you smoke, but orders from upstairs say, 'No'. So, what's with Pentram?"

"You're making it sound more complicated than it is. He has an idea for a real money machine. We can use some of that good stuff. What's wrong with wanting to share the wealth?"

"Is that a reason to knock off his collectors?"

"Think of it as a warning. Or better yet, a way to really get his attention."

"But, that's not the real reason, is it. After all, you're a tough character, so is Pentram. He won't stand still for some outsider trying to muscle him into giving up the golden pipeline."

"That's why we wanted Frane to be on our side. He has the old-man's ear and that could make all the difference in the world."

"And, once you got his ear, next you take his face, then his heart. Got it all worked out."

"N0. We're not pigs. Just need some of the access. After all, when you're involved the way we are, anything goes. That's the difference between us. In our work we do what we have to."

"That sort of brings us back to square one. Who is the 'we' you keep referring to?"

"Yes," answered Abate, "That does bring us back to square one. And that's the point. No way I can tell you who I work for. No way indeed."

Rogers stood, took a few steps around the small room, twisted her head as if to work a kink out of her neck, and then faced Abate. "Since kidnapping is federal, I am going to place you under arrest. You know the pitch, anything you say can be held against you and all that stuff. The point is, we're going to hold you until the Feds can come and get you. I don't want to talk to you any more. In fact, I'd be happy if I never saw you again. Have a good life; probably in Leavenworth."

Smiling, "And to make sure you don't disappear this time, I'll have you moved around town. Maybe even lose the paper work. Could be days, maybe weeks until we find you in the system. Have a nice day."

66

For peace and quiet, when some important talk is called for, there is no place like a stand-up bar. Some have high stools to allow drinkers to stay longer. Background noise includes music a little too loud and low chatter from others seeking to share information. "What did the market do today?" "How you making out with Martha?" "Leno was funny as hell last night." Just ordinary conversation between two people that holds little interest. Unless you speak in guarded terms.

"Is it all over?" asked Frane.

"Yep. The lady, if you can call her that, is now safely tucked away."

"The three people offed, are accounted for?"

"All wrapped up. One guy still nursing sore ribs. His partner long gone. And the third man safely stashed out of town. Plus, the two heavies in suits are now residing in the local lock-up. My first really big case," Rogers said. "All tied up with a fancy ribbon."

"What about Marmaduke?"

"Still making lots of noise, but it's out of my hands now. You know the routine, we catch them, somebody else takes over."

Frane signaled the bartender. "Want to do it again?"

A small nod.

"Good to see you here, Loo. Heard you were retired. Guess the oversized drinks we serve keep you coming back."

"Nah, it's really your smiling face."

"That's pretty good. Nobody's said anything like that since I was a baby."

Turning back to Rogers he said, "So, you figure this case is over now?"

As the fresh drinks arrived, she squeezed the lime in her G and T before stirring it with her finger. Then she licked the gin off her finger, smiled, and asked, "Want a taste?"

"Cut it out, GG. There's people in here who may be underage. You want to give this place a bad name?"

"RC, you're not on the force any more. This case is wrapped tight because I got kidnapped. Not a bad way to solve a couple of murders."

"Except for one very important point."

"Oh?"

Taking a little sip of his drink, Frane answered. "All those murders simply interfered with the real case."

"That's great. Death interferes."

"Good that you wrapped up your part, but you know there's a lot more to this than a few simple murders."

Rogers swiveled around on her seat and looked at the crowd forming for an end-of-the-day alcohol escape. Men who usually wear ties had removed them in preparation for pre-dinner revelry. Small groups of women laughing; recounting the day.

"RC, where are we going with this conversation? You saying there's more to this case than all those juicy murders?"

"Nothing juicy about murder, but, there's more to it than meets the nose. I smell a bigger, much bigger issue."

"Like what?"

"Thought maybe you had some idea. For instance, I've been doing security thinking for Star. They bring in lots of containers, from all over the world. So, who wants whatever is in those containers? Abate said she wanted a piece of the action, the money. I don't think so. Keep in mind, I know a lot about the money. Even a big piece would be bubkas to some of the people involved."

"Bubkas? What the heck are bubkas?"

"It's part of my new language in the consulting world. In English we might say, 'peanuts.'"

220

"Peanuts? Bubkas? Am I missing something here?"

"How about 'small potatoes'? Does that work better for you?"

Rogers gulped the rest of her drink. Closing in on ten years of police work, she had learned what her father had looked forward to at the end of the week. Significant amounts of liquor to smooth the nerves and take the edge off the problems the world piled on during the week.

"RC, I guess I have more to learn about this here profession. Now it's bubkas. Who knows what else I have to learn. Maybe another drink, and then we can go to my place and talk about more important matters. Like you and me."

The laughter and talk around the room obscured the need for some quiet conversation. Touching fingers and moving a hand across her back didn't seem proper is so public a setting. Despite the antics that take hold during the early-bird festivities, the open snack table and the two-for-one drinks, Frane retreated into his rigid upbringing. Rogers, once removed from her overpowering family, had lost all inhibitions.

She let her fingers do a tap dance on Franes' right knee. Then along his upper leg, just far enough to make sure he knew she was there. "Sure you don't want to go to my place?"

"You're missing a beat, here. What I'm trying to say in my most solicitous manner is there are some bigger issues. Did you know that ninety-five percent of the containers coming into the country don't get inspected? National Health agencies are scared to death thinking of what might be in those containers. Defense people can't get over imagining a bomb going off in New York harbor. Or, how about one big blast under the Delaware Memorial Bridge. Where do you think all the traffic would go? Think the Three Mile Island leak. How about a little explosion at that nuclear plant down near Salem?"

"Look, RC," Rogers said, her voice soothed. "I got no idea what you're talking about. My job is murder here and now in Philadelphia. If you're into something bigger than that, fine. Knocking my work down doesn't help us. If the world is about to blow up, I'll just go along for the ride. In the meantime, I'm trying to keep my head above the Delaware. You want to join me, that's good. If not, maybe it's time to let me know."

Head bowed, RC answered, "Trouble is, I don't know what's going on. Remember I told you before, I got different bosses, all pulling me in different ways."

"You're a big boy. Better get you scene together."

67

The driver waited in the long car while Fish accompanied by three men entered the offices of Star Distributing. One carried a thin red leather brief case. The other two concentrated on security, scrutinizing every car, truck, fork lift and particularly people intent on going about their jobs.

In his most impervious manner, Fish said to the woman behind the bullet proof cage, "Tell Mr. Stark that Fish is here."

"Does he expect you, Mr. Fish?"

Lips curled, he repeated, "Tell him Fish is here."

Half mesmerized, half frightened, she immediately pressed number one on the automatic dialer. "Mr. Stark, there are four men here. One said to tell you, 'Fish is here.'"

After a pause, "Tell him I'll be out in three minutes. Have to clear my desk."

The four men were dressed in dark business suits, striped ties, and wore hats. Two concentrated on their furtive looks, while Fish and the man with the red brief case stood quietly.

In less than the allotted time, Star appeared, shook hands with Fish and acknowledged the other men. "You brought lots of company," he said.

"Troubled times. Requires certain precautionary measures."

Star led the men down a long hall to his private office. He had arranged several chairs around the small conference table. Only Fish and brief case entered the office. The other two men remained outside, trying not to look like guards. In the busy environment of a distribution center, they stood as obvious beacons of watchfulness.

"You knew I would be visiting," said Fish.

"Well, yes. I suppose I felt it was inevitable. However, I'm still not certain what this means. Have you checked our deliveries, found them in order?"

Eyes riveted on his leader, the man in charge of the brief case slowly selected a single page which he handed to Fish.

"It appears," Fish intoned, "that everything is in order." With that, he nudged the page toward Star.

Glancing down the page of numbers and a few single line comments, Star nodded. "Seems like a duplicate of what I submitted to Washington."

"In fact, it is a duplicate. It suggests that you are making the necessary deliveries in good order. Your evaluations are quite high."

Now relaxed, Star asked, "So why the heavy weight visit? Something not going the way it's supposed to?"

Without answering, Fish continued. "When you accepted the government contracts to deliver food to military installations it was fairly well understood that you would do a good job. The report confirms that. Now it's time to move to the next step."

Rising to the occasion, Star said, "Does that mean more deliveries? We cover several large military bases within our distribution area. In fact, we're more than ready to duplicate our existing prices and begin to schedule as many deliveries as needed in less than 30 days."

Again, disregarding Star, Fish admonished, "There are certain services you can perform within the framework of our existing arrangements. That is the purpose of this visit." Signaling brief case, he accepted another sheet of paper.

After reviewing the page, he handed it to Star. "This is a partial list of containers you will be receiving in the next three months."

Star studied the list. "How did you get all this information?"

"Not an important question. The list is accurate."

"Near as I can tell it is. I'd have to ask the people in the purchasing department. But, I don't understand. What's your interest in the containers coming in?"

Fish took a silver Tiffany pen from his coat pocket and laid it on the table. "Before we go any further, I want you to look at this security pledge." Again, he signaled his associate, who was already pulling another sheet of paper from the red brief case. Without looking, he pushed it towards Star along with the pen.

It was a simple statement committing Star to secrecy. The stationary had an official stamp and the initials at the top had an official look, like CIA.

"If you agree to hold the next part of our conversation secret, please sign the bottom and my associate will bear witness to the signature."

"How can I sign anything like this without my attorney being here?"

Despite every attempt to remain calm, Fish could not conceal his dissatisfaction with this response. "Mr. Star, you have done a great deal of business with the Federal Government." He emphasized the last two words. "This represents further commitment. There is need for much security in these troubling times. What I am asking, no, what I am telling you to sign is your word that further business relations with you and the United States Government will remain of the utmost confidence."

This is very upsetting Star thought. All of a sudden they want some kind of legal statement in addition to ones I have already agreed to. Something doesn't sound right. On the other hand, there is a lot of business to be considered. And, it isn't as if they are asking me to do anything illegal.

Star read the brief statement. It was simple. Any requests made with regard to future shipments were to remain secret. "Okay. I'll sign. Can I get a copy for my files?"

"As soon as I am back in my office, you will receive a copy."

"Can't I make a copy here, in my own office?"

"No. Because I want to register it in my records, add the registry number and they we'll send it to you, in a confidential way. Probably by messenger."

In an attempt to change the tone of the meeting, Fish asked, "Think we can get a cup of tea?"

Startled by the question, Star answered, "Would you prefer regular or decaf?"

"My preference is herbal."

68

"Chief, I'm not sure what to do with this tape."

"Before I listen to it, tell me what I'm about to hear."

"You'll love this," said Frane. "After we found Sergeant Rogers at the apartment where she was being held prisoner, I took her next door to get some breakfast. While we were eating, this woman, Muriel Abate, signals me through the window and sends me a message with a table server to meet her on the corner of 15th and Locust."

"You knew this woman?"

"Oh yeh. In fact, she had two of her toughs pick me up one day and take me to her office for a meeting. But, to get back to the tape; when I got to the corner the phone rang in a kiosk. I picked it up and she gave me instructions where to meet her. So, I walked back to Pine street and sure enough she pulls up to the curb and orders me to get in. Fortunately, I was carrying at the time, so as I slid into the front seat I immediately covered her. Now, here's the tricky part. I used the automatic dialer on my cell phone and called my home number. By the time I was in the car, my answering machine was recording our conversation. That's what you're about to hear."

"That was very clever, RC."

Together they listened to the conversation. It only lasted a few minutes when the Chief said, "Doesn't make a whole lot of sense. She keeps talking around the bush. Has she got both oars in the water?"

"My personal opinion; I don't think so. She keeps pushing the idea that she answers to some higher authority, like the head of the CIA or maybe even the FBI. I don't know which is worse."

"Isn't she in custody? She's the one who Sergeant Rogers fingered for kidnapping her. That's a pretty serious charge."

"Right; but, if she really is working for the feds, then do we have enough muscle to keep her under wraps? In the meantime, my sources tell me she got a walk."

Smiling, the Chief said, "You've been away only a couple of months and you seem to have forgotten how we can move a suspect around in the system for quite a while. Who knows, she might wind up in deep South Philadelphia where people haven't been heard from for years."

"What's the use?"

"Maybe none. I'm just thinking she may really be a loose cannon. Have you found any other information about her?"

"Chief, I'm in a bit of a quandary. May have overshot my mark. Anyhow, I found out through some sources I'd rather not mention, that Abate flew down to Norfolk and had a meeting with Fish."

"Fish?"

"That's another part of my quandary. A week ago, Pentram and I took a ride down I-95 and met with Fish and a couple of suits. Pentram knew these guys and I was along for the ride."

"Fish."

"That's all I know. That's what he wanted to be called."

"What did he look like? Can you describe him?"

"Close to six feet. Maybe 60-62. Grey hair, strong face, lots of lines. Dressed in a classy suit, you know Brooks Brothers, that kind. Cuff links. Might pass for a diplomat or a high level government official. You know him?"

Chiefs learned long ago how to keep a straight face. No way to read surprise or interest or anything. Frane looked, but picked up nothing.

"What else is on your mind?"

"Guess that's about everything."

Rising from the couch, Chief added, "Good idea to see me at home. Be careful nobody is following you."

69

Inconsistency rules! Well thought out plans for retirement, falter in the face of inflation. Diet plans collapse when a mushroom-topped steak and a baked potato larded with sour cream appear on the table. Savings for retirement never takes into account Saturday nights at the local pub. Making a date with Greta Rogers doesn't always lead to fun and games. I don't even know who I work for or who I report to. People succeed in misleading and unadulterated lying. What the hell am I doing?

Disconcerted by his own meanderings, Frane almost missed the little man headed his way. When he left Chief's house he drove to Chesterbrook Village and found the macadam path. It was late afternoon, the day was clear and he decided a brisk walk would help clear his thinking.

The man stopped, waiting to be seen.

"I've been waiting for you."

"You know me?"

"Everybody knows former Lieutenant RC Frane."

As the hackles rose on his neck, Frane knew what was coming. Early training signaled trouble. No thinking was required, only the need to react.

With a perfect whirl, the little man spun counter-clockwise, gaining momentum and raising his right leg that was directed at Franes' left arm.

Frane rotated in a clockwise motion, moving swiftly so that his right arm caught the raised leg and threw the little man onto the ground. As he bounced off the path, Frane continued in his rotation while reaching for the .22 he carried for emergencies.

Feeling no match for the little man who was obviously expert in karate, he took aim and shot his left ankle; a damaging wound but certainly not fatal. His only concern was whether this would put an end to the attack. Trained assassins learn how to deal with pain. Trained police officers learn to observe and wait before committing to a disabling shot. It all happened in seconds.

"Move and my next bullet will do your right knee cap."

The little man coiled like a snake and rushed forward on the strength of his right leg. His fingers stiffened, prepared to thrust into Franes' chest. The second shot crippled his right knee and he once again fell to the ground.

"The next bullet will go between your eyes. Want to try?"

Disabled the little man snarled, even while clutching his knee. Few joints in the body are as complicated as the knee, and the bullet that crushed the cap caused the pain to travel through his entire body. No amount of training could stop the flood of agony.

He finally muttered, "Get me a doctor, you bastard."

"Two conditions," answered Frane. "First, say 'Please'. Second, tell me what this is all about."

Teeth grinding, the little man said, "Okay. Please get me a doctor, you bastard."

"And second?"

"Just following orders. You know the routine. I do a certain kind of work, sell my services."

"Good. Now, give me the name of your employer."

"He didn't mention his name."

"How much do you get paid for disabling a person?"

"Did you call the doctor?"

"As soon as you tell me more about the man. How much did you get paid?"

"It wasn't a man, it was a young boy. He handed me a note with your name and where to find you. And $150."

"Where's the note?"

"In my pocket."

"Take it out and lay it on the ground."

"Screw you!"

"Sorry you're being so stubborn. I'll see you later." With that, he backed away and headed for his car.

"Wait. Aren't you going to call for a doctor?"

Turning, Frane smiled, "Of course. As soon as I get home and have my dinner, I'll call. Hang loose."

As he passed out of sight, Frane moved toward his car. Once there, he paused, waited for two minutes and then edged back to look over the rise. Still writhing, the little man had extracted a cell phone and was calling. He tried to struggle to his feet, but the knee kept him down. Returning to his car, Frane settled in.

Within ten minutes, a dark blue Ford Taurus pulled into the curb about half-a-block from where he was parked. Two men in equally dark blue, double breasted suits got out of the car and walked towards the path. Slinking down in his seat, Frane watched as the two men carried the little man and urged him into the back of the car. As they drove off, Frane cautiously followed. Concentrating on keeping track of the blue Ford, he missed the black Ford following him.

After a short ride south on Route 202, the Ford pulled into a tree-lined street dotted with large brick houses. It pulled into a driveway where the garage was located along the side of the house. Frane drove further down the block before making a U-turn. As he passed the house for a second time, he saw the two suits lift the little man into the garage.

He paused long enough to note the address, before pulling away.

Waiting at the end of the block, the black Ford continued to follow Frane.

70

"Sometimes I think we're wasting our time," Roberta Mercado said.

"I look at it in a different light," answered Robert Vogt. "First off, any time we spend together is good. After all, we're still getting paid and we do enjoy doing what we do." He reached out to touch her hand even as it rested easily on the steering wheel of her Mercedes.

"And?"

"Well, this talk with Harry Waterhouse was not very successful. However, I truly believe we can capitalize on what we already know."

The early morning meeting in Trenton at The Diner on Olden Avenue was less than helpful. Waterhouse arrived with two of his people, who sat in a distant booth. He seemed determined to agree with nothing they had to say. The prospect of being part of a very large public company passed over him like an unwelcome breath of garlic.

"I thought after our joint meeting in Atlantic City that he would be more receptive to a positive, profitable relationship. Guess that means we go it alone. There is no way to stop the forward momentum."

"At least Pentram and Arthur are on board. Think we should get in touch with Marty Seelman in Camden?"

Mercado asked, "What do you know about him?"

"Mostly just his name. Camden is a tough town. But, he also covers a lot of the surrounding territory, through the whole county. With Pentram and Arthur we cover Philadelphia. With Seelman we include most of South Jersey. In terms of population, we're talking a whole big bunch."

They took the "scenic" road home, traveling on Route 1 until they reached Interstate 95, all the way to downtown Philadelphia. There, they turned off to stop at the Hyatt for lunch.

"Not exactly an out-of-the-way spot, but a big bowl of chowder, half a sandwich, glass of wine, what could be better?"

"Think they rent rooms by the half-day?" she asked.

"Don't you have to go back to your office?"

"Oh," she said, disappointment dripping.

Realizing he had asked the wrong question, Vogt backtracked, "What I meant was why only half-a-day? When we finish lunch we can adjourn to a suite, have some interesting and pleasurable time, come down for dinner, and see what that leads to."

"Late afternoon movie, a nap, and a shower. Can we look forward to a drink before dinner?"

"Pretty much what I had in mind. You want to talk business at all?"

"What for? We know what we're doing. When they're ready, we'll swing into action."

71

Frane knew he was being followed. Driving slowly through the crowded streets, he did what he told everyone else not to do; he slid the cell phone from his pocket and punched in a number.

"I think I can use some help."

"Trouble?"

"Right now I'm being followed by a black Ford. Guy's been tracking me for about an hour. Not sure what it's all about. You have any idea?"

Without answering, Pentram said, "Go to my street, ring the bell of the corner house on the west side. We'll talk."

The phone went dead.

Picking up speed, he joined the heavy stream of traffic on the Schuylkill Expressway, and exited left on Passyunk Avenue, turned right when he got to 17th Street and pulled next to the curb in front of a "No Parking" sign. Casually looking back, he spotted the black Ford slowly cruising, almost not moving as he started for the porch.

Immediately, the door eased open and a man in a dark blue, double-breasted suit, with a bulging chest that outlined a shoulder holster complete with an oversize piece, greeted him. "Come with me Mr. Frane."

The house was typical of the row houses built in an early era. Frane knew the layout; it reminded him of his own home growing up in the Eastwick section of Philadelphia. There was little light as he trailed the man to a door leading to the basement. An overhead uncovered bulb only made the shadows deeper. At the bottom of the steps, he was led to the area that was known as the coal bin. Delivery trucks brought heavy canvass bags of dirty black coal that were poured through an open window. Only later did they use metal chutes to send streams of coal into the bowels of the home. Now, a clean gas heater did the job of bringing warmth and hot water into the house.

To the left of the heating unit was a door. Frane asked no questions, only followed as the burly man led him through an underground passage that moved in a diagonal direction as it crossed under the street. He counted thirty steps until they reached another door. Bright light shone once the door opened. This basement was paneled in mahogany and covered with a deep carpet. Against the far wall was a small bar topped with a coffee maker and six sets of cups and saucers. Easy chairs and an oversized leather couch were neatly arranged, along with a round poker table and six Captains chairs.

"Have a seat. Mr. Pentram will be with you in a minute."

Frane was disbelieving, wondering how far the tunnels might extend. He was almost flattered that he had been allowed to know of the existence of the secret networks, reminiscent of spy novels. He fully expected he would have to take an oath of silence. Only this was not exactly a high school fraternity initiation.

From yet another secret passage, John Pentram entered the room. "Welcome, Lieutenant. Would you care for a cup of coffee?"

Seeking to conceal his amazement, Frane responded, "Yes, coffee sounds good. I thought since we were involved in a business way we might get down to a first name basis."

"What you say is true. However, men of my age and position prefer a fair degree of decorum. You can certainly understand that. Sugar? Cream?"

"Straight, please."

"You see, there are only a few things people really respect. Money for example. If it is known that you are the possessor of a significant business worth many dollars, people react accordingly. Physical prowess always tends to inspire respect. Over the years, I have learned that maintaining a more formal environment commands all the respect one could hope for. That is why I prefer to address you with your well-earned title, even though you no longer work for the Police Department."

"Point well made. I shall be glad to conform to your desires."

"Good. From time to time we may be in a more relaxed setting. Our concern today is quite serious and I am glad of the opportunity to be of assistance. You were quite disturbed when you called. So much so, that I felt it would be appropriate to share this small resource that we have developed over time. For all intents and purposes, whoever is following you is now under the impression you are across the street. Do you think we should intercept them?"

Frane eased into one of the Captain's chairs. "I'm not sure. What do you think?"

Pentram took a seat on the opposite side of the table. "If you wish to leave them behind, your car can remain where it is and you can have a substitute car. On the other hand, whoever is following you will probably park. It would be relatively easy to invite them in for a cup of coffee. Whatever is your pleasure?"

"How would you do that?"

Smiling, "Not to worry. We can be very convincing."

The coffee was hot and strong. He sipped slowly. "I'd really like to know who's on my tail. Just for the record. There are so many things complicating my new work, that I'm not sure who are the good guys and who are the bad guys."

"Welcome to the world of intrigue."

"If that's what it is, I prefer to keep you out of sight. How about if I just take you up on the offer of a car, and arrange to exchange cars later."

With that, he laid his keys on the table.

Pentram walked to the door and signaled one of his men to come in. "Please show Lieutenant Frane to a car." Turning to Frane he added, "Of course, there is no need to tell you that how you disappeared must remain our secret."

Nodding assurance, he answered, "I wouldn't have it any other way."

72

"Can we keep this conversation in the utmost confidence?"

"Depends," Frane answered.

"Okay. If that's the best you can do, we'll just have dinner, drink some wine and call it a day."

"You invited me to dinner. I didn't know this was going to turn into something serious."

After a day filled with massive surprises, including his encounter with the little man, a shooting, being followed by an unknown person in a black Ford, the subterranean passages in South Philadelphia, and now an invitation to come to the apartment of Greta Rogers for dinner, Frane had reached a point of high anxiety.

"I'm making baked chicken. Kinda harmless, basted with apricot preserves and a dab of orange juice. Rice, and a side of green beans. Why don't you pour us a glass of this Pinot Grigio."

He examined the bottle carefully, read the label and then filled two glasses half way. Handing one to Rogers he offered a mild toast. "To good times."

"I wanted you to come over so we could talk about good times. Maybe not exactly what you had in mind."

He stood, walked around the room, took note of the new curtains, the pictures on the walls, and the table set with purple napkins, and what appeared to be brand new flatware.

"This is quite an event," he said. "We seem to have gotten off the social track. Nice to be able to get together, have a comfortable dinner, good glass of wine, and who knows what."

"You still didn't answer my question."

"I forgot the question."

"Damn it, can we have a confidential conversation!"

Doesn't sound like this is a night for fun and games. Serious talk. Confidential. I always thought everything we did together was confidential.

"Alright, Greta. Let's have a confidential talk. Shall I pour more wine?"

After taking a long sip, she said, "A very high authority instructed me to keep an eye on you. Not so much to discover what you were doing, but more important, as a safeguard."

"What?" demanded Frane. "Gimmie that again."

Rogers turned the heat down on the baking chicken and moved into the living room of her small apartment. "Let's have a quiet talk for a minute. You should feel good that somebody up there is interested in you. That's why this talk is confidential. I'm not supposed to tell you anything. But, our history is pretty important to me. I hope it's important to you."

Angered, Frane said, "Why should I feel good about a woman with whom I have been seriously involved, now tells me that she's tracking my every movement."

Retreating, Rogers answered, "It's because we are involved that I am taking a big risk in telling you anything. If you want to end this conversation, this would be a good time for you to leave."

This is getting out of hand. Maybe I over-reacted; Frane thought.

"Look, GG. I'm sorry. But, how would you feel if I was tracking you?"

"Matter of fact, I'd feel pretty good. It would be a sign that you have some heavy-duty feelings about my welfare. Particularly when you're playing in a game where the rules are a lot different that just being a cop."

"Let' start over. Who told you to track me?"

Shying away from a direct answer, she said, "Let's just say somebody high up."

"Bigger than Bailey?"

"Guess you could say that."

"Does Bailey know?"

"I never discussed it with him. So, I don't really know if he knows."

"What have you learned so far?"

"This is pretty uncomfortable. Let's just say I know you almost had a big problem when you were walking down the path."

"You know what happened?"

"Sort of."

"What the hell does that mean?"

"It means that our people were prepared to step in, if necessary."

"They saw everything."

"In a word, yes. No need to report what we saw."

"And you followed me after that."

"All the way. We lost you when you went into that house. We're still trying to figure that one out."

Laughing, Frane admitted, "That was pretty neat, wasn't it."

"How'd you do it?"

"Smoke and mirrors, like any good magician."

"What does that mean?"

"You know how magicians work. They do something with their right hand, so you don't notice what they're doing with their left hand. I think they call is misdirection."

"Go on."

"Well, you saw me go into the house on the corner. But, whoever was in the black Ford kept on watching my car. That was one of your people following me, wasn't it?"

"They were looking out for you, making sure nobody was going to do anything to you. That's why this meeting is confidential. Just so I can tell you we're interested in your welfare."

"How was I supposed to know I was being tracked by the good guys?"

"Are we confidential?"

"Yes. Tell me everything."

"There's not much to tell. Somebody upstairs wants you to be safe. I was called in and given very vague instructions. Something like, don't let anything happen to him."

Frane refilled the wine glasses, this time to the top. "Did you tell them about the little man?"

"Only a bit. They didn't really want to know all the details. If he turns up in a hospital, which I doubt, we may get a call. You know the routine, gun shot

wounds."
    "Do you know the house he was taken to?"
    "We're looking into it now."
    "What else do you know?"
    "Nothing. What do you know?"
    "Twice as much as you."

73

Deliveries into distribution centers usually take place during the day. Outgoing orders are loaded at night, some departing in the early morning if customers are a couple of hours away. That means that the night shift can leave after all the trucks are loaded. When the warehouse teams arrive in the morning, their job is to get ready for in-coming merchandise.

For large facilities such as Star Distributing, the twenty loading docks become receiving docks. Fork lift trucks stream in the gapping rears of forty-foot long trailers and exit with a pallet load of cases. Depending on the product, the fork lift may go right to a proscribed location, raise its cargo and slide the pallet into position. Some modern distribution centers reach heights of fifty feet. Just like the shelves in a super market—only much larger.

Ronald Star was giving RC Frane a tour of the facility. They had walked through the purchasing department, marveled at the complexity of the data processing area, and reviewed the sales room where rows of carrels replete with telephones and computers stood silent because the reps were, "on the street."

"How many outside people do you have?"

"Last time I looked, I think over fifty. And they are backed up by ten inside salespeople. Lot of ordering takes place on the phone."

This is all very interesting. Guess it's part of being a consultant, letting people do all the talking about stuff that doesn't seem important. Time's running out, I'm supposed to be watching the unloading of a shipment of olives within the next ten minutes. At least that's what I was told to watch.

"How about the main event, the warehouse?"

"Right through that door over there. Got to get you a hard hat."

"Pretty impressive," Frane said as he considered almost three hundred feet of space needed to accommodate the yawning doors, all open like a set of teeth ready to chomp on the food coming through.

"When all the trucks are lined up we have special high-power lights to play on the interiors of the trailers. Come on down here, there's a container of Olives just coming in from Spain."

"All the way from Spain?"

"These are green olives of all kinds." Signaling to a foreman, he said, "Have you got the manifest. Like to look at it."

Showing Frane the papers, the mix of items included cases of quart bottles of Cocktail Olives, four-gallon cases of Stuffed Manzanilla Olives, Colossal Stuffed Olives, Jumbo Olives, Pitted Olives, including various sizes. The entire container held over eight hundred cases. Plus one case of samples.

Very casually, Star told the foreman, "When you come across the case of samples, please see that it gets to my office."

Bingo. My information was right on target.

"We'll take a fast walk through the freezers. More than a few minutes and we should put on some heavy clothes."

Frane knew a little about freezers from his earlier experience chasing down the killers of Chef Robert Doritt. That was a case he and Greta Rogers worked on when the chef was found in the freezer of the restaurant, buried under eight cases of frozen shrimp. The investigation led to a frozen food distributor only a few blocks from Star's facility. Several walks through that freezer added new meaning to crime solving. That very chilly, first hand experience helped Frane when he "convinced" Marmaduke to tell him where Rogers was being held captive.

A five minute walk through the freezer and I'll tell Star I'm chilled and we should return to his office for a cup of hot coffee.

"What I want to show you," Star said, "is the variety of cold storage. We have a number of different areas for maintaining the quality of different products. For instance, bananas require one temperature, lettuce something a little different, and even peaches and grapes from Chile something else. It's just not a matter of one refrigerator suits all."

Frane nodded, silence would lead him where he wanted to be, Star's office.

As they walked, Star pointed out the large area where the fork lift trucks were recharged each night. Proudly he waved his arm and explained how much time and effort was solved by "wrapping" outgoing orders. "Some of the new technology cost us heavily at the outset, but now saves us tons of money."

"Very impressive. It's easy to see how you can take on an account like the Food Buying Group at such competitive prices. I appreciate you're taking me for this tour. Helps me understand better what my job is."

Star was a little surprised. "I didn't know you were helping to sell some of the restaurants in joining the Buying Group."

"I do all manner of strange things. Whatever it takes to get the job done." Then quick to add, "All within the ethical constraints of consulting."

"Still, you work for, shall we say, a man who marches to the beat, oh, you know the rest."

Taken aback, Frane responded, "The most important person I work for is the one I have to confront every day when I shave."

"Sorry," answered Star. "Let's go have a cup of coffee."

74

On the way to his office, Star led Frane into the test kitchen. "Since you have some contact with our new customers, those joining the Group, you ought to have a sense of how seriously we take our quality."

"I thought that was all taken care of by government standards."

"There are really two issues. Yes, there are government standards for most food products. That's for one. The other thing is that the standards are flexible. So, we have to verify that we're getting what we're paying for."

"Something like quality control."

"It goes a little deeper than that. Here's a brief picture. Grade A, sometimes called 'Fancy' can score anywhere from ninety to one hundred."

"What does that mean?"

"Let's say that a product like Applesauce is being graded. There may be five or six factors, things like color, consistency, absence of defects, sometimes even weight."

"Sounds like tests we used to take in school. When they're all added up, you get a grade for the year. But, what about taste?"

"Taste is in the mind of the taster. So, not too many things can be graded that way. Again, it depends on the product. Tomato juice can be sweet or maybe tart. Depends where it comes from, California tends to be richer than Jersey."

"But, if the government has standards, why do you have to test them?"

"Wait till I get us a cup of coffee."

After they were seated in front of the stainless steel work table, Star continued. "Let's say our buyer orders 'Fancy' canned corn. If it had a score of ninety-one, how would it compare to another brand that scored ninety-six?"

"You mean this equipment can measure the difference?"

"Well, using this equipment, our Quality Control person, usually assisted by our Chef can do that kind of measuring."

"You have a Chef?"

"Oh, yes. And a top talented man he is."

"And the quality control person?"

"We were very lucky there. The woman who heads our Health Care department has training in quality testing. It's very important in her work and we're able to couple her with the Chef and test anything we want to look at."

This is really interesting and maybe I can use some of this when I'm doing things with the Food Buying Group. But, hell, there are much more important things on my mind. Like what's in the box of samples.

"Thanks, this is pretty good. It can sure help me if anybody out there questions me. How about we take a look at your box of samples?"

As they walked down the hall, Star continued to point out other departments. "Over there are the people who work on major bids. Next to them is the Human Resources department. Those rooms at the far corner are the Marketing Department. All in all, what we have here is a far cry from what I found when I joined the firm."

"That was when you came back from Vietnam?"

"How'd you know that?"

"I used to be a detective."

When they entered Star's office, Fish was waiting for them.

"Didn't want to leave without paying my respects," he said.

"How'd you get in here?" asked Star.

Without responding, Fish reminded Star, "Part of our earlier conversation. I'm here to pick up the box of samples."

Frane interrupted. "It's good to see you again, Mr. Fish. A little surprising, but still good."

There were two double-breasted suits standing quietly off to one side. One moved to secure the box. Hefting a forty-pound weight didn't seem like any problem.

"Hold on a minute," demanded Star. "You can't just walk out of here with this box of samples."

"I don't think you understand. I can do whatever I wish."

Frane hesitated, then joined in. "Mr. Fish, the last time we spoke I thought we were on the same page. I came here today to follow through on some instructions I received. Now there seems to be, shall we call it, a difference of opinions."

"I remember our meeting very well. So, to make matters easy, let's do two things. First, I am empowered to pick up any incoming samples from certain specified origins. Spain is one of those origins. Second, to prove that there is nothing untoward in my actions, we'll take a look at the contents."

With a slight hand signal, one of the suits took a small pen knife from his pocket and slide it around the sealed edges of the box. A nod from Fish and he opened the box and started to place the contents on the floor.

Both Frane and Star stooped to scrutinize the pile of books. They thumbed through some pages, even stopped to read a few lines. Searching for anything that might be incriminating defied them.

"Satisfied?" asked Fish.

75

"He's not playing with a full deck."

"Over his head in a puddle."

"He only rows with one oar."

All descriptions of John Pentram, Jr. Finally, "He has a gold card for dumb."

Frane tried to set aside all these warning signs. Not that he didn't care, more that he only wanted to answer to one boss; John Pentram himself. The police department wasn't the right place to learn this lesson. There, you always had to know who was over your current leader, and who might be right behind you, waiting for you to tumble. As a private consultant, working alone, he accepted the new found freedom at the same time he was on his own. No guaranteed work, an agreement to depart on twenty-four hours notice, and no pension plan. After twenty years on the force, he was experiencing the fears that attend any free-lance operator.

Pentram was as good as his word. The healthy check arrived by the second day of each month. Still, he never knew from day-to-day if he was still employed. What started as a noble effort, began to look like a recipe for disaster. Especially when Junior saw fit to exercise an authority he did not possess.

"What kind of arrangement do you have with the old man?"

"What old man?"

"Cut the crap, Frane. My old man."

They were driving to Atlantic City to keep an appointment with a well-known steak house, a restaurant that was brought to their attention as an excellent prospect for the Buying Group by the Sales Manager at Star. "They buy tons of meat and we sell tons of meat. You start talking fillets, rib eyes, and sirloin, you're into big bucks."

"John, I don't want to tell you how to drive, but eighty on the Expressway is a little heavy."

"That's right. Don't tell me how to drive. Now, let's get back to the deal you made with my father."

This is a big problem. My deal is only with Mr. Pentram. Junior doesn't register on the Richter Scale. Still, he is heir apparent. So many people pulling at me. Time to change the subject.

"Did the boss tell you about the books?"

"What books?"

"Okay. Here's what happened. I was visiting with Ronald Star. You know, he gave me a tour of the facility, trying to teach me something about the business. Thought it would help in negotiations with potential customers."

"I'm supposed to be running that part of the operation," demanded Junior.

"Absolutely. That really has nothing to do with me. But, here we are on our way to meet with a possible customer, and it just makes sense for me to have some idea of what it's all about."

Grudgingly, Junior agreed. "Maybe I ought to let him take me through his operation. I haven't had any trouble so far. Usually I set up a meeting then bring along another operator so the two guys can talk to each other. Who cares how Star runs his business. We're just interested that he does everything we want."

"I'm just following orders. Anyhow, the other day when I was there, a man your father knows, in fact a man he introduced me to, stopped in to pick up a box of books."

"They sell books over at Star's?"

"I'm still working on that. So far I have come up blank. Anyhow, what do you know about this place we're going to?"

"All I know is the Old Man gimmie a note to go see this guy. Called for an appointment. He didn't sound too happy. But, he says, c'mon down."

"How big is the place?"

"A hundred seats. Bar. Sells mostly steaks, a little chicken, and a little sea food."

"Is it a worthwhile prospect?"

"I can't do all the figuring. What'dya you think?"

Frane took out the pad from his jacket. Repeating an exercise that Mr. Pentram taught him, he turned to a blank page and started. "Suppose he sells fifty steaks a night. That's 350 a week. Each one weighs ten ounces. That's 3500 ounces, plus some waste, comes to maybe 240 pounds a week. At nine bucks a pound comes to about $2,200 a week. Must use a lot of baked potatoes and French Fries. That means oil or shortening for the deep fryer. Plenty of fresh vegetables, dressings, fancy frozen deserts. May not reach the ten thousand a week we're looking for. Depends on the other stuff."

"You're way off," blurted Junior. "Three hundred and fifty a week is peanuts. Must be serving twice that number and the same number of other things. I figure he serves maybe a thousand dinners a week at $25 a pop. What's that come to?"

"You forgot drinks, liquor and wine. Sounds like it could go to forty thousand a week. That should be more than enough for us."

The big Lincoln was heavy and held the road. Even at eighty miles an hour, the ride was smooth. A clear sky and mild temperatures made for a comfortable ride. Only the conversation stalled.

This isn't exactly what I had in mind when I became a consultant. The money is good, the Old Man is interesting, but this guy is an idiot. A few more days traveling with him and I may have to clarify a few things with the boss. Besides, there is something big going on and I have to find out what those books mean. Wonder if the Chief has any ideas?

"When we finish with this restaurant guy, maybe we can go over and drop a few coins at one of the casinos."

"Sounds good, but I'll tell you, I have to be back in the city by three o'clock."

"I'll just drop in for a fast couple of pulls on a slot machine. They got some new models."

"Let's see how long this call takes."

76

Leonides Andros controlled himself. He realized there was no humor in Frane's story, only a search for some element of truth, or understanding. At the minimum, a man reaching out for help.

The two were drinking Ouzo, that clear Greek liquor that turns into a milky haze when mixed with water. Even diluted, it had a subtle clout that grew with each fresh glass. They punctuated toasts with occasional bites of pita bread dipped in skordalia. By the time the bottle was half empty, the two men had moved to a first name basis.

"You know, Leonides is a strong name. It has a certain resonance; it defines you as more than just a person."

Andros was surprised. "I'm not sure what you mean."

"It's a dignified name and it fits you. It carries weight."

"Well, how does one offer similar compliments to a man with initials for a name? I hesitate to ask the significance. We know each other for five, six years and we have shared some deep experiences. Still, I would not impose on our relationship, RC."

"Here's the story. My mother was enchanted with the story of Robinson

Crusoe. Overcoming all possible obstacles and surviving. Of course, with the help of his man, Friday."

"Interesting," answered Andros, pouring another drink for each of them. "Good thing the dinner hour is over so we can talk."

After his trip to Atlantic City with John Pentram Junior, Frane called ahead to see if Andros was free. The owner of the Sand Box restaurant had become a friend, even though Frane and Rogers were never able to solve the murder of his daughter. They had a serious suspicion that the killer was sleeping in an ancient deep-sea diving suit at the bottom of the Delaware River. Somehow, they could not dismiss the notion that he arrived there with the help of Leonides Andros. Friendships grow in strange and fertile places.

Frane arrived after nine and immediately the older man led him to a table far into the restaurant. Waiting for them was a deep dish of skordalia, the garlic-oil blend that sparked the tongue and suggested more Ouzo. It only took a few minutes for Frane to reveal his problem.

"In the past we often spoke in confidential terms. Those conditions still exist?"

"If you wish."

"Basically, you know I'm working for this man, Pentram. And you also know that I'm on a different kind of assignment. Highly secret."

"Yes."

"Anyhow, the man I report to in this secret assignment told me to take a look at a shipment of olives coming in from Spain."

"Olives?"

"Yeh, olives. A whole container of olives. All kinds of olives. Maybe eight hundred cases of olives."

"You were supposed to examine them?"

"That's the part that doesn't make sense. No way I could do that. The kicker is there was a case of samples in the container. Just packed like a case of olives, only marked, 'Samples'."

"And?"

"This case was taken into Mr. Star's office. You remember, we talked about him before. Anyhow, we go into the office and there are three men. Strong men. They wanted to take the box of Samples. We objected, so they opened the box and it was full of books."

"What kind of books?"

"Fiction. Titles I recognized, but not my kind of reading. We thumbed through some of them and couldn't figure it out."

"You let them take the books?"

"Don't forget, I don't have any authority. And there were three of them to the two of us."

Pouring more Ouzo, Andros asked, "So, why have you come to me?"

Before answering, Frane took a long drink. The glasses were fairly small, hold only five ounces. A long drink was two, three ounces. Even diluted with water, the alcohol content is still formidable.

"The problem is this. In fact the problem is two-fold. First, how do I tell my 'secret' client what I discovered? which is almost nothing. More important, I think I'm missing a beat. That's what led me to you. I need some philosophic approach to this part of the problem."

It was at this point that Andros sought to control himself. Laughter was out of the question. He pondered over a proper response; sought refuge in his own long swallow of Ouzo.

"When I came to this country I was still a very young boy, maybe ten. It was war time and one of my uncles worked at the Frankford Arsenal. He used to tell us stories about what was happening there. Nothing secret, of course. One of his favorites was about the guards. You're too young to remember, but every worker had a badge and the guard would inspect the badge when you entered and when you left."

"Is this going to help me?" asked Frane.

"That's up to you," smiled Andros. "Anyhow, one night as he was leaving the Arsenal, the man ahead of him was pushing a wheel barrow filled with sand. Suspecting something, the guard pulled him aside and poked his night stick into the sand and stirred it around. Finding nothing, he passed the man through.

"Well, the next night the same thing happened. This time the guard poked many more times. Still, he couldn't find anything. After two more nights of the same things, the guard pulled the man aside and said, 'Dump all that sand on the ground.' This time he spread the sand over a large area until he had a small beach. Still, there was nothing.

"My uncle was intrigued. So, he followed the man as he wheeled the barrow down two blocks before turning the corner. It was then that he stopped the man and asked, 'What's going on? What are you doing with all the sand?'

"The man looked at him and shrugged. Again my uncle said, 'What are you doing with all the sand?'

Finally, the man answered, "I throw it away."

"So, what are you doing?" said my uncle.

Again, the man shrugged. "I'm stealing wheel barrows."

Frane stared. A laugh almost crossed his lips. "Good story. But, what has that got to do with my problem?"

Andros signaled to a table server. Pointing to the now empty bottle of Ouzo, he beckoned for more.

"My dear friend, when you dumped the books, maybe you were missing the message."

77

"Can I have about fifteen minutes?" Rogers asked.

Bailey looked at his wrist watch. Something resembling a growl passed his lips. "Yeh."

I wonder if Frane ever came to the 'boss' with a wild idea? Rogers thought. Wish he was available to advise me. This could put me behind the eight-ball. On the other hand, it may be my opening to head for lieutenant's bars.

"If it's okay, Captain, I want to offer a different view of the murders that we seem to have solved."

"What'dya mean, seem to have solved. Two murders, you caught the Three Jimmies, then another murder and capture the two Fancy Suits. What's your problem?"

"Chris DeLeon is working this case. The DA thinks this is a push-over. But, here's what bothers me. It's just too easy to say these people were hired by their bosses because some small player was skimming. Just not enough money involved. You don't bring in some top talent and pay them ten— maybe fifteen thousand to take out a couple of runners."

"Your point being?"

"How much skimming can you do? You're covering five or six customers a day, picking up a couple of thousand; how much can you take? A hundred bucks? In the whole week, with luck you can pick up maybe five hundred dollars. And that would take a lot of luck. From what I have learned, the records are pretty strong."

"Where did you learn that?"

Retreating slightly, Rogers continued. "I had a little talk with RC. He didn't tell me much, but he spoke very highly about how Pentram keeps his records."

Bailey bristled. "How can you use RC as a source? Guy walks away from the department, and then goes to work for one of the best known crooks in the city."

"Hear me out, boss," Rogers implored. "I'm not talking about what RC did or didn't do. He tells me Pentram runs a clean shop. RC is involved in a new business deal with Pentram. I don't understand a whole lot about running a business, but RC says Pentram is straight. Income tax and all."

"You believe all this crap Frane is telling you?"

Oh boy, this is dangerous territory. Just because RC told me some stuff, I figured my own game plan. Bailey is one tough guy. Can't cross him.

"Captain, let's just say for the moment that Pentram is clean. No way he is going to off two of his collectors cause they're skimming. All he has to do is bring them in, tell them they have been stealing from him, get them to sign an IOU and fire them. That way he may lose a couple of thousand bucks, but he doesn't open the door to a heavy duty Uncle Sam investigation."

Bailey scratched his jaw. His lined face resembled one of those ads for razor blades. He looked like five-o'clock shadow was his nemesis. "So, what's the rest of your theory?"

"Here's where I get a little fuzzy. I need your help. Because we know somebody hired the two gun slingers to hurt the Three Jimmies, who were brought in to do the two collectors. If Pentram wasn't involved, who was?"

"You're beginning to sound like a detective, Rogers. These shooters may not even know who hired them. Word goes out; somebody pays them; so they have to take the rap. If it wasn't Pentram, who was it?"

"My theory is that all this killing was intended as a diversion. A road block set in place to interfere with the real purpose."

"Which is?"

"That's the part where I'm stuck. Off the record, RC won't tell me, but I think he has another client. And, then we have that wild card, Abate. She wants Frane to do something and he says, 'No'. So, among other things she has me kidnapped."

Bailey leaned back in his worn swivel chair. "Rogers, if you're making sense, I missed the last turn. Two people get shot, three bad guys are captured, one of them gets shot in the meantime, you catch two more bad guys, you get kidnapped; I am lost."

Rogers felt a drop of perspiration in her arm pits. When she first considered talking to Bailey, all the pot holes weren't visible. One more shot.

"The thing is this. I got a feeling that Pentram's relationship with the Star Company has something to do with the overall plan. Remember, Abate wanted Frane to get her to the inside. She as much as told Frane and even me when I was kidnapped, that she wanted a piece of the action."

"Let's get this straight. Abate wants to be partners with Pentram? No way! No damn way."

"I appreciate your insights, boss. It still leaves the question, why did she want to be partners? It's got to be more than money. So, what I think is there is a big reason to be his partner, and it involves big bucks, and getting rid of two lowly collectors was like a 'shot across the bow'."

"A warning to frighten Pentram. Ha, that's a joke. Don't they know the man was born with cast iron cajones?"

"One last part of my observations. When big deliveries come into Star, they often arrive in containers from out of the country. These things are hardly inspected."

"What are you saying, somebody's trying to sneak a nuke into the country?"

"I could think of a lot of things coming in. Your guess is probably better than mine."

78

The house was just a big old house. What went on inside was cloaked by heavy drapes that were closed in the early afternoons. A six-foot fence of time-worn pickets guarded two sides and the back. Concrete steps led to an oversized front door and an outside porch lacking furniture. The double driveway along the side was home to three cars. A delivery entrance in the back led into a substantial kitchen, including a breakfast area to seat at least six.

On one counter was a coffee maker that held one pot of regular, one pot of decaf and a third pot of constantly hot water. Ten white commercial cups with big handles were neatly arrayed. A tray of fresh donuts and bagels were waiting.

"What shall I do about our Karate expert?"

Fish looked disturbed. *Losing one of my people is painful. Little Joe has been with me for a long time. It's never easy to make a hard decision. The mission takes precedence. There's a lot at stake, including how I have engineered this entire operation.*

"Find a place for him where he won't do us any hurt."

"The ultimate?" asked the guard.

"As straightforward as possible. Make sure it's done."

Fish nodded to the other guard and motioned him to the coffee pot. Then he sat at the table and drummed his fingers, planning the next move. As his coffee reached the table he said, "Here's what we have to do. Have the cleaners secure the house. I want all fingerprints removed; no mistakes. Then pack up anything we brought in. We're going to move. But, first, get a new box for the books. I'll take them with me. And burn the remains of the original box."

In the dark of night, secreted in the basement, Fish had dismembered the sides, top and bottom of the corrugated box that held the collection of books. As he peeled the panels apart, there were sixty-eight neatly packed slots, each containing ten-one hundred dollar bills. Sixty-eight thousand dollars in all. And, a single page listing chemicals and other requested supplies. An order for materials not normally available. An order Fish had successfully intercepted.

"Any other instructions, boss?"

"Yes. I want Abate brought to Norfolk. See that she is in one of the cars. Don't tell her where she is going and keep a close eye on her."

"Will you be joining us?"

"There are a few matters to be completed here in Philadelphia. You and the others can pack up and go whenever you're ready. Shouldn't take more than a few hours. If you have too much, store some in one of those rent-a-garage places. We can always retrieve whatever we leave behind. Too early to tell if we shall return."

As his people moved into action, Fish reached for his cell phone, the one that was bought and registered in Miami Beach. He dialed Juliani's Restaurant. "I'd like to make a reservation for dinner. Can you tell me if Mr. Pentram is expected today?"

By the time Captain Bailey and a squad of police arrived, the big house was empty. Four cars with sixteen officers were deployed around the building. The booming bull horn resounded through the neighborhood. Two SWAT sharpshooters were positioned; one across the street and another overseeing the back of the house. Empty houses make no response.

Signaling to his troops, Captain Bailey motioned for three men to crash through the front door. They were followed by two more men who rushed into the house. Finally, all the officers except the sharpshooters were in the house, searching all the rooms.

Frane remained outside, leaning against his own car. As a retired cop, he could only observe. Bailey approached him and said, "Looks like we're late. When did you say you were attacked?"

"It wasn't so much about being attacked. I think the man who came after me was badly hurt. This is where he was brought." *No need to talk about a shooting. If he's gone, that's it. Keep forgetting I'm supposed to be a civilian. Not nice to go around shooting people.*

"I'll get the house dusted for prints. So far we haven't been able to find a damn thing."

Frane shrugged. "Some days are better than others."

79

Ever since the murder of Chips Brewer behind the restaurant, Juliani's had taken on an aura of mystery. Customers from out of the neighborhood were drawn to the site of a real-life murder. This was not the scene of a household crime, rather the place where an assailant led the victim to the rear of the restaurant, where the accumulation of wasted food awaited the massive compacting machine, and sent two bullets into his head.

It was the kind of publicity that Dennis Angelo hated. When he bought the restaurant from his uncle, his plan was to attract, "my kind of people," friends from the immediate neighborhood and the executives from the Food Distribution Center. After ten years, the clientele increased, and his success lay in serving good food in a comfortable setting. The sudden influx of strangers who sought after the excitement of dining where someone had been murdered caused him personal anguish. Once, he knew the names and families of his customers; now the tables were filled with unfamiliar faces. Once, only a select few could reserve a seat. Now he had to hire a hostess to maintain a semblance of order. Despite the additional income, he was not happy. Even John Pentram expressed concern with the increased clatter.

"Your place has changed, Dennis."

"Mr. Pentram, I'm at a loss. Used to be a nice, quiet, friendly restaurant. People like you would come in two, three nights a week just because it was like home. All these foreigners from other parts of the city are destroying the place."

"Price of success," said Pentram.

"Hey, some guy called a little while ago; wanted to know if you were coming in for dinner."

"Interesting."

Before getting out of the darkened car, Fish said, "There he goes, right on time. If you boys want to come in and have something to eat, pick a table where you can keep an eye on things."

The bright neon sign stood out in an otherwise dark block of stores. A few overhead lights flooded down on the crowded parking lot. Fish took in the scene before moving toward the front door. Inside, a hostess asked him, "Alone tonight, sir?"

As he scanned the dinning room and spotted Pentram, he said, "I'll sit over there."

"Oh, but that's Mr. Pentram's table."

Without a smile, he answered, "Exactly."

Before he reached the table, Pentram looked up. "Ah, Fish. I thought you might be the one who called. Please, sit." A glass of wine had already been poured.

"Thank you." After a small sip, he added, "Nice."

"Will you have some dinner?"

"That's a wonderful idea. All the pressures of the day suggest a quiet, friendly meal would be appropriate."

Without waiting, Pentram signaled Jo-Ann, his favorite waitress. With a slight nod he sent the message to double his order. "Hope you like Veal Marsala. It is truly one of the specialties of the house."

"It's amazing how many things we have in common. Including our taste in food. Marsala is always good."

"We always seem to meet in restaurants."

"Why not?" asked Fish. "Isn't that where so many important business deals take place?"

"Indeed. So, how are things progressing?"

"I had an excellent meeting with your Mr. Star. Picked up a case of books, mostly literature. It was worth the effort."

Pentram patted his lips with the napkin. "He's not my Mr. Star. Just happens we have a small business arrangement."

"Which brings me to Ms Abate. We have decided to withdraw her efforts to persuade you to allow us to participate in your venture."

"After all she has done to involve me? Where is she going?"

Avoiding the question, Fish continued. "We completed our trial run. All that remains is full implementation of our project."

"Which is?"

His lips pursed, Fish said, "No need to go into that. Suffice to say, we won't be needing your assistance as we move forward. The proper authorities will be notified. It may not be possible to get you a letter of appreciation. That's why I came by tonight. To express our gratitude for all you have done. You understand."

"What more could a man ask than to have had the opportunity to serve."

"There may come a time when your services will be appropriately acknowledged." He raised his wine glass in a show of respect.

As the meal arrived, the two men sat silently. Jo Ann returned with a large serving of sauteed spinach and a platter of linguine. "Compliments of Dennis Angelo."

"Nice touch. Hope you like spinach."

"As you can imagine, my work has taken me all over the world. I have learned to enjoy indigenous foods wherever I am. Better than the last time when we met at the Maryland House on Interstate 95."

When they finished dinner Pentram offered, "I'm not much for dessert. But, don't let me stop you."

"No, this was fine. Do you they have any Galliano?"

"Just what I was about to suggest," said Pentram. "And a cup of good hot coffee."

"Perfect."

When the cordial arrived, they raised their glasses and added, "Salute."

"You will forgive me if I don't take a second coffee. Business calls. It's been a pleasure working with you."

Fish rose, moved naturally toward the door. From the corner of his left eye, he spotted his two men, who dropped a fifty dollar bill on the table and followed him. The three men walked across the street and got into the car. They drove off, toward the ramp that led to the intersection that would take them south for the long trip to Norfolk. A dark blue Chevy and a black Ford trailed close behind, at a respectable distance.

Frane watched from the shadows. Then, he turned and entered the restaurant. As the hostess greeted him, he waved her aside and joined Pentram. "I was taping your conversation. Didn't sound incriminating."

"No need. We know what he arranged. Taking out those two collectors wasn't necessary. He is a bad person."

"No comment."

"Things are going to be settled soon."

"What does that mean?"

"You're the detective. What do you think?"

"I think there were two cars following Fish and his helpers."

"Oh," said Pentram. "Care for a coffee and a Crème Brule?"

"What's that?"

"A taste treat to sweeten a rather tasteless day."

80

Interstate 95 is a long, fast highway. It runs down the east coast, skirts Wilmington, Delaware, skims along toward Baltimore where it passes through the Fort McHenry Tunnel, heads toward Washington, down to Richmond and on to Norfolk and beyond. From Philadelphia to the Maryland House just before reaching Baltimore takes about two hours. That is where the meet was scheduled.

Another Ford and another Chevy headed north from Washington had arrived and were waiting as the three cars from Philadelphia eased into the rest stop. When Fish and the two men entered the restaurant, the eight FBI agents took their positions. Simple hand signals were exchanged. Three men moved toward the exit door to wait for them to leave. The other five, three men and two women agents, lined the walkway.

When the door swung open, the beefy lead agent stepped forward holding his badge in clear view. "Just a moment, we need you three to come with us."

Fish straightened up as he sought to remind them who he was. "You don't really intend to arrest us, do you?"

"Sir, we're taking you to headquarters in Washington. You can call it anything you wish."

"Do you have any idea who I am?"

Disdaining to answer, the agent said, "Please hold still while my associates frisk you."

"You can't do this!"

Signaling to the three agents who stood behind Fish and his bodyguards, the pat down began. "Don't do anything foolish." Fish was clean, but his guards each had a 9mm Glock and a snub nose S & W.

Two agents directed travelers to move rapidly away from the arrest that was taking place. "Step around, please."

"Do I get a phone call?"

"Not my orders. When we reach Washington, they will tell you whatever you need to know. In the meantime, put your hands behind your back and the agents will handcuff you. Then, two agents will take each of you to a car. One agent will drive your car. Please, hand me the keys to your car."

"Do you think this is an appropriate way to treat members of another government agency?"

Smiling, the lead agent said, "Ours not to reason why."

It was cut and dry. Eight to three didn't seem like winning odds. FBI agents are well-trained.

With another hand signal, the lead agent appointed one man to take the Lincoln Town Car. "Check the trunk. See if there's anything interesting."

"Just some books," Fish interrupted.

"Nice to know you like to read."

81

Dinner time at the Maryland House Restaurant on Interstate 95 is a crowded affair. Milling people hinder easy movement. Some holding sandwiches, or ice cream cones, or those big puffy cinnamon buns covered with white icing. A perfect place to cause chaos.

Two of Fish's men escorted Muriel Abate to the entrance to the Ladies Room. She offered a back hand wave as she disappeared.

"Think I'll stroll over and get a hot dog. You want one?"

"I'll stay here and keep an eye out for Abate."

"You better. She's one tough banana."

"Fish just said to deliver her to Norfolk, to the beach house."

"It's a long ride, but, she's not going to give us any trouble."

"You ever work with her?"

"Not really, but I've heard stories. She screwed up that kidnapping bit."

"Glad we work for Fish."

"Okay. I'll be back in a couple of minutes."

Abate, entered a stall. Inside, she released the catch on her oversize shoulder bag. "Wise guys, they searched it good. Just that they're not so smart."

From the stiff frame at the top of the bag, she twisted the ornament and slowly withdrew the business-end of a six-inch long ice pick. *Not my favorite choice, but more than enough to do what I have to do.*

She edged toward the exit and peered around a corner. Standing casually was the one remaining man. As three or four woman moved through the door, she filed along side. When she reached her captor, she feigned a trip and as he reached to help, she plunged the ice pick between his ribs.

"Help, help," she screamed. "He attacked me!"

Then came the chaos. Women, men and children gathered around as the man fell to the floor. Yelling and shouts filled the air.

"Get a doctor!"

"Call the cops!"

"Did you see what he did?"

"Tried to grab her!"

"Watch him. Don't let him get away!"

Standing in the hot dog line, the second man hardly glanced at the forming crowd. *Not much gonna happen in a crowded restaurant. Just some kids raising a ruckus.*

Slowly, Abate eased to the edge of the pack. Then, she quietly moved aside as more people forced their way toward the action, trying to get a better view of what was happening. Without notice, she waited at the door as newcomers entered the building, and then slipped through the open door.

She walked quickly to the parking lot on the south side of the restaurant, spotted the dark car and went to the driver's side. There, she inserted a hairpin into the lock and with a few twists, opened the door. Inside the car, she jiggled the hairpin in the ignition. After using an in-and-out motion and then bending it three times, the car started. *The last time I did anything like this I was in Prague. The Agency certainly taught us good.*

Pulling into the south bound lane she realized the distance to the next exit was about ten miles. That meant she had ten minutes to get off of Interstate 95. If her captors gave the license number to the state police, catching her would be easy. Her plan was simple. Find a small motel, check in, and then call for a rental car. On second thought, she decided to find a bus stop, park the car and make her way to the bus terminal. Better yet, find a way to the Baltimore-Washington Airport, and catch a flight to Norfolk.

Staying on the back roads, it took almost two hours to get to the airport.

Then, irony of ironies, Abate barely caught the 7:50 p.m. flight, only to find it backtracked to Philadelphia before leaving for Norfolk. *This doesn't matter, she thought. I'll have a drink, a sandwich and then another drink.*

Car rentals were closed when she arrived at midnight, so she went to the curb and picked up a cab. In less than forty minutes, she reached the beach house. She knew someone would be on duty, so the loud knock on the door brought a fast response by a man and a woman.

"It's okay," said the woman. "It's that Ms Abate. Remember, she was here a couple of weeks ago. Let her in."

"Thank you," Abate said. "Mr. Fish is supposed to meet me here. Has he arrived yet?"

"No."

"Well, I'll just take my usual room and see him when he gets here. Probably tomorrow morning."

"You need anything?"

"Just a bit of quiet. By the way, what time is breakfast?"

With a look of condescension, the woman replied, "When you want to eat, we serve."

82

They each entered a different restaurant. Bob Vogt traveled all the way to Northeast Philadelphia to the Home Plate. He sat at the counter, ordered coffee and a piece of pumpkin pie. Before the food arrived, he went to the Men's Room. The corridor had a third door that opened into the kitchen. Barely paying attention to the kitchen staff, he headed for the back door. Waiting at the bottom of the steps was a black Ford Taurus. With a simple nod, he got in the passenger side for the ride downtown.

Tom Jenkins, owner of the Uptown Diner kept an eye out for Thurman Arthur. Identifying the imposing, well dressed black man was no problem. With a simple gesture, a slight tilt of the head, Jenkins led Arthur through the swinging doors into the kitchen and then to the back door. He pointed to the dark blue Chevy, and held the door open as the big man left the diner and slid into the rear of the car.

Roberta Mercado was greeted by Larry Warren, the manager of the Orchid Room Restaurant. He even offered to carry her brief case. She refused. On the way to his office, they detoured through the kitchen where none of the staff paid any attention. People were always coming into their kitchen. At the rear door, she spotted the waiting black Lincoln Town car.

By prior arrangement, RC Frane was dining with John Pentram at Juliani's. At exactly nine o'clock, the two men finished their coffees and headed for the kitchen. Angelo Dennis was waiting for them. The special room hidden behind the kitchen, reserved for special occasions had been set. A round table with six seats, a silver water pitcher, six crystal glasses and several bottles of Evian were appropriately arranged.

"Why six chairs?" asked Frane.

"Good question," replied Pentram. "If any of the players think we should add someone to the team, we show that the opportunity exists."

"Are you sure I should be here?"

"You are my main consultant. As we have discussed in the past, I don't usually avail myself of outside assistance. You are a special case. Don't we work well together?"

Frane spoke cautiously. "Quite frankly, our time together has been most educational. It would be nice if it could continue."

Pentram nodded.

Angelo Dennis knocked on the door before opening it so Mercado could enter. Exactly as planned, the other two arrived.

Pentram said, "Mr. Arthur, I don't know if you have met Ms Mercado, she is one of my lawyers. And this is RC Frane, Ms Mercado. Mr. Frane, do you know Mr. Vogt?"

"Only by reputation," Frane added.

"How's that?"

"He was one of my heroes when he played football at West Philly. Years ahead of my time; but a classy quarterback."

"Nice of you to remember."

Arthur asked, "Who is the extra chair for?"

"We don't know yet," answered Pentram. "Maybe nobody."

"Lady and gentlemen, let's get down to business. Both Mr. Vogt and Ms Mercado have been working on a proposal. So, let's leave the initial discussion to them."

"Before we get to that," Arthur said. "I understand you and me, and I understand your lawyer and my lawyer. No offence, by what is Mr. Frane doing here?"

"Let me just say," began Pentram, "that the success of our business is paramount, and being able to raise questions is an integral part of getting along. So, it is good you raised that issue, Thurman. You don't object to our reaching a first name basis?"

"I don't object," Arthur responded. "However, you are the senior person and I still don't feel comfortable in calling you, John. However, I have no problem with you calling me, Thurman."

"Very gracious. Now, to answer your question. You know that Mr. Frane used to be Lieutenant Frane. His credentials are of the highest. He has also been my personal consultant during this time. If this group decides his services are no longer required as we go forward, so be it. On the other hand, I have other businesses, as you all know, and I still might want to have him at my side."

A combination of shrugs and nods ended the discussion.

"Let's hear from the lawyers."

Vogt and Mercado opened their brief cases. Each extracted a single sheet of paper, one to Arthur and one to Pentram. Frane sat quietly.

Finally, Pentram spoke. "This is the barest outline of what we are about. Tell us a little about this last item. 'Going Public'."

Mercado started. "There's lots of detail to go with this presentation. However, where we're headed is to a large organization selling shares to the public. Takes time and effort. The pay-off is enormous."

"How do you feel about that, Thurman?"

The big man twirled a multi-colored Cross pen. "For me, it's going to take a little getting used to. So far, I have always been my own boss. Don't do too bad. What kind of money you talking about?"

Vogt joined in. "If we can build the Food Buying Group to a critical mass, one that warrants going public, we're talking multi-millions. More than enough for everybody."

"So, who would be the boss?" asked Thurman.

"This is a very simple plan," Mercado said. "Even before going public there would be plenty of money. Just look what has been accomplished so far. The Pentram people have already signed up more than twenty operations. How many have you lined up Mr. Arthur?"

"Maybe fifteen."

"That means our combined efforts have created a business already doing more than forty million dollars a year. We haven't even scratched the surface. Do you have any idea how many prospects we have in Philadelphia alone?"

"Lots."

"A conservative estimate, about five hundred."

Pentram went to the door, and signaled to Dennis. He led two table servers into the room, one with a tray of five crystal flutes, the other wheeling in a Jeroboam of champagne. When the glasses were filled, the group stood in solemn tribute.

"Salute."

83

"I think your mission is over."

"It seems to me there are still some loose ends," answered Frane.

"Let's just say you have done a masterful job. Of course, we expected nothing less than the best. Are you ready to return to your job?"

"Do I have a choice, Chief?"

"When you reach my age, you realize that life is filled with choices—always. You were asked to do some very important investigating, that required you disassociate yourself from the police department. As the head of a special unit closely allied with certain federal agencies, I sought you out as the best man for the job. You understand, that my role is not clearly defined, almost like the role, say of the CIA. For several reasons, we cannot offer public recognition for what you have done."

Frane nodded. "Chief, we have known one another since I became a cop. People in the department regard you with high esteem. The fact that my meetings with you have been in your home borders on the scary. After all my years hearing and knowing about you, I was and am willing to do whatever you say."

He reached for the crystal decanter. "Ever had 15-year-old single malt scotch?" With that, the Chief of Police, who heads up the Inter-Agency Relations Department, poured an inch into the two glasses. "It's interesting, when I first tasted Glenfiddich it was served at room temperature. No ice, no water. Took a little getting used to. Now, it seems quite natural."

"Thank you, Chief." Raising his glass in respect, he took a sip.

"That's good, RC. Let a little roll around on your tongue. The first small swallow is not the best. The next is better, and pretty soon you'll drink it like water. Only better."

Frane laughed. "Sounds good. You won't take advantage of me after a couple of these?"

The two men were sitting in the study of the Chief's home. Deep, comfortable easy chairs facing the unlit fire place. Too early in the season for heat. Shelves of books and piles of magazines. The room had no windows, a design intended for complete privacy.

"That trick you pulled on Abate, taping her on your own answering machine; that was neat. How'd you come up with that idea?"

"You gotta do what you gotta do. She's a wild card, you never know what to expect. When she signaled me while we were having breakfast and took me through the paces, going to a phone booth, getting picked up in her car, I just didn't have time for planning. The idea of calling my apartment and then leaving the message on my machine seemed like a good idea. Turned out to be very effective."

"You did a lot of innovative things on this assignment. Of course, you know we can't put anything in your record. Just that you were on a special assignment and you did a superb job."

"That's nice of you to say. But, I'm not sure exactly what I did that was so important."

Pouring another inch of scotch, the Chief said, "RC, when I asked you to take this job, you were skeptical. But, like a good officer, you did everything that needed doing. You were our eyes and ears into everything that was happening. The Spanish Connection will prove invaluable, out of our area, but very significant. It was almost laughable when Fish dumped books out of that fake box."

"I was really stunned," said Frane. "Now you want to know if I'm ready to rejoin my department."

"I've already talked to Captain Bailey. He understands you were working, shall we say, undercover. I'm sure he'll welcome you back."

"May I ask a few questions?"

"Sure. You understand I may not answer all of them. Fire away."

"Who is this Abate woman?"

Pursing his lips, the Chief took a deep breath. "When people work for some of the secret government agencies for a long time they forget there is a world out there. She had nineteen years of active duty before she was cashiered. That's a fancy word for 'fired'. Well, it's hard for these kinds of people to reorient themselves. They go off half-cocked. She had big responsibilities in her day and she never got over the idea that she was reduced to just being a citizen."

"So, what you're saying is she had no real authority. Just organized a bunch of like-minded people and acted like she was still in business."

"That's about the size of it. She was free-lancing. That's why she wanted to get her claws on some of Pentram's businesses. She needed money."

"Where is Pentram in all this?"

"You've been involved completely. However, I have to say that this conversation is confidential. It never happened."

"I figured as much. So, do you want to tell me about Pentram?"

"This is as much as I can tell. His business is clean. He is clean. There may come a time when I can share more than I have said. Let's leave it at this. He was doing some things for us."

"What about the money he paid me?"

"You earned that. You're entitled to keep it. And, of course, you're still on the payroll even though I have arranged to hold your checks for the past couple of months."

"Suppose he wants me to continue to be his consultant?"

"That's a tough question. If he does, and you want to really leave the force, that's your decision. As a friend, stay with the force. With this assignment over, you're probably in line to make captain."

Frane finished his drink and twirled the empty glass. The Chief reached over and poured more scotch. "You're beginning to like this stuff.

"Oh, by the way," he laughed. "Would you like to tell me how you got Stanley Rankin to do what you wanted?"

"Who's Stanley Rankin? I don't know the name."

"The guy who told you where Rogers was being held. You didn't know his name?"

Frane swallowed the rest of his drink. "We gave him a code name. Called him, 'Marmaduke'. Chief, I'm not sure you want to know how I persuaded him to give me the information."

"That's okay. Our conversation is confidential." He reached out and poured more scotch in Frane's glass.

"Well, remember, I was operating as a civilian. This wasn't police business."

"So?"

Frane shook his head. Then smiled. "I locked him in a freezer in his shorts."

The Chief recoiled, then burst into laughter. "You what? You froze his ass off. Damn, you are a clever devil, Frane."

Together they raised their glasses. The scotch was taking hold. Smooth, easy going done, and wanted more.

"Can I ask you about this Fish character?"

"He's real. In fact, he was playing Abate. He paid her to do some dirty work. At the same time, I'm not sure of his title or his job description. Only that he is clear. You know the FBI picked him up after he left Pentram at Juliani's. As soon as they got to Washington and verified his credentials, he was turned loose."

"What about all the killing, the two collectors, the guys from Trenton?"

"Nothing to do with our work. Rogers and Bailey have that all wrapped up. It was just a diversion as far as you and I are concerned. In one way, it interfered with your investigation."

"Just what did I do?"

The Chief tried to answer without divulging too much. "RC, you were there when Fish picked up that case of books that was delivered in the container of olives. Did you ever figure out what was happening?"

Leaning back in the easy chair, Frane felt good, despite all the drinking. He knew that standing to leave would present a problem. For the moment, he was safe. "I had some conversation about that with my philosopher friend. He told me a strange story and I never completely figured it out."

"So, you had the help of a philosopher? Care to share his name?"

"Can't I have a couple of secrets?"

Smiling, the Chief said, "Sure, as long as they don't impinge on what we need to know. Anyhow, maybe I can help. The books didn't mean a thing. But, the box they came in was key. Once again, this is strictly confidential. When the box was stripped, there was sixty-four thousand dollars and an order for chemicals. I'll leave it to you to guess what that was all about. Here's a clue. What would you do with a truck load of explosives?"

Head whirling, Frane asked, "Chief, can I get a lift home?"

84

Captain Bailey wasn't happy. "RC, we've been together a long time. You could have tipped me off."

"George, you're absolutely right. But, you have no idea what I had to go through. I'm still not sure about all the papers I signed and the deep background checks they did on me before I was tapped and after I agreed."

"Okay. I'm trying not to take this too personal. I know all this stuff was at the highest authority. There's still some things I'm not certain about."

Changing the subject, Frane asked, "What about the little man? What happened to him?"

"Here's the deal. I don't tell you what happened to him and you don't tell me how he got in the condition he was in. Deal?"

"Message received."

"Speaking of messages, there's one for you. Note from Fish asking for a meeting. He mentioned the cafeteria where you and Abate met. Wants to go over a few things."

"When?"

"As soon as we're done here."

"Thanks."

"Consider this meeting as an official welcome back to the job. I assume that's what you want to do."

"Can I have a couple of days off. Gotta get my head back where it belongs."

Rising from his seat, Bailey put out his hand and said, "It'll be good to work with you again, RC."

Frane strolled through the corridors, reacquainting himself, even glancing into his old office which he intended to reoccupy. He took time to breathe deeply, recognizing the different aromas of a police station where so many diverse people bring their individual tang to add to the mix. He was home again, glad to be back.

Outside the sun was bright. A cab had just discharged a fare and he signaled the driver. "Take me to 18th and Market." He wanted to walk that last block to the cafeteria.

He got in the short line and picked up a cup of coffee, black. Glancing around, he spotted Fish. *I see he has company. My old friend Marmaduke.*

"Hello, Fish. Hi, Rankin."

"You know my name?"

"Doesn't everyone."

"Don't give me any crap, Frane. I still got a score to settle with you."

Fish interrupted. "This is neither the time nor the place. You know better than to hold grudges. Man was doing his job, just like you were doing your job. I didn't bring you together to argue. I just want to chat with the Lieutenant."

Turning to Fish, "So, what's on your mind? Understand they turned you loose in Washington."

"You were only in on a small part of the story. I have no intention of telling you more than you need to know. What surprised me in this entire operation was how little you really knew."

"Guess that's because I'm an amateur in your business. But, seeing as how I did some good things, I made out all right." With this he turned to smile at Rankin.

"We're not done," snarled Rankin. "Since you know my name, where'd you come up with this Marmaduke moniker?"

"You really want to know?"

"Yeh."

Frane laughed. "In my line of work, whenever we come across a congenital liar, we call them 'Marmaduke'. I guess you have something like that in your work."

"I'll get you, you bastard!"

Fish spoke in anger. "I thought I told you what happened is history. Gone. Over. Forget it."

"You don't know what he did."

"I don't want to know. You know better than to carry a grudge."

Rankin reached across the table, intent on grabbing Frane. "I'll tear you apart."

Frane held up his hands, palms open and said, "Before you do that, take a look to your left. See that attractive black woman sitting at the next table. She's nursing her ice tea. Can you see beneath the table where she has her .22 aimed at your right testicle."

"You crazy bastard."

"Then, look to your right and you'll see that tall skinny man in the t-shirt and dungarees. His .22 is aimed at your left testicle."

Fish fought to contain himself. "Listen, Frane. Maybe you shouldn't go back to being a cop. How about joining my organization. Tough to get in, but life is exciting."

"Is that what you wanted to see me about?"

"Not really. Just wanted to close the gap. We were both working the same side of the street. For the record, I knew everything you were doing. Including Pentram. He's a hell of a man. Helped us with a lot of details."

"And Abate?"

"I'll tell you what you already know. She used to be part of the organization. When she turned sour, some of us old-timers took pity. I farmed out some work so she could keep her hand in."

"So, where does Rankin fit in?"

"He always worked for me. Abate didn't know him, so he was undercover staying close to her. Make sure she didn't go crazy."

"But, she did go crazy. She had her own team."

"They are a dedicated group, but not dangerous—in the deadly way."

"Wish I had known that back then."

"To make sure we understand each other, the job I was instructed to complete worked fine. We have the information we need, and a way to follow-up what could be a touchy situation."

"So, you just wanted to tell me everything is okay."

"Let's put it this way. Your work was admirable. It may happen that I can call on you sometime in the future. You know, do a little free lance."

I'm not cut out for this kind of work. These people are dancing to tunes that haven't been written yet. If I ever leave the force, this is one place I don't want to be. No way.

"I appreciate the nice words. They don't come my way too often." Rising to leave, he looked at Marmaduke and said, "When you had Sergeant Rogers you had no idea what you were messing with. I did what I had to do. If it didn't work, you would be, as they say, 'sleeping with the fishes'. Rogers is a special person in my life. Go near her again and I'll kill you. Is that clear? Do you understand?"

Fish answered for Rankin. "He understands. He's a professional."

85

"This is my party. No more picking up the check. Okay?"

"Just this once," answered Leonides Andros.

"The table looks good. Two other people are coming; Peg Wilson and Milt Thomason. Sergeant Rogers and Chris DeLeon you know."

"Who are the two new faces?"

"They're street cops who have been assigned to Homicide. Good people."

"You want to order from the menu? Or leave it to me for something special?"

"Either way. I assume we'll have the usual variety of drinks?"

"My pleasure. I'll come up with something extra."

"While we're waiting, might as well have a drink. What would you suggest?"

Andros considered. "Perhaps a small glass of Sherry to quiet the nerves."

"Whatever."

Rogers and DeLeon arrived a few minutes early. "Welcome," Frane greeted. "We're having a glass of Sherry. Would you care for a drop?"

It was close to seven o'clock and the evening stretched ahead. "Of course, always nice to start slow and warm up in good time," DeLeon said.

With an easy laugh, Rogers added, "I'm all yours."

"I must say, you two look splendiferous."

"Is that a real word, or did you make it up."

Frane was saved as Wilson and Thomason were being led to the table.

"This pretty nifty," said Wilson. "Not too often I get to such a fancy event."

Thomason joked, "How can you say that. When we're on the job don't we go to some pretty nice places, Burger Chef, Taco Bell, and on a good day, TGIF."

"You two haven't met Leonides Andros. He is the owner of the Sand Box and we come here a lot for advice."

"It's good to have you here. As to the advice, I'm not so sure about that. For now I advise a small Sherry before we sit down to dinner."

"Sounds good."

Andros had cordoned off a section of the restaurant so the small group could have some privacy. Even though he was seeing to the meal, he was also an invited guest. The mood was congenial and convivial. A table server pointed them to a separate setting where an assortment of delicacies were arrayed. At the same time she took orders for drinks.

"Martinis all around?" She remembered Frane was partial to a gin starter.

"Why not a large pitcher of the good stuff while we nibble on a few shrimp."

Andros motioned to the table server and whispered, "Just enough for one drink each. We're going to spend the evening drinking. Better to go easy."

"What's the occasion Lieutenant?"

"Later."

Sipping their drinks, dipping pita bread in the Tzatziki, creamy yogurt blended with cucumbers, garlic, olive oil and seasonings, and sampling Dolmadakia, grape leaves stuffed with rice and herbs was almost enough to kill the appetite. Until Andros called a halt. "Time for food."

Wisely, they skipped salad and moved to Ouzo. Then two table servers circled their table. One offered large halves of Mediterranean Chicken in a Hellenic sauce of garlic, lemon juice, olive oil, and spices. The second brought a tray of small Porgies and filleted Red Snapper. Before they could finish what was already on their plates, another platter of Pork Chops and

Lamb Chops appeared.

It was at this point that Frane rose and walked slowly around the table, filling the wine glasses with Mouton Cadet '88, a classic French Bordeaux White Wine. Returning to his place, as he remained standing, he began. "My friends, my team, this dinner prepared by my favorite philosopher-restaurateur, Leonides Andros is my way of saying thank you to you all. These past weeks have been trying because I didn't know what I was doing. As it turns out, I have been told I did it very well. Whatever that means.

"I want to pay tribute to each of you for your help and advice. There is one person not here. However, you should know that John Pentram, despite his past, is a committed citizen. As I have been told, he made an important contribution.

"You have stood beside me and behind me and in front of me. For that I am grateful." Turning to Andros, "For your wonderful way of enlightening me. And now, let's eat some more and drink some more. Because tomorrow I'm going back to work as a Lieutenant on the Philadelphia Police Force. No more undercover work for me."

Rogers stood, "Just one question, boss. Are we having Metaxa tonight?"

"It's on the way," said Andros. "Shall we have some dessert?"

"Can I have some of that Baklava?" asked Wilson.

"Sounds good."

"To make the evening complete," Andros announced. "I have ordered four taxis to see that you all get home safely."

Printed in the United States
63921LVS00003B/253-255